ISOLATION

ISOLATION

A NOVEL

TRAVIS THRASHER

Faith Words

NEW YORK BOSTON NASHVILLE

FaithWords
Hachette Book Group USA
237 Park Avenue
New York, NY 10017

Visit our Web site at www.faithwords.com.

Printed in the United States of America

First Edition: September 2008
10 9 8 7 6 5 4 3 2 1

FaithWords is a division of Hachette Book Group USA, Inc.

The FaithWords name and logo are trademarks of Hachette Book Group USA, Inc.

Library of Congress Cataloging-in-Publication Data

Thrasher, Travis, 1971–
    Isolation : a novel / Travis Thrasher. — 1st ed.
        p. cm.
    ISBN-13: 978-0-446-50554-3
    ISBN-10: 0-446-50554-4
    1. Missionaries—Fiction. 2. Psychological fiction. I. Title.
    PS3570.H6925I86 2008
    813'.54—dc22   2007047218

To my mother, Mary Jo Thrasher,
for passing on to me a fraction of her writing talents
and a love of really scary stories

Nineteen Years Ago

It was the sort of hot summer night that made a young woman abandon her fears and jump into the lake with barely anything on. And the sort of night that made a man in the nearby woods watch.

He heard their voices first. Laughter, conversation, even shouts, as if there wasn't another soul in the surrounding countryside. The night air was thick and the forest full of aged trees and wild growth. It was easy to be swallowed in the black pit of the woods.

He watched as one thing led to another and a bet turned into a splash. Then the girl shouted as the boy ran off, leaving the swimmer all alone.

She didn't seem to mind. The moon lit the murky waters of the lake, the ripples gliding out from arms and feet that stretched out calmly. She looked peaceful. Peaceful and very naïve.

He watched from behind a nearby oak tree, wondering when she would come out, knowing that would be the time to make his move. He was used to walking in shadow, walking without sound, walking without anyone knowing.

For several moments he held his breath.

He waited, his eyes unmoving, his hands flexing.

He had killed before. And tonight he would kill again.

Nobody knew. Nobody understood the hunger, the need, the curiosity. What it felt like to hear the screams.

The sound of water spattering fell over the backdrop of the Michigan night. Summer nights were supposed to be carefree, just like a picture in a travel brochure. Nobody expected people like him to be out there, to be watching.

But there were plenty of people like him. People with hunger. People with need.

He watched carefully.

Waiting.

"Hey."

The voice came out of nowhere. It didn't jolt him, but merely annoyed him. He turned to the darkness behind him.

He couldn't see anybody.

"Yeah, you. I'm looking at you." The voice sounded young but undaunted, defiant. "Having a nice little time hiding out here?"

The figure came into better view, then spoke. "What do you think you're doing, spying on that girl?" The light of the moon reflected on the high forehead, the intense eyes, the strong cheekbones.

"You'd be wise to sneak back into those woods and never come out again." He could feel his hands flex, getting eager, getting ready.

The tall figure came closer, standing over him. "I know about you," its voice said, suddenly different, lower.

Lower. Or fuller.

"I know all about you."

And then the looming figure was upon him, swiftly, just like that—a shadow blurring and suddenly up against him, over him.

He didn't feel the knife until it plunged deeply into his gut. Again. And again.

"I know all about you," the deep, guttural voice said. "And you're no longer needed."

He dropped on his back and looked at the face of a man who looked like a boy. He could see the smile. Then he looked further up into the heavens. Even though the stars were out, all he could see was a growing flood of darkness. For a brief second he felt a dread come into him worse than any feeling in his life. He knew that he was done, but the terror had just started.

PART ONE

Division

1

The Stranger in the House

A loud crash woke her. It came from outside their bedroom, but she wasn't sure where. Stephanie jerked and turned onto her back, opening her eyes and adjusting to the pitch black. Next to her Jim's heavy sleep floated somewhere between snoring and ragged breathing. She called out his name twice, but he wouldn't wake at this hour unless she tugged at him. He was a big man who didn't go to sleep easily, but once he did, he stayed asleep.

She slipped out from under the bed's massive covers, and the chill of the winter night greeted her. The wind blew hard against the house, and she wondered if it was still snowing. The first few days in January had been particularly brutal, and they were forecasting another round of snow for Chicago that weekend.

I know I heard something, and I know I'm awake this time. I'm not sleepwalking.

The doorknob felt hard and cold as she turned it and opened the door. She walked down the hallway, a small night-light illuminating the floor.

This house had four bedrooms, and they had put Ashley in the room closest to theirs. Ash and Zachary were still adjusting to separate rooms after being cramped together in their tiny room in Dambi. Sometimes Ashley still wanted to sleep with them, a habit that was hard to break and even harder to argue with now that they were in a new house.

They had been here since September, but it still didn't feel like home. The furniture had been picked out by someone else years ago. The house itself felt like a model home, one of those you toured but never *lived* in. It looked like it was trying to have the feel of a home but didn't really get it.

One day they might know what it felt like to have their own home. Not someone else's house they were borrowing or a house they were renting or a temporary house they built themselves on the mission field. Stephanie wanted stability, something she could see every day for ten years, maybe something she could grow old in.

Ashley lay in her bed with half the covers off. Stephanie put them back over her and made sure she could hear her breathing. She always did that with her kids, even though they were five and eight. Ashley was her baby and always would be.

What about another one?

She could hear Jim's question but knew she was through. She dearly loved her children, but she didn't want another. Men just couldn't understand the pain and the emotional journey of having a baby. Maybe it was selfish, but she knew she couldn't go through another nine months of that if she had doubts.

She walked down to Zachary's room. It felt colder than the rest of the house for some reason, and she couldn't help shivering as she entered the room.

Zach breathed heavily, but that was because he was coming off a nasty sinus infection. Everything in the room looked fine. By the glow of the small night-light, she could see him tucked under the covers—his eyes closed, his dark brown hair messy.

Her heart leaped a little as she looked at him. Even though she wasn't supposed to have a favorite, she knew she loved Zachary a little more than Ashley. She would never tell another soul this, but she knew God could see. She couldn't help it. Zachary was her first and had been an answer to prayer and was just . . . he was Zach. He was special.

He's so much like you, it's scary.

That's what Jim said, but sometimes she didn't know. Zach was restless and outgoing and inquisitive, so, yes, sure, he took after her more than after Jim's quiet, deep persona. But there was something about Zach that was nothing like her, that wasn't like anybody.

He's a fifty-year-old man in the body of an eight-year-old.

She lost herself looking at her son when she heard another noise. This one came from downstairs, in the kitchen. It sounded like something had fallen.

That's twice now. Someone's in our house.

Her heart raced and she tiptoed to the top of the stairs, where she just stood and listened. She wondered about racing to get Jim, but she knew he would think she was sleepwalking and would tell her to go back to bed. Sure, she had dreams—nightmares—every now and then, but this was real. She was awake. Her bare feet could feel the soft carpet underneath them, a foreign luxury that took a while to get used to after coming back from Papua New Guinea. Her eyes adjusted to the darkness. She looked downstairs but could see nothing.

She slowly made her way down the steps, one after another. *Someone's there.*

She knew, she believed.

So why was she walking down there? She was the mother of the house. This was crazy. *If* someone were there, she shouldn't be going to greet them.

She reached the bottom of the stairs, then held her breath and listened. Nothing. Her hands shook, and she couldn't see anything except the light on the old VCR showing the time of 3:14 AM.

She flipped the light switch, expecting to see a man in black standing in the middle of the kitchen. Her heart raced as she stood at the base of the stairs, the light illuminating the family room and kitchen.

Nobody.

Stephanie walked over to the kitchen and stood in the middle near the island, looking around. There was nobody to see, nothing on the wood floor. No stray pot that had fallen or pan that was out of place.

She needed to calm down. She opened the refrigerator to get some milk, then saw something out of the corner of her eye.

Something shadowy and black and big and quick.

Something heading for the stairs.

She stiffened, not sure what she had just seen.

She heard movement on the carpeted steps, as though it were Jim heading up the stairs. The footsteps were quick, like someone was running.

Stephanie's body froze, and she could only turn her head. She spotted the set of knives she used for cooking, one of the few things she enjoyed doing in this house. For one brief second, she couldn't move or think or do anything. But then she heard the steps find their way to the hallway

to the kids' rooms

and with the creaking sound in the hallway right outside Zach's room, Stephanie jerked into motion.

She grabbed the largest knife in the set and clenched it as she ran up the stairs.

She rushed into Zach's room and held the knife out in the darkness. She turned around. Nobody there but her child.

She ran to Ashley's room.

Same thing.

I know what I heard and saw. I know it.

She stood in the middle of Ashley's room, looking quickly toward the doorway and to the hallway outside.

Suddenly she saw a figure glide by.

She felt very cold, a cold deep under her skin.

Stephanie charged out of the room and rushed down the hall back to Zach's room. This time, the bed was empty, the covers turned over, the room deserted.

For a second she just stood there in horror.

He's gone somebody took him the darkness took him he's gone he's gone forever

She felt her legs grow weak until she had to kneel on the floor. She took in a breath and felt light-headed, but kept the knife tightly clenched in her hand.

Where'd he go? Where'd they take him?

As she panted for air, a sound rose from behind her. She jerked around with her knife to face the doorway and suddenly found herself blinded by bright light. She squinted and discerned an ominous figure in the doorway.

"Don't! I swear!" she said, waving the knife toward the doorway.

"Steph—what the—Stephanie, drop the knife!"

She looked up and saw the beard first, then the eyes, bigger than usual, then the balding head. The voice hadn't just asked her to drop the knife. It had issued a command, a deep and booming command that jerked her

awake?

and made her drop the knife.

Jim stood at the doorway. The light to Zach's room was on. He came to her side and picked up the knife.

"What are you doing?" he asked as he helped her up.

"It's Zach. I saw someone—heard something—then I looked and someone was coming up—I didn't know—"

She turned to see Zach in his bed, his hair shaped like a mushroom, his eyes wide open and adjusting to the light.

He's there.

"He wasn't—I looked and he wasn't there. Jim, I swear. I saw something. I know I did. I don't know what—"

"What were you doing with this knife?"

"I was scared somebody—"

"Steph. You've got to get some help. This is really—"

He stopped, obviously noticing that Zachary was hanging on every word. Jim laid the knife on the small dresser and went over to their son.

"Hey, buddy. It's okay. Mommy was just having another dream."

But I wasn't dreaming this time. I swear I wasn't dreaming.

"It's okay. Just go to sleep. All right?"

Zach nodded and looked at her. "Mom, are you okay?"

She stood, and she could feel her legs shaking. "I'm fine. I'm sorry, sweetheart. I'm just tired."

As she went to kiss Zach, she saw his frightened look.

He's afraid of me. Oh dear God, my son is afraid of me.

"Get some sleep, buddy. Okay?" Jim tucked him in and took the knife from the dresser. He turned off the lights and went downstairs.

Stephanie found her way back to bed. She lay on her back, feeling as awake as she had been when she first heard the noise.

Jim came back into the room and didn't bother turning on the light. He climbed into bed and laid there in silence.

"Jim?"

"Yeah," he said eventually.

"I'm sorry."

There was more silence, and she wondered what he was thinking.

"Jim?"

"Let's just get some rest, okay?"

"I heard something. I know you think I was sleepwalking, but I heard something."

She could tell he was thinking, wondering whether to say something.

"James?" she asked, trying to get him to respond.

"I just found you in our son's room, hovering over him with a knife. *With a knife.*"

Fear raced through Stephanie, and it wasn't at Jim's words. It was at the way he said them. He spoke them as though he was angry at her, as though she were a stranger and not the woman he loved, who had given birth to these children.

She could hear the fear in Jim's voice. And that scared her the most.

Jim was never scared. Of anything.

And now . . .

Jim sounded scared.

Of her.

2

Father–Son Talk

You know I think it's a bad idea."

Jim stared across the kitchen table at his father. Gary Miller was sixty-seven years old, retired, and usually kept his opinions to himself unless they were matters of life and death. Or matters of the soul. Jim loved his father and knew that at thirty-four he took after him in many ways. But sometimes he hated that deep reservoir of contemplation and stoicism. Sometimes Jim wanted his father to sit across the table from him, pop open a couple of beers, and toast to whatever the situation called for.

Not Gary Frederick Miller. Not Pastor Gary Frederick Miller.

His father was a few inches shorter than him and at least fifty pounds lighter. Jim took after his mother's side of the family. Still, Gary Miller didn't look like someone you'd mess with on a street corner. He kept himself in good shape and had an intense look about him, the kind that made Jim determine never to deliberately disobey him for fear of what might be behind that intensity.

"You've said that before," Jim said.

They had just finished the lunch his mom had made them—ham sandwiches, milk, and potato chips. It didn't matter how old he got. Whenever he was in this house, Jim was still their son. Sometimes, many times, he still liked being the son.

But he knew this invitation to come over meant more than sandwiches.

"It's not as though there are just Stephanie and you to think about," Gary said.

The lines around his eyes seemed more deeply etched than Jim remembered.

"You don't have to remind me," Jim said. "You forget we were in Papua New Guinea for two years."

"I didn't forget. This is different."

"How is it different?"

"You've always had people around you."

Jim shook his head. "Sometimes, in the village, we were very much alone."

"You weren't that isolated, Jim. This is different. And there's no reason for it."

He wanted to tell his father the whole story. Everything. He wanted to just get it out, put it on the table, and let him know everything.

Having people around doesn't necessarily mean you're not alone.

But to tell his father that would mean a theological discussion and an opportunity for his father to give a spiritual lesson, and Jim wasn't in the mood.

"I've told you guys. We need to get away."

"Get away from what?"

Jim sipped his milk. Where was this going? He didn't have the energy. Not today. Not now.

"I've been busier in these last four months than I've been in my entire life. That's not what a furlough is supposed to look like."

"It's just the season you're in."

Jim laughed and shook his head. They sat at the same table where his mom had toasted bread for him and cut off the ends so he could pour butter and syrup over them every weekday morning when he was a boy. The same table they'd had in the kitchen for most of his life. The Millers—Mom and Pop Miller, that is—were not big on change. If something worked and made sense, why change it? And if you didn't *have* to move to North Carolina to get away from the busyness of life (not to mention to get away from your parents), why do so?

"I hate that expression," Jim said.

"But it's true. This is a very busy season for you as a father and husband and someone doing God's work. When I was your age—"

"Oh, here we go," Jim said, a resigned smile rising on his lips.

"Now hear me out and don't give me a hard time. When I was your age, our small church was growing by leaps and bounds. And I had four of you to deal with."

"Wait a minute, there are four of me?"

Gary laughed at his son's joke. "Sometimes I think it would have been easier if we'd had only two children, as you do."

"I was a model son."

"You were. No complaints there. Now Luke is another story."

"Yes, he is."

The Millers had been as methodical in their family planning as they were in everything else. First came James, then two years later came Debra, then two years later came Rick, and then an amazing two years later came Luke. Each sibling had a completely unique personality, and all the birth order traits were in full view. Luke was still the lost child, the prodigal son, the boy who hadn't grown up even though he was twenty-eight years old.

The last they had heard, Luke was in Seattle living with a girl, trying to get his band going, and still not buying into what he called "the God thing."

The God thing.

Jim would like to talk to his brother about the whole God thing. It would be an interesting conversation.

"James, you've never been known to make a hasty decision."

"This is not a hasty decision."

"It came about only recently."

"And it's a great opportunity."

"You've never even visited the place. You hardly know anything about this Charles Wolfcott or his brother."

"I'd never visited Dambi either."

"It's just so far away from anybody."

"The closest town is an hour away. So what?"

Gary gave his son what Jim called one of his "heavy looks." Somehow the weight of the world was transferred from that look into Jim's heart and soul. When he was younger, sometimes Jim would look at his father and see the heaviness there as his father went on about Christ's suffering and all the sin in the world and the destination all of us face without the atonement. All of that was somehow transferred with one look, leaving Jim miserable and wretched and lonely.

God is not just about judgment. He is also about love. He is also about grace.

Jim knew his father knew this, but the thing was, Gary never spoke about such things.

I wonder what Dad would think if he knew everything that happened back in Dambi. What sort of spiritualizing would he do after hearing those stories?

Jim knew he would never tell his father what happened. He was still processing it himself, and it would be some time before he would be at peace with everything. If ever.

"We're worried about Stephanie."

There it was. The crux of the issue. Two important words in his father's sentence: *We're* and *Stephanie.*

"And why is that?" Jim asked, baiting him, feeling instantly defensive, feeling the back of his neck tingle and the knot in his gut tighten.

"You know why. We think it's better if she—if all of you—stay around here."

"And why is that?" Again, he knew the answer.

"Just in case you need somebody."

"No, just so you guys can keep tabs on her."

"That's not true."

Jim shook his head and stared at his father without blinking. For years Jim couldn't look at the stern man across from him without backing down, but he was different now.

"Mom checks up on her all the time. It's ridiculous."

"She just likes seeing the children."

"Yeah. And she wants to know how Steph is doing."

"You know Stephanie's had a few episodes."

"They were months ago. I keep telling you they were no big deal. I shouldn't have said anything to begin with."

"We still think it would be good if she got some help."

"She's fine," Jim said. "Look, this isn't about her."

"Yes, in some ways, it is."

"And how's that?"

"There are pressures both of you are under—"

"And you guys add to them."

His father stopped, tightened his lips, then looked down at the table, apparently searching for the right words. Gary Miller didn't lose his temper. That wasn't how he got to people. It was the way he paused, the way he carefully calculated his words, the way he almost seemed to leave you hanging before going on.

"James, you know we love Stephanie."

"You can't run our family the way you run the church."

His dad looked puzzled by the comment. Puzzled and hurt.

"Is that really what you think I'm trying to do?"

"It's hard for you *not* to run anything in your life."

"I'm not trying to control this, Jim. I'm just afraid for you. I've been praying for a long time now, and I feel led to ask you to reconsider."

"How can you 'feel led' when the bottom line is you just don't want us to move away?"

"That's part of it. But there's something else."

"Don't say anything about Steph, okay? Just—that's not really your business. She's fine. She just—she needs some space. All of us do."

"It's not about space," Gary said.

"Then what's it about?"

"I feel that some of these things—that you two are going through a spiritual battle."

"We're just tired. I'm overworked, and I need some time off."

"But things haven't been the same since you came back."

"They're fine," Jim said.

"Satan strikes at us when we're tired and let down our guard."

"I know."

His father's eyes narrowed. "Don't let down your guard, son."

"I won't."

"You need support."

"I have—*we* have plenty of support."

"But you're moving away from all of it," Gary said.

"We're moving away to find some sanity. I'm going to do some writing and a whole lot of reading, and I need to find time to reconnect with my family. Since coming back here, I've barely spent a moment with them."

"You've barely spent time with us either."

"Dad, come on."

"What?"

"This isn't up for discussion. I told you guys before Christmas that we were moving."

"Jim—"

"And we'll be fine. It's going to be like a mini-vacation. I showed you the pictures. The house is beautiful. It's huge."

Jim knew his father would let it be. At least for now. He had broached the issue of Stephanie and voiced his concerns and could now at least say to God that he had tried to do what he "felt called" to do.

How does anybody really truly know God's will?

Moving the family to North Carolina was a good thing. They needed to get away. From his hometown of Wheaton, from his parents, and from the busyness and their five support churches and the work. And, somehow, from the shadow of their last month in Papua New Guinea.

His parents were worried for Stephanie. They wanted her to get "help" before moving.

It had started with the nightmares, then had grown into irrational behavior. At first Jim had talked to his parents about it, but recently he had kept things from them. Things like the other night with Stephanie and the knife.

They overspiritualized things. And they were worried enough as it was. They didn't need to know things like that.

The opportunity to stay at Edge Hill in North Carolina was almost too good to be true. Jim saw it as a chance to get away, to reconnect with Stephanie and the kids, and to sort out the battles that had been waging inside him for the last few months. Dad would call them attacks by Satan. To Dad, the fact that Jim was struggling with faith issues could only mean sin and Satan and all those bad things that happened when you actually started asking questions.

"We'll be praying that God will watch over your family," Gary said as Jim rose to leave.

I'm his son, Jim thought. *Why does he sound like he's speaking to a member of his church?*

"Thanks," Jim said.

In his car, thinking about their conversation and the last thing his father had said, Jim wondered if God was indeed watching over his family.

It was nice to say and nice to hear, but it was one of those things he wondered about. As a missionary supported by five churches and overseeing God's work in the small village of Dambi, Jim wasn't supposed to have such thoughts.

But they were becoming more and more common.

And God was becoming more and more quiet.

3

Zachary

Zachary watched the houses pass by as he sat in the front seat of his parents' Volvo wagon. He missed Dambi—the freedom of the nearby jungle and the river that ran through the village. He missed the people, especially Tawi, who was like a second dad to him. Looking at these lawns and the large houses, Zachary couldn't get over how crowded everything seemed.

"You're quiet today," Mom said.

He nodded. They passed the elementary school he had attended since moving to Wheaton in September. He was going to miss this school and his new friends, especially Bobby and Taylor and Sam. But he missed Dambi even more.

"Everything okay?" she asked.

Sometimes if he was really quiet Mom got worried and made him talk. Dad wasn't like that. Dad liked the silence and could be around Zach for a long time without saying a word.

"Yeah," he said.

"What're you thinking about?"

"Nothing."

Zachary looked at his mom. She was beautiful. She was tall and thin and had long, straight, dark brown hair. He liked it when she smiled. He liked her in jeans too, something she hadn't worn back in Dambi.

"Are you looking forward to the movie tonight?"

He nodded. He didn't want to say he had forgotten about it. Zachary loved seeing movies. Normally he'd be dying to see this one. But he couldn't help worrying about everything, about Mom and Dad and the upcoming move.

"Mom?"

"Yes?"

"Why don't you want to move to North Carolina?"

Mom looked at him for a moment, as though searching for words. Her face seemed pale and her eyes troubled.

"I never said I didn't want to move to North Carolina."

"You told Dad that the other night."

She glanced at him with a look that said, *Got me.*

"It's not that I don't want to move. It's just—sometimes Dad and I disagree on things."

"Are you scared of moving?"

"No, of course not. Not at all."

Mom took his hand and clenched it, as if that action would prove that she wasn't scared. She was quiet again. Zachary wondered why adults sometimes worked so hard at trying to say the right thing.

"Your father and I want what's best for all of us, Zach. And sometimes we need to talk things through."

"Dad's excited about it."

"I know he is. He's been very busy. And he wants all of us to have a chance to get away and spend more time with each other."

"Are you worried because of the nightmares?"

His mother cleared her throat and tightened her lips, looking at Zachary and slowing down the car as they approached a stoplight.

"No, that's not why I'm worried, Zach."

"Why do you have them?"

"We don't know. I think—I'm not sure. I'm going to see if a doctor can help me get better sleep."

"Is that why you don't want to move? Because there are no doctors around there?"

"I didn't say I don't want to move. And I'm sure there are doctors around there."

"Dad said the nearest big city is a couple hours away."

"But there are doctors that live closer. There's a small town only an hour away."

"What if something happens to one of us?"

He saw something in Mom's face change, something that gave her away. Something that said, *That's exactly why I'm scared*.

Zachary could read his mom well. Most of the time she told him what she was thinking, and the other times he simply had to ask enough questions to get an idea.

Dad wasn't like that. Zachary rarely knew exactly what his dad was thinking.

"Nothing is going to happen to us," Mom said, the worried look gone.

"But what about everything that happened in the village?"

She grew more stern.

"Don't think about that anymore," she said sharply. "That's not anything we want to talk about."

She turned down their street and pulled up in the driveway. As Zachary opened the car door, she took his hand again.

"Zach, things are going to be fine. And Mommy's going to get better."

"I know," he said, believing her.

"It will just take a little while to get used to the idea of moving. Again."

He nodded and wanted to say something but didn't have the words. She kissed his cheek and let him go.

4

Scared

All she wanted was to be able to tell somebody what she was feeling. Somebody. Anybody. But she was afraid of what the reaction might be.

Stephanie looked at the tall caramel mocha in her hands. She'd drunk only half and already felt nauseated from the sugar overload. She glanced at Michelle's small cup of coffee as she waited for her friend to come back from the ladies' room.

It was January 5, and they were a week away from moving. She felt anxious. Actually, anxious was putting it mildly, but that was all she allowed herself to reveal to others. What she wanted to say was that she had been dreading the move ever since they decided months ago to go ahead and do it.

Jim decided. Just like he decides everything.

It wasn't like she was some delicate wallflower who did whatever he told her to do. And Jim wasn't the sort of man who made things all about himself and his way. But once he decided on something, it was pretty much final. Who was she to argue when she didn't have any other ideas? Soon the house they occupied now would no longer be theirs to rent—another missionary family was moving in two weeks from now. The opportunity to move had come up suddenly, and at first Stephanie had been excited just like Jim. The unease came shortly after, and for some reason it had grown.

There are reasons why, and they don't have anything to do with the move.

She didn't want to think back to their last few weeks in Dambi, to the events that occurred right before they left. Sometimes she woke up in the middle of the night thinking about them, only to have Jim touch her arm and tell her she was okay. Those were the good nights. The nights that scared her were the ones she didn't recall the next morning, when Jim asked her if she remembered wandering around in the crawl space in the basement or sitting on their front lawn in her pajamas.

Then there was the other night. When she knew someone was in their house. She still believed someone had been there. But how could she make Jim believe her?

Michelle touched her on the shoulder as she passed by, then sat across from her. "Sorry, there was a line."

"That's okay."

"This place is always busy."

"Isn't there another Starbucks five minutes away?"

Michelle nodded her head as she sipped her coffee. "In Danada Square. I think this one is more crowded since it's downtown."

Stephanie could see the train tracks running through the heart of Wheaton. The day outside looked gray and cold. The forecast had predicted snow, but so far there was nothing but chilling winds and bleak skies. The Monday afternoon traffic was getting busier the closer it got to five o'clock.

"So how are the in-laws?" Michelle asked.

"They've been giving us privacy, believe it or not. But they're not very happy we're moving."

"How come?"

"They think the house is too remote. They don't like the idea that we'll be up there in the middle of nowhere."

"You said there's another family staying in the house already, right?"

Stephanie nodded. "An older couple. It might be like staying with Jim's folks."

They both laughed, giving each other a knowing glance.

Michelle and her husband, Tim, had been Jim and Stephanie's friends for the last ten years. They met in a newlywed class and quickly developed into close friends. There were three other couples in their small group as well, a support team who prayed for and helped them. It felt good to share a common history and understanding.

"How's Jim doing?"

"Okay, I guess."

"Steph."

"What?"

"Come on. What's going on?"

"What do you mean?"

"You look worried and tired. Are you okay?"

No, I'm not. I'm scared and I'm fed up and I want Jim and the kids to move away and I want to stay here by myself.

"I just wish things weren't so hectic. Especially for Jim."

"But that's why you guys are moving, right? Things will be better."

Michelle's no-nonsense quality was one of the reasons Stephanie loved her. *Why aren't there women elders in the church, and why can't they serve Communion, and what's the big deal with having a beer every now and then, and why can't Christians get off their high horses sometimes?* Michelle's ideas didn't always fit in with some of the other women in their church. Neither did her unconditional concern, a care that still surprised Stephanie on occasion.

"Do you want to know something horrible?" Stephanie asked, looking around to see if anybody they knew sat nearby.

"What?"

Just say it. Go ahead and say it. She'll understand.

"Sometimes I wish . . ."

"Wish what?"

"I wish—sometimes I wish I weren't with Jim. That we weren't . . ."

Michelle waited for a moment, then asked, "That you weren't what?"

"Together."

Michelle's gaze didn't waver. "I understand."

"That's such a horrible thing to say. It's not like I don't love him; I do. It's just—sometimes. I don't know. I wonder. I wonder a lot these days."

"About what?"

Stephanie licked her dry lips. "I wonder where I would be if we hadn't—you know—gotten married. I sometimes thought that when we were in Dambi. I just felt—I've felt so alone. Even with Zach and Ashley. It's just not the same. And Jim can't understand sometimes what I need—what a woman needs. He's so busy, and he leaves so many of the family duties up to me, and sometimes I get so overwhelmed and tired. I feel like we're going right back to somewhere that's in the middle of nowhere, with nobody around to talk to or to have coffee with or . . ." Stephanie's eyes filled, and she brushed away the tears.

Michelle reached across and touched her hand. "It's going to be okay. *You're* going to be okay."

"I don't know. Sometimes I wonder."

"You need to get Jim to understand that it's not just about him."

"It's just that he's so busy—he's got this book project, and he knows he shouldn't have taken it on, but we needed the money and now it's taking so much of his time—"

"You don't have to defend him, Steph. It's okay. I know Jim. I know what he's like."

"He's a good man."

"I didn't say he wasn't. But you're a good wife. A good mate. He needs to realize there are two of you in the marriage."

Stephanie wiped her eyes again and looked around the coffee shop. "I'm just worried that the move will make things worse."

"How would it do that?"

"Maybe instead of connecting, we'll be driven further apart."

Michelle nodded. She and Tim weren't the perfect couple, and Stephanie knew they had gone through a couple of years of counseling.

"Jim loves me and the kids so much," Stephanie said.

Michelle smiled. "I know. And you love them too. You guys are going to be okay. The trip is going to be good for all of you."

I'm scared of leaving.

Stephanie knew she could tell her friend a lot, but she couldn't tell her everything.

Does anybody ever share everything *about themselves?*

There were a lot of things even Jim didn't know.

SNOW STARTED TO FALL. The heavy kind that looked almost un-real—thick flakes that filled the sky and stuck in your hair and on your arms and shoulders. Stephanie hugged Michelle good-bye and got into her Maxima. For a moment she didn't move, just sat in the sanctuary of the car, the flakes covering it and shielding her from the outside. She wept and tried to let the emptiness and awful sorrow flow out of her.

"God, why is this happening?"

Was that even a prayer? She was tired of praying and wondering and hoping and trying and waiting.

Stephanie knew she hadn't prayed a sincere and deep prayer for some time. All she could offer God were the cries of her heart. Cries like *Where are You?* and *What are You doing?* and *Why is this happening?*

But there was no answer. No word and no nothing.

She started the car and began to drive. Suburbia had suddenly been painted all in white. Their house was only ten minutes away. She drove down Main Street and stopped at a light and waited, watching her windshield wipers brush away the heavy flakes. They were coming down hard now, and she could barely see through her windshield.

Stephanie turned up the heat in the borrowed Maxima. It belonged to a church family. Jim had the station wagon today.

When were they not borrowing or renting or taking as a gift? When would something be theirs, legitimately theirs?

She needed to think about dinner and talk to her mother-in-law, who was babysitting the kids, and then see what sort of mood Jim was in when he came home. Recently, he had been unusually distant. Part of it had to come from her "episodes," as they referred to them. Jim knew something was up, but he couldn't fix it and couldn't get Stephanie to do something about it.

Suddenly a dark smudge spotted her windshield. *That's weird.* It was almost as though a clump of mud had landed on the glass.

She looked ahead, visibility strained as snow pounded against her car.

Again something hit the windshield, splattering and dripping until the wipers brushed it away. This time it left a dirty coating, streaks of something dark and grimy.

Stephanie slowed down and concentrated on the windshield to see what was happening.

A loud smack startled her. Something dark red and almost meaty clumped against the windshield.

What the . . .

It loosened, and small clusters dropped and smeared across the windshield. Even before they could be wiped away, another thick mass struck the windshield and scattered all over the glass.

They were almost like clumps of snow-dampened mud. But not exactly. More like . . . like . . . *flesh.*

The thought was ridiculous.

Another thud struck the windshield, this time harder, as though it had been thrown. It disintegrated into wet, dripping grime. Stephanie slowed the car and stopped.

Something hit the top of her car. Something else. More. As though it was hailing. Her windshield was grimy and disgusting and covered in something—something she couldn't recognize.

A thick, gooey mass hit the side of her window, and something that looked like intestines slithered down the glass.

God, what is happening? What is this?

The snow falling no longer looked white, but dark red and melted as soon as it hit the window. It looked like blood seeping down and making streaks as the wipers moved back and forth.

Stephanie was paralyzed. She breathed in and smelled something horrible.

death that's what I smell I know that smell well

For a brief second she saw something from a long time ago, and it made her sick with fear.

Suddenly the smell and the grime and the light-headedness and the knot in her stomach were all too much. She keeled over and threw up on the floorboard of the passenger seat.

The car shook loudly, and she saw a huge, hulking mess in the middle of the windshield, leaking and oozing, red and wet.

God, help me! What's happening? What's going on?

Her eyes watered, and she shut them tight and breathed in through her nose until she coughed.

Another loud bang made the car shudder.

She kept her eyes closed.

Help me God help me please God

Her hands and her body shook, and she didn't want to look but she knew she had to. She imagined her entire car surrounded by these—things—whatever they were. They looked like flesh and blood, and Stephanie knew it was crazy, but she couldn't stop seeing and hearing and feeling.

Please God help me please God please

She opened one eye and saw the street in front of her, the snow still falling hard, the trees covered in white. Nothing was on the windshield or on the window next to her. Nothing except snow.

What just happened?

She looked at the seat next to her. Her vomit was real. The pungent acrid smell filled the car. For a second she thought about unrolling her window, but then decided against it. A car passed her, driving slowly down the slippery street.

I'm losing my mind. I'm seriously losing my mind.

Her eyes started to tear, this time out of fear and terror.

I can't tell anybody. I'm going crazy, and I can't tell a single soul.

She put her hands on the steering wheel and saw them shaking. Finally she put the car in drive and started moving again, slowly. She stared at the windshield, the flakes coming down, the wipers brushing away the snow.

Nothing abnormal. Nothing dark or red or gross. She drove slowly, and at the stop sign where she should have turned onto her street, she continued to go straight. This wasn't her car; she needed to stop at a gas station and clean it up before Jim came home.

Her hands wouldn't stop shaking. She tried to get control over herself. But control was something she had not had for a very long time.

5

Morning

A staple for every Christian man in the suburbs was the 6:00 AM breakfast meeting. It was something every good, up-standing, faith-filled man needed to do with another brother on a regular basis. If he did it on a weekly basis, well, that was almost a sign of sainthood.

Jim couldn't help his thoughts as he drank his third cup of coffee and listened to the well-dressed man across from him talk about the struggles of trying to find prayer time every day. Todd Baker had asked Jim several times to do breakfast, and Jim finally ran out of excuses. Todd did financial consulting and was very well off, yet even with his busy schedule he somehow made it a point to take out the church's missionaries, to get to know them, and to pray for them. Jim appreciated the man's heart and his upbeat attitude, but he wished it could have been a later breakfast. Or maybe a lunch. But who was he to say no? And how could he tell Todd that Stephanie had had another night of uneasy sleep, that she had gotten up several times, and that Jim hadn't been able to go back to sleep for fear of what Stephanie might do?

"Edge Hill is really going to be amazing once it's up and running," Todd said suddenly, out of the blue.

The statement surprised Jim. "How do you know about Edge Hill?"

"I'm on the missions board. But even before that, I'd heard of Charles Wolfcott. He's a big name on Wall Street. The guy is legendary, but a little strange."

"How so?"

"Didn't they tell you about him?"

"No. I mean, not really. It was purely accidental that I heard about the lodge. I was preaching at a church in Fort Myers, and a guy approached me afterward and asked how long we were going to be in the States. Turns out he's Wolfcott's brother. Said there was this large cabin—a mountain lodge—that was empty, and that he was planning to use it for missionaries on furlough. He had only been there once, and he said they planned on fixing it up. I didn't even realize until later that his brother was *the* Charles Wolfcott of Edge Communications."

Todd pushed his plate away and took the last sip of orange juice. His eyes had gotten more intense as he looked at Jim. "Wolfcott was eccentric. Owned ten or fifteen houses. The last house he ever built was the lodge in the Smoky Mountains. Have you been there yet?"

"No, I've just heard about it. And seen pictures."

"Supposedly it's massive. It's on a large stretch of land that Wolfcott bought for privacy. He wanted to make a place where he could retire, get away from the world, but he never had the opportunity. He was only in his fifties when he died."

"What'd he die of?" Jim asked.

"They didn't say."

"Who are 'they'?"

"I know a company that used to work with Wolfcott. They knew a lot of things about him. They knew how weird he was."

"Weird how?"

Todd shrugged, seeming uncomfortable. "It's just guys I know talking. They said Wolfcott was into some strange stuff. Dark stuff, you know?"

Jim nodded. "I did some looking online about Wolfcott. Found a lot of interesting information. For a while I wasn't sure—but I spoke to a local pastor from the area who personally went to the lodge to pray over it and bless it. I also talked with the couple staying there—they're good people."

"It's awesome that God is using something for His glory that was initially made for the glory of man."

"Yeah."

"I've seen pictures of the place too. It looks amazing. The deck stands around four stories tall and seems to go on forever."

"My parents think I'm crazy for moving there because it's in the middle of nowhere."

"It's not *that* remote."

"Our village in Papua New Guinea was far more remote, obviously. I think they just want us to stay near them."

"Are you looking forward to moving?"

"Very much so." *Stephanie is another story.*

"Do they get a lot of snow?"

"Supposedly. The Pattersons—they're a missionary couple in their sixties who've been there for a couple of months—said they've gotten a few heavy snows. There's one road up the mountain and that's it. When it snows, they're stuck."

"So what are your plans going to be the next few months?"

Jim rubbed his face and thought for a moment. "I'm looking forward to relaxing, to be honest. I've got a few projects—a writing project, along with some research I'm wanting to do. Reading, of course. But the main thing I'm looking forward to is spending time with my family. Just—just getting away from the busyness of everything."

"Edge Hill sounds like the perfect place to do that."

THE SNOW FROM YESTERDAY'S storm had mostly melted away, leaving everything damp and dirty. Jim loved snow, and he hated it when the temperature rose just enough to melt most of it. The plowed piles turned into muddy ice on the edges of the streets. Everything looked barren and cold. To make things worse, it was still overcast, with no hint the sun would be shining through today.

Jim turned up the volume of the classic rock station. It was nice to be back in the States, to drive down the road and grab a burger at McDonald's or turn on the radio and hear Zeppelin or anything he recognized. It was nice to be back in civilization. He hadn't minded being far away in an isolated part of the world, but sometimes he'd missed the conveniences Americans lived with every day.

Even staying at the lodge in North Carolina would have its benefits. There was still Internet and cable and satellite and cell service. In Dambi there was hardly anything like that. They could send e-mails, but they had to conserve energy. During the day it was fine because the generator was solar powered, but there was only a certain amount they could use at nighttime.

The music reminded him of his brothers. He wondered how they were doing, especially Luke. He thought back to the last time he saw him. They'd talked over a beer at a local pub, and Luke said he believed God was dead or at least acted like it and that he wanted nothing to do with Him. Nothing whatsoever.

"You can have your beliefs, that's fine, and I'm not going to give you a hard time for moving halfway around the world for them, but you'd better not try to shove them down my throat."

That was one of Luke's last comments to him—a fairly drunk Luke who was being driven home by Jim.

How many years ago had that been? Three? Four?

Time passes too quickly.

He glanced at the clock. 8:30 AM. He would be home for a while and then do a list of errands, most of them pertaining to the upcoming move. His stomach still felt full from breakfast, and his mind was racing from the cups of coffee he had consumed.

People said he was into some strange stuff. Dark stuff.

He wondered what Todd meant by dark stuff. Sexual deviance? Demonic activity? "Dark" could mean a lot of things. It had to be more than simply being a control freak or a germaphobe. He'd seen a lot of darkness in the world. He thought back to his last few weeks in Dambi. His body tensed up, and he felt goose bumps. He didn't want to think about it, but sometimes he couldn't help it. He could still feel the presence of the enemy and how strong he had been during those last few weeks.

Jim pulled into the driveway and instantly buried the thoughts. They were his and his alone. At least he could spare Stephanie and the children from seeing or feeling any of it.

Even though Stephanie was going through her own struggles recently, he knew they were different from what he'd gone through right before their move back to the States. It's one thing to be stressed and anxious; it's another to be attacked on every spiritual level possible.

He went inside, and immediately he could hear Ashley's cries. "Steph?" he called out.

He passed the family room, then followed the cries toward the kitchen. They were shrill and panicky, as though Ashley had been crying for some time.

God no God no

He felt a wave of fear rush through him as he entered the kitchen and saw Ashley sitting on the kitchen floor, wailing and red-eyed, looking at her mommy passed out on the wood floor.

"Steph!"

Jim grabbed Ashley up with one hand and touched Stephanie's face. It felt cold

she's dead

and he looked around to see if there was blood or vomit or anything like a knife, but there was nothing to be found.

"It's okay, sweetie. It's okay," he said, setting Ashley down next to Steph on the floor. "Daddy's here. Daddy's here."

He held Stephanie's face and felt sick and overwhelmed. He called out her name over and over.

"Steph, Steph, come on, Steph."

He felt her neck, but forgot where to find a pulse. He held his wife in terror.

God she feels cold she's dead Stephanie is dead

Then he saw her eyes move and her eyebrows raise the way they did in the morning when she woke up.

"Steph? Steph, are you okay?"

Ashley was still crying. Where was Zach? Jim breathed in, forcing himself to take one thing at a time.

"Steph, hey, come on—are you okay?"

His wife was opening her eyes. That was good. She wasn't dead.

Ashley continued to cry.

"Where's Zach?" he asked his wife, but she just looked at him, groggy and out of it.

"It's going to be okay," he said as he laid her back down and went for the phone to call 911.

"Steph, what happened?" Jim sat back down on the floor and held her in his arms, but she didn't say anything; she just continued to look around as though she didn't know where she was.

Ashley continued to cry.

And Zach—where was Zach?

6

Stress

Jim looked at the woman in the bed, the closed eyes, the straight brown hair falling to one side, the slender but strong hands resting at her sides. He stared at her and wondered what was going on inside her, what was causing her nightmares and sleepwalking and now this blackout. He worried it was something to do with the move . . . that ultimately it was something to do with him. Sometimes Jim wondered if in the last few years of serving in Papua New Guinea, the two of them had lost something. He wondered if the passion and the care and ultimately the love that had been there from the beginning had evaporated in the stress of trying to be parents and spouses and missionaries.

He took Stephanie's hand and held it. He wanted to say so much to her. Then again, he wanted to say a few things to God too, but he couldn't. He wouldn't. He shouldn't. All those things and more, and here he was, unable to look his wife in the face and kiss her and tell her he loved her. It was the same way with God. He couldn't pray because he felt like he had no right to ask for anything. Could he knock on a stranger's house and ask for a favor?

"Jim?" a soft voice spoke.

Her eyes weren't open, but she had felt his touch.

"I'm right here, Steph."

"What happened?" she asked, her eyes slowly opening, looking around the hospital room.

"You blacked out."

"Where are Ash—Zach—"

"They're okay. My parents are with them."

Stephanie groaned.

"It's okay. I told them you had a fainting spell. They think you're pregnant."

"It's just more . . ." She trailed off, looking as though she was trying to make sense of her surroundings.

"How are you feeling?" Jim asked. He had let go of her hand.

"Tired. And really groggy."

"Do you remember what happened?"

Stephanie frowned. "I was in the kitchen and—and I don't know. I just remember feeling light-headed and hot and dizzy."

"Have you felt that way before?"

"Maybe I am pregnant," she said, trying to make a joke.

"I think that would be impossible."

She nodded. "I was just kidding."

He wanted to say more, to ask more, to see if it was the stress of the upcoming move or the busyness of being around Wheaton or if he had caused any of this. But he didn't want to overwhelm her or add to the stress.

"Look, you need to rest."

"The kids—"

"They're fine. Seriously. I'll call Mom and Dad and tell them you're okay."

"What about the doctor?"

"I'll get him. It's okay. They're going to do some tests and see what's going on."

Jim got up to go find the nurse. Before he could leave the room, Stephanie called out his name, and he turned.

"I'm sorry," she said, a look of embarrassment and confusion on her face.

"It's okay."

"I'm sorry I've been acting so—so crazy lately."

She looked so pale and desperate and lonely. He wanted to go to her and embrace her and tell her he loved her and tell her that everything was going to be fine.

But he stood, his six-foot-three frame immovable.

"It's going to be fine," he said to her, giving her a conciliatory smile.

∾

"WELL, I GUESS it's official. I'm losing my mind."

Jim looked at Stephanie and had to laugh. At least she could make jokes about it.

"You're not losing your mind."

"No, I guess I lost my mind some time ago. I've finally given up trying to find it."

"Would you stop?"

"Jim, it's fine. I'm fine. Really. Let's just get back to your parents'. I can't *wait* to hear what they'll say."

"They're not going to say anything," Jim said. "I promise you that."

He had spoken with his father before leaving the hospital and had specifically told him not to say anything out of line: *You know, Stephanie, if you took better care of yourself* . . . Or to make it into a spiritual matter: *Perhaps you need to be praying more and letting go and letting God.* Jim had warned him, and he knew his father would heed his request.

"I wish I had something to tell them," she said, looking out the passenger side window. "Something. Anything."

"It's just a combination of stress and fatigue."

"Everybody gets stressed and fatigued," Stephanie replied. "Not everybody passes out in the kitchen in front of their children."

"The doctors said everything appeared normal."

"And you say it's good news."

"Okay, I'm sorry. Too bad they didn't say you've come down with cancer."

"Jim—"

"Well, what do you want me to say?"

"I don't need to go to a shrink."

"It's a psychiatrist, and there are reasons people go to see them."

"Do you want to go see one?"

Jim gripped the steering wheel. He didn't want to argue. "Just think about it," he said.

"Don't tell your parents the doctor suggested I go."

"You really think I would?"

"I don't know."

"Maybe you can go talk to a doctor before we leave."

"I don't need to see a psychiatrist. I'm fine. I'm just—I'm just tired and not sleeping. When you don't get sleep, a lot of things can happen."

"But this has been going on for some time now."

"It's just been the last few months."

"Don't you think that's long enough?"

She gave him a sharp look. Perhaps if she felt stronger, Stephanie might have made a defensive comment back at him. But the look on her face spoke of resignation. And fatigue.

"Steph, I just—"

"It's okay. I'll go. I'll talk to a doctor or whoever. It's fine."

He slowed down the car and reached to take her hand. But she moved her hand to stroke back her hair. Jim awkwardly drew back, trying to act nonchalant.

"What?" Stephanie asked.

"Nothing."

"What? I said I'd go. You don't have to have that look on your face."

He wondered what she saw. He couldn't help the intensity on his face sometimes. What she and others sometimes saw as anger or frustration was really deep down hurt or sadness.

"I'm not angry, Steph."

"Yes, you are. You're angry all the time. Angry or frustrated or overwhelmed."

"Not all the time. I'm not angry now."

She shook her head and glanced out the window.

At least we're talking.

"Steph . . . ," he began.

"What?"

Jim gazed at the pretty houses belonging to the pretty families in this pretty neighborhood. He felt empty and exhausted.

"Nothing."

7

The Phone Call

Zachary knew something was wrong.

For some time now he had known his parents weren't okay. But he was beginning to think it might not be all about the move. His mom and dad were getting worse, and ever since he had found his mother passed out on the kitchen floor, Zachary had been scared.

Something bad is coming. I can feel it.

When he saw Mom on the floor, he ran upstairs to his room.
To pray. That was where he felt most comfortable praying, and
he didn't know what else to do.

I should have done something else. I should have called 911.

Dad asked him what happened, and Zach said he had been
in his room playing when Mom fainted. Dad didn't ask what he
was playing. Of course he trusted Zach. And Zach wasn't lying.
He just didn't want to get into a discussion with his dad about
praying. He knew that might not go so well.

Something's wrong with Mom. With both of them.

But it was nothing, they told him. It was just her fainting, her
not feeling well, the strain of a variety of different adult things that
made her not sleep well and feel stressed. They still spoke to him
sometimes as though he were a little baby. There were things he
understood about his parents, things about them they didn't have to
say or even do. He knew they were worried and bothered, his mom
especially. He knew about her nightmares and her sleeplessness. He
saw her in the mornings, saw the look of fear on her face.

She's had it ever since Dambi. Both of them have.

They hadn't talked to him about the last few weeks in Dambi,
the sickness that had torn through the village, their arguments
about whether or not to leave. Zach had tried to talk about it a
few times with Mom, but each time she had made it clear not to
go there. As if avoiding it would make everything better.

Nothing's getting better. Things are just getting worse.

It was 8:40 in the morning, and he was watching television. Dad
had gone to the college to do some work while Mom was upstairs
with Ashley. Watching television was one of the good things about
being back in the States, though Zachary still enjoyed reading more.
He had read some books three and four times in the village, including the entire Chronicles of Narnia. His dad said he was almost old
enough to start reading *The Lord of the Rings* by Tolkien.

The phone rang, and Mom called out for him to get it. She
must be busy with Ashley—maybe giving her a bath or helping

her get dressed. The only phone was a cordless in the kitchen. Zachary stood up and found the receiver.

"Hello?"

"Is Jim Miller there?"

It was an adult voice, strong and deep and slow.

"No, I'm sorry."

Say he's busy. Don't say he's not here.

"He's busy," Zachary added.

"Is this Zachary?"

"Yes."

Zachary wasn't paying attention to the voice. He could still see the television from where he stood. It was a cartoon he hadn't seen before.

"Are you ready to move, Zach?"

The question got his attention, and he suddenly wondered who was calling.

"Yes."

"That's good. When do you move?"

Zachary suddenly felt uncomfortable. The voice sounded friendly enough, maybe a little too friendly. Mom and Dad had told him about strangers, about being careful when he was on his own. They hadn't said much about unknown callers. It wasn't like they got a lot of prank calls in Dambi.

"Who is calling?" he asked, trying to be polite in his response.

"How old are you, Zach?"

The question scared him. The tone and the deliberate, slow words . . .

"Eight."

"Do you want to know something, Zachary? Do you want to know something I know?"

Hang up the phone. Hang up the phone and call Mom.

But he couldn't say anything or do anything. He just froze, his hand gripping the phone, listening to the eerie voice on the other end.

"You're never going to see your ninth birthday, Zach. You're never going to get off that mountain in North Carolina. Do you know why? Because you're going to die up there, Zach. I've seen it. You're going to—"

He dropped the receiver and heard it crack as it hit the wood floor. He ran to the bathroom and locked the door behind him. Everything in him felt sick and dizzy and petrified. He didn't cry. Zach didn't cry very often. But he was afraid, and his whole body shook.

The man's voice had changed at the end, had turned rougher and deeper somehow.

That's your imagination.

It had sounded pure evil. Sick and twisted and dark.

You're going crazy just like Mom.

Zach sat in the bathroom, breathing in and out, trying to stop shaking, wondering what to do.

He couldn't tell Mom. Of course not. She wasn't able to handle something like this. It had to be a joke, right? But how did the caller know his name?

It had to be a prank or someone who didn't like Dad or someone from the church being stupid.

He closed his eyes and started to pray. Just as he had when he'd found Mom. He asked God to protect him, to watch over all of them. He knew God heard his words.

"Zach? Where are you?"

He stood up and breathed in and knew he had to be strong for Mom.

"Did you drop the phone?"

He couldn't tell her what happened. Maybe he would tell Dad. But not now. Not when things were so bad with both of them.

Zach knew they needed to move, to get out of the town and to finally not be so busy.

He opened the bathroom door.

"I'm sorry—I just really had to go," he said.

As she lectured him about taking care of things that didn't belong to them, Zachary thought of the caller and the words he'd said.

He felt cold and wanted to hug his mom, but he couldn't. He didn't want to show his fear. He wasn't crazy. He knew what he had heard, and he would tell Dad about it. Later.

8

Dreams/Memories

Even though Stephanie knew she was tucked underneath the covers of her king-sized bed next to a snoring Jim, she found herself walking through her old house in Michigan at the same time. She was eight years old and had been awakened from her sleep and was walking down the carpeted stairs to see where the noise was coming from.

Don't.

This wasn't a dream or a nightmare. It was a real memory, and she was replaying it like a scene selection from a DVD. It was the movie of her life, and she hadn't selected this scene or even thought of it for some time.

Don't go down there.

Her bare feet touched the cold linoleum tile. A night-light lit up the hall as she walked toward the kitchen.

The door to the basement was cracked open, and she could see the sliver of light coming from behind it.

Don't go down don't open it go back to bed

But the little girl didn't hear her and couldn't turn back.

She touched the handle of the door and slowly opened it. Voices came from downstairs.

This was the house she had lived in her whole life, the house both she and her brother had been raised in, the house at the end of Willoughby Drive. It was in Grandville, a neighboring city of Grand Rapids. She and Paul went to the elementary school a few minutes away from their house. Paul was three years older and in sixth grade.

The voices sounded strange. Adult, distant, secret.

She stepped on the top stair and started to go down.

Don't go don't go please don't go

But the eight-year-old Stephanie continued down the stairs while the noise continued to get louder.

It wasn't just her mother and father. There were other voices, other people.

When had others come to the house? she wondered.

God please don't please little girl stop walking go back to bed

She heard strange sounds. Sounds she had never heard before. Sounds that scared her, that made her want to turn around, that made her feel slightly sick.

These are adults and Mom and Dad have told me about adults and it's not for me to see yet.

She was almost near the bottom. They had a full basement downstairs with thick carpet and an area to "entertain" as her parents called it. There was a pool table and a bar and a stereo, and she and Paul weren't allowed down there unless her parents were there.

She stepped onto the carpet.

No don't don't go back close your eyes close your eyes Stephanie don't

She looked across the room to see the pool table and the figures around it and the sheet placed over it.

What is that?

She saw the face of her mother, looking at her, not with surprise or anger but with a delirious grin that scared her more than anything else she saw.

No no no no no

The thirty-three-year-old Stephanie finally willed herself to wake up with a gasp and a jerk. She sat up on the bed and felt her heart racing and tried to get the picture out of her mind. It didn't really happen. It couldn't have.

She stopped thinking of the images in her head. Maybe she really did need to talk to a doctor. She heard Jim snoring next to her, and she lay back down on the bed, her eyes wide open, staring into the darkness.

It never happened. It never happened and I imagined it and no matter what I think of my parents this never—it couldn't have. It didn't happen.

She thought of her family and suddenly wanted to call her brother. It had been a while—several months in fact—since she had spoken with Paul. It had been a few years since she'd seen him. She missed his protective presence. She needed to call him. Maybe she could get him to come to North Carolina to visit. Maybe she could ask him what happened at the house at the end of Willoughby Drive.

But she knew he would say nothing. He would say they had a childhood like a lot of other kids, with stupid selfish parents who no longer cared about them.

But Paul cared. And that was enough for her.

Late Night

The next night it was Jim who couldn't sleep. It was past midnight, and he sat at the kitchen table, one lamp in the corner of the family room providing dim light. He turned off his old laptop that had seen better days. Sometime in the next six months he hoped to replace the ancient thing before they headed back to Papua New Guinea.

He had been checking e-mail and had gotten one from a teammate in Dambi. Their close friend and coworker, Tawi, was still sick even though there had been a bedside vigil going on for him the last week and a half. So many prayers offered up from the little village, and so many of them unanswered. Other villagers who had recently come to faith were now starting to lose it, asking questions of this God who had been deemed mighty and powerful. The teammate out in Dambi reported another demon possession.

Other e-mail included family issues and prayer requests. Jim eventually had to stop reading. So much sadness. So much heaviness. In the silent semidarkness, he wanted to pray. He really did. But he felt so distant from God. He knew God was above, watching, waiting, but he wondered how he could approach Him with full faith. Jim felt a heaviness beyond anything he'd ever experienced.

God, what do You want of me?

He felt like he had given the Lord his life. All of it. But now, somehow, he was holding back. He wanted to pray, but he was afraid of what God might say. He was afraid that God might urge him to do something else. Maybe not move. Maybe reconsider being a missionary. Maybe reconsider a lot of things. Sometimes he wished he didn't live in a Christian bubble where the expressions and sentiments of believers all took on the same flavor. *We're praying for you* and *You're doing the Lord's work* and *God is watching over you* and a hundred other trite clichés he'd heard time and time again.

How about this one? I'm afraid God doesn't really care. I'm afraid I'm doing all of this for nothing. That this faith and love and hope I talk about and try to show others doesn't really have any meaning in my own life.

Jim closed his eyes. He was tired. Worried too. Worried about the move in three days. Worried that their car wouldn't make it, that the kids would get sick on the drive, that something would be wrong with the house, or that they wouldn't get along with the older couple at the lodge. He was concerned mostly for Stephanie and her state of mind. He wanted to do something for her, but he could barely talk to her about it. About anything.

He was worried and fearful of the growing rift between them and knew a move wouldn't solve it.

Lay all your troubles before the Lord.

And then what?

It was just another tired Christian cliché.

Jim had laid a whole lot of troubles before the Lord in Dambi, and it hadn't done much good. Prayers went unanswered. It was almost like each prayer had a reverse effect.

Jim wanted this trip to be good for himself and his family. He would reconnect with Steph and the kids, and they'd have time to themselves without the busyness of Wheaton and all its churches and people. They could concentrate on themselves and their family.

But now Jim wondered if the move would only make things worse.

He wanted to pray to God for safety and for help and to restore hope inside him. But he didn't know how. This was Jim Miller who had gotten behind the pulpit just a week ago to talk about his ministry overseas, and yet he couldn't even manage a simple prayer.

All he felt was fear. And he knew it wasn't going to go away anytime soon.

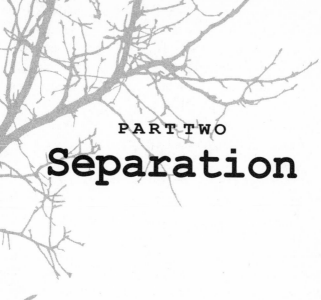

PART TWO
Separation

10

Monster

There is strength in numbers and, God, You know we're strong.

In the darkness of the rented car, he waited patiently. The four-door, nondescript Ford sat parked in the lot next to a Denny's facing the two-story apartment building. The engine was off, and he listened to music from his iPod, which had more than seven thousand songs in it. Quite a variety, depending on his mood and his mission. Tonight, it was appropriately loud. Tonight, the tunes were violent.

He closed his eyes and saw her face, her rolling eyes, her enticing outfit, and her dismissive gestures. He heard her smug laugh. He hated women like her. The way they lured men and got exactly what they wanted, then laughed and left them without a thought. She had gotten two drinks out of him until someone better came along.

She's stupid, and stupid girls end up dead.

It was close to three in the morning, and he stared across the lot just as he had for the last two hours. Waiting patiently.

She'll be back. Messy and tired and needing a shower.

He knew the type. It didn't matter what city or state he was traveling through. They were all the same.

Most people were weak. Most people were insecure. And the ones he hated the most were those who tried to hide under looks or smarts or, worst of all, faith.

Stupid pigs, one and all.

He adjusted to try to get feeling in his backside, which had started to fall asleep. There was an empty sixteen-ounce bottle of Coke on the seat next to him. He felt like getting another, but he didn't want to miss his opportunity. He knew he wouldn't fall asleep; he didn't need anything to keep him awake. His eyes stayed on the highway in the distance and the side street that ran to the apartment building, the restaurant, and the gas station.

Virginia. Some town in Virginia. He was just passing through. Just making a pit stop at a local bar and grill. He wasn't even drinking, but he'd decided to have some fun with the blonde and buy her a few drinks. Two, to be exact. But as she finished her second, the bimbo had the gall to call him a handful of names and move to the group of truckers who had just meandered into the bar.

She had called him a freak. She said it wasn't his looks that bothered her. They had actually brought her to his table to talk. It was what he was talking about.

Some girls are more adventurous. Some try to look adventurous, but when push comes to shove and when you actually tell them what sort of fun stuff they might have, they instantly go cold and get all scared.

His eyes didn't move, didn't blink. They just stared ahead.

She will understand the meaning of scared. Before she takes her last breath—and by God she will take her last breath tonight—she is going to know the meaning of the word scared *and she is going to look into my face, my eyes, my hands and know that what she fears is a mere taste of all the fear that can and will come and it will come tonight.*

He breathed in.

Perhaps Nancy would be too drunk to know what was coming. That was okay.

Nancy Jennings.

She had been stupid enough to show him her license. One brief look was all it took.

That was before the talk and the rejection.

The music blasted as loud as it could, but it wasn't loud enough.

He didn't really need the aggressive industrial music to fuel him. He didn't drink, and he hated smoking. Those vices killed you. And so did strangers that you angered and rejected and called a freak.

A car raced down the side street and veered into the lot outside the apartment. It was the first car he had seen in at least an hour.

It was a red Camaro.

Yes.

He knew it was her. He felt it.

Some things simply needed to be felt. He could close his eyes and see it. It was a power he had enjoyed since childhood. It wasn't the ability to see things. But he could feel them. And the sensation was stronger when he closed his eyes and let his senses take hold.

The smoke from the bar still lingered. The pounding, pounding music pressed against his skull. The rubber of the steering wheel he was gripping too hard. The taste of sugar on his lips.

His senses were about to experience something else and something soon.

He opened his eyes in time to see the car lights go off. He took off the iPod earphones and rested them on the seat next to him, then opened the car door.

The night was clear, and the moon looked bold.

You don't scare me. Not now and not ever.

This place felt desolate and empty, and he knew that God was around but not around in full.

Places had different feelings. And most people couldn't tell. Sometimes the feeling was so overwhelming it was like a dead body in the middle of a sunny, summer day left in the garbage to rot. That's how bad the stench and the irritation were when he was around a lot of them, when the presence was full. But in the middle of nowhere where the loose prevailed, the loose and the hopeless and the wandering, that was where he thrived.

I was just driving by, and I don't need and don't want, but tonight I will have. I will show. I will control and nobody can do anything about it.

He walked toward the apartment.

Nothing can stop me now 'cause I don't care I don't care and God doesn't care either because He's a liar He's a liar and all those He's lying to aren't around

The rocks moved under his boots.

He could see the figure walking up the stairs, stopping by the apartment door, taking time to open it.

She'll open the door without thought. Stupid ignorant trash.

The man knew this was a late-night diversion. By mid-morning he would be out of the state.

There were other places to go and other things to do.

He passed her car and touched the rust on the side panel.

So many going nowhere and content in their simple little ways. Never looking at the big picture of life and death and eternity and heaven and hell.

He walked up the same stairs the long-legged woman in the painted-on jeans had climbed.

This is nothing in the big picture. This is like running over something on the highway on the way to Disneyland. A minor diversion in the big circus of life.

He knew where he was going and what he was going to do and he felt good because he knew this was what he had been meant to do all his life. Some people didn't know their calling, but he knew his; he knew that all the pigs were lined up for his choosing, and all he needed to do was arrive and find them and let God *try* and protect them.

The faithful are one thing. But this, this insect, is another. She will cry out, but not to God.

She would cry out and then realize *he* was her master. And

then she'd realize not every single act ended up meaning something and that she would have an eternity to be scared and frightened and ultimately sorry.

He reached the door. The numbers he'd memorized were on it.

It was the middle of nowhere, and she probably wouldn't be found for another day or two. If she had family, they wouldn't be surprised, and then it would be a little sidebar in the newspaper and her useless life would be over and would mean absolutely nothing.

He knocked gently.

I'm not a monster. I only act like one.

The door opened, and the blonde behind the door approached, looking at him with a drunken grin. She laughed out loud.

It would be her last.

11

Edge Hill

The Volvo wagon drove slowly down the unpaved road. Certain patches were slippery with wet, untouched mud. It looked like there had been snow recently that had melted and left everything soft and damp.

They divided the trip to North Carolina into two legs. The first had been from Wheaton, Illinois, to Lexington, Kentucky, where they stayed at a hotel with a swimming pool. Stephanie had slept maybe an hour in the uncomfortable queen-sized bed. Today, the trip would be easier and shorter.

She still felt weary and had a nasty headache. She continued drinking water and held on to the handgrip above her as Jim steered them down the winding roads. They took an exit off the highway that went past a gas station/convenience store. An unmarked road continued through the wooded mountains. For some time they drove upward, the road becoming more and more remote. A side road with a barely noticeable sign reading McKinney Gap signaled their turnoff, and Jim steered onto the dirt road they had been driving on now for fifteen minutes.

"How in the world did that rich guy ever find this place?" Stephanie asked.

The reality was beginning to hit her that they were in North Carolina, the remote woods of western North Carolina, high up in the Smoky Mountains. It was beautiful here, but extremely secluded.

"I think someone found it for him. There was a log cabin at the end of this road. He supposedly tore it down and built the house himself. I think the house was originally built in the early eighties, and he added on to it around 1995 or so."

"But why here?" she wondered.

"If you want to get away, this is the place to come," Jim said with a laugh. "Works for me."

Zach asked them how much longer, and Jim said just a few more minutes. The drive continued upward, and at certain points the mountain on Stephanie's side dropped steeply. Because of the bare trees, she could see out to the horizon and couldn't help noticing how high up they were.

"So if we get a lot of snow . . . ," she started as the road suddenly narrowed to little more than a path.

"We're stuck. Especially with this thing. You don't see a lot of station wagons driving on snowy roads like this."

She knew her husband was excited to finally be here, at the place they had spent so many hours talking about. She could see the animation on his face and in his eyes. She could also see something in him that had been missing for some time.

Peace, she thought when it finally hit her.

The car slowly climbed a steep hill. Jim stopped when it came to the top.

"Maybe this is the 'hill' Edge Hill is referring to," Stephanie said.

On each side of the road were stone barriers that looked as though they were designed to hold a gate between them. They drove past the six-foot-tall monuments and continued ahead, the road leveling out for a hundred yards. Then it dropped downward and circled alongside the mountain until it reached the entrance to the driveway leading up to the massive "log cabin" Charles Wolfcott had built.

Jim stopped the car, and they all gaped at the scene before them.

"Is that where we're going to live?" Zach asked.

"Yeah, is *that* where we're going to live?" Stephanie echoed.

Jim laughed. "I guess so. Maybe someone somewhere is about to realize they made a mistake."

"I've never seen anything so . . . so big."

Jim had showed Stephanie an aerial view of the lodge taken from some magazine reporting on Wolfcott. The house consisted of three large sections, almost as though three houses had been built and attached to one another—the main lodge, then another lodge at its right side and left side. While the view from where they sat gave the appearance that the lodge was only three stories tall, the look was deceiving. The lodge faced out over the hills, and since it had been built against the side of a steep mountain, the front of it went down several stories.

"It's incredible," Stephanie said.

"I told you this was going to be fun."

The road wound around to the back of the lodge. There wasn't a garage, but there was plenty of parking space for vehicles. Thick beams lined one side of the hill like a tall fence. They saw a small, white truck parked in the corner of the lot.

They stopped the car in front of the massive house. Jim looked at Stephanie, and both started laughing.

"What are we doing here?" she asked him.

"I don't know. Wait until the villagers see this."

"Wait till the *church members* see this," she answered. "We'll stop getting financial support."

Ashley demanded to get out, so they climbed out of the wagon into the noticeably colder air.

Outside, with Zach at her side, Stephanie looked up at the lodge.

Mammoth—that was the only word to describe it. Mammoth and stunning. The huge, natural stained pine logs sprawled against the gentle terrain of the hills in the background. The dark red-brown metal roofing spread a canvas over the logs, shimmering in the glow of sunlight through the trees.

She couldn't help but shiver at the grandeur.

Behind the wing facing west, a large atrium occupied the area between the adjoining north and south wings. The evergreen trees and holly berry bushes placed throughout accented the neutral color of the logs. Even in the deadness of the winter weather, Steph could imagine what a beautiful space this was in full bloom.

As Stephanie walked toward the house on the stone path, weaving through the courtyard filled with strange stone structures, her eyes scanned the length and breadth of the lodge. Her heart quickened as she realized there were dozens of windows staring down at her with glassy, monstrous eyes.

How sad it seemed. All those vacant rooms.

Not anymore.

The thought of some multimillionaire building this immense lodge for himself and himself alone made no sense.

God works in amazing ways.

The fact that this building was going to be used for missionaries in the future was purely a miracle.

There was a stone bench on one side of the walkway. It faced a small statue of some sort of creature—a gnome maybe. Staring at it, Stephanie felt a chill that had nothing to do with the temperature or the fading light of day.

She felt distant and remote and alone.

The sidewalk ended at an immense door that seemed more fitting for a castle. There were steps leading up to the door, which featured an ornate emblem. She looked behind her at Jim trying to guide the kids through the open area.

Before she could knock, the door opened.

A friendly faced man with white hair and even whiter whiskers greeted her.

"You made it," he said. "You must be Stephanie."

"I am."

"I'm Bob Patterson. Welcome to our humble home." He gave her a firm handshake as he let out a funny little giggle.

Okay, I'm just being dramatic, she told herself. *This is the start of something good. For all of us.*

"How was the drive?"

"A little queasy, but I'm better now."

"The roads can do that to you. This is high up here too. It takes some people a while to get used to it."

Jim came up behind Stephanie then, holding Ashley in his arms. "Bob, nice to finally meet you."

"Great to have some guests here," Bob said. "The space is going to be a little tight, as you might notice, but I think we'll manage."

They all laughed.

"My better half is somewhere inside. It might take a day or so to find her. But come on in. I'll give you the grand tour."

The house, if one could call the immense lodge a house, was more impressive in person than any photo could convey. They entered the main hall that opened up to a vaulted ceiling. A ledge with a railing overlooked the hall from the second story.

Mr. Patterson led them through the wide-open area that revealed large staircases on both sides. "Everything was here just like this when we arrived," he told them as he walked into what he called the great room. "This section of the house is the west wing. We don't come over here too much except when we want to go outside. We live over in the south wing—that's big enough to house several families."

The great room lived up to its name. An immense fireplace and vaulted ceilings were the first thing Stephanie noticed, and then a wall full of windows three stories tall, flooding the room with light. Paintings lined the walls and expensive furniture filled the room. The walls were the same pine logs as the outside, and two massive chandeliers hung from the ceiling.

"That door leads to the north wing. It's locked, and they say it's the older section of the lodge and still has personal items the family needs to go through. I assume it's just as big as it is over here."

"Mom, can I go upstairs?" Zach asked.

"No, stay with us."

"For now, it's probably best to stick together," Mr. Patterson said. "Not that there's anything wrong with exploring the house—I still have fun coming upon a room I haven't seen here and there. They must've had a field day designing these wings—every room has a different look and feel to it. You'll find rooms with every possible theme you can think of."

"Cool," Zach said.

Bob showed them the hallway that led to the south wing. "I'll take you to the kitchen and introduce you to Evelyn. Are you hungry?"

"I'm hungry," Ashley said, still in Jim's arms.

Bob smiled. "Well, aren't you beautiful? How old are you?"

"I'm five."

"We have four grandchildren. Two live down in Florida and two live in Wisconsin. This is sort of a middle point between the two."

He led them to a large living room with several couches. "This is the south wing. I'll show you all how to use the intercoms. They're the only way to really be able to find anyone around here. Evelyn still can't figure them out, but at least I can let her know where I am."

They entered the roomy kitchen with a large island and chairs. A round woman with short, gray hair greeted them with a huge smile. Without hesitation, she gave Stephanie a big hug. "I'm so happy to meet all of you," she said.

Stephanie released a breath and relaxed. It was just a house. A massive house, but just a house nonetheless. And the Pattersons looked like a sweet older couple.

Maybe things will be fine after all. Maybe there's no reason to worry.

12

After-Dinner Conversation

So you said things got a little tough the last few weeks you were in Papua New Guinea. Care to talk about it?"

Jim glanced at Stephanie, then at the kids as they worked on their apple pie and ice cream.

"There's a lot to tell," he said.

Stephanie took his cue. "Evelyn, let me clear some of these plates. The roast was delicious."

As his wife started clearing the table with the help of Zachary and Ashley, Jim wondered how much to tell the Pattersons. They seemed like an amicable couple, familiar with the missionary lifestyle and the difficulties that created for family, marriage, and even self.

"We'll do it together," Evelyn said.

They had eaten the meal Evelyn prepared in the fancy dining room off the kitchen. She and Bob seemed pleased to have an excuse to use the ornate china and eat at the mahogany dining table in the stately room. The surroundings kept things a little stiff and formal at first, but gradually the conversation and company became natural and easy. Evelyn was a good listener, and Bob was introspective and took time sharing his thoughts.

With the women and children cleaning up in the kitchen, Jim felt even more comfortable talking to Bob. He knew this would come up eventually; he just hadn't thought it would be so soon.

"I think that, ultimately, we were under spiritual attack in Dambi," he began.

"How so?"

"Something was going around. A virus or something—we don't know. The doctors, the villagers, nobody seemed to know what it was. But it killed several people in the village. And people started looking at us—at me—for guidance. Then, shortly before we left, they started blaming us. There were some difficult times."

"And nobody knew what was causing it?"

Jim shook his head. There were so many details he could get into. But he didn't want to share his anger and questions and doubt. He didn't want Bob to try to answer his feelings.

"When we were in the Philippines, Evelyn and I saw the work of Satan." Bob recounted a typical missionary story about the horrors of demon possession and a family under spiritual attack. "That village is now being used in a mighty way."

Not all stories end so happily, Jim thought. But they never tell you those stories in church. Jim couldn't get up in front of his supporters and tell the truth. *Well, folks, we lost a village. We tried, but ultimately we failed.*

Because saying "we failed" meant what? It didn't mean that God failed because of course God couldn't fail. So what did it mean?

It means I failed.

Evelyn came in and refilled their coffee cups.

"So when do you see yourself going back to Papua New Guinea?" Bob asked.

"This summer, if everything goes well. How long are you guys staying up here?"

"Probably toward the end of spring. Then we'll spend some time with our kids in Florida. It will be hard leaving such a beautiful place, though."

"It is amazing," Jim said. "I look forward to checking it all out tomorrow."

"Tell me again how you guys found out about the property. Our son goes to the church that Wolfcott's brother attends."

"Oceanside Baptist?" Jim asked, remembering where Harry Wolfcott first approached him to let him know about Edge Hill.

"No, it's actually Faith Community Bible Church."

"You sure?"

"Been there many times. Our son introduced us to Harry."

"I just assumed he went to Oceanside. I guess we were fortunate to meet him."

"He has high hopes for this place, but he's a relatively new Christian. He's a very ambitious, energetic guy."

"Yeah, I could tell that even from our brief meeting."

"That's why he felt compelled to open up the lodge even before they had a chance to go through all of it. We volunteered to do some work, but he just wants us to relax. Which we've done for the last few weeks."

"The timing for us being here is perfect," Jim said.

"God's timing always is."

Jim took a sip of his coffee and didn't respond.

"Amazing to think that Wolfcott built the house of his dreams only to have it end up being used for God's glory. I can see a dozen families or more living in a place like this. Especially if they open up the north wing."

"So what's over there?"

"I didn't ask," Bob said. "Wolfcott's brother hasn't even been over there, so he's not sure. The whole thing fell into his lap rather quickly, and he's very busy—he's hoping to come here this spring to look things over. I've been corresponding with him the last few weeks."

Stephanie called out Jim's name from the kitchen.

"What is it?"

"Want to play a game with Ashley?"

Jim smiled. "Excuse me, but my daughter needs to beat me at checkers."

13

Midnight Trail

Stephanie walked down the carpeted hallway from the room where Zachary slept. They were in the south wing of the lodge on the second floor. They had chosen this because the main bedroom was close to several guest rooms on this floor. The Pattersons' bedroom was downstairs below them, a medium-sized room done in a Confederate theme, complete with a life-sized bust of General Robert E. Lee on the dresser.

Zachary picked the "awesome" hunting room with animal heads adorning the walls and African-themed furniture and decorations. He wanted to take pictures to show his friends.

Ashley had wanted the nautical room on the first floor, but Stephanie and Jim didn't want her so far away from them. She ended up choosing a small bedroom done in a star theme with a ceiling that glowed with lit stars after the lights went out.

As Stephanie entered their bedroom, she thought about *Trading Spaces* and wondered who had designed this house. It seemed as though several decorators had come in and been allowed to do whatever they wanted. She had a feeling the owner of the house had not been involved in the decision process to make rooms like "the star room."

The focal point of their room was a large, four-poster bed. Everything was designed in dark colors, from the wood to the comforter to the painting on the wall of the Victorian woman looking very alone.

Jim sat at a desk in the corner of the room, checking his laptop. "There's wireless Internet throughout the whole house. I can get it from here."

He seemed almost more excited about the house than Zachary. From the full furnishings to the state-of-the-art technology, Edge Hill was truly amazing.

"This wasn't what I was picturing," Stephanie said.

"You need to trust me more."

She sat on the edge of the bed and faced Jim, who was still busy at his computer. She could see the top of his balding head and his large frame.

"It's not that I don't trust you," she said, wanting to say more. Wanting him to know that it wasn't necessarily about him.

The sound of his typing meant he was probably on e-mail. It was a new late-night habit he had gotten into. She looked at him for a long time.

I'm here, right here, and for once it'd be nice if you knew that.

Finally she stood up and headed for the bathroom attached to their room. The walk-in closet she passed on the way was almost as large as their room in Papua New Guinea. Over the running faucet she could hear Jim say, "I'm just sending my parents a quick e-mail."

There was nothing quick about Jim. Nothing he did in haste, nothing he did trivially. She knew she would crawl under the sheets without him, would close her eyes without seeing his, would go to bed without feeling his touch.

On a night like this, feeling cold and strangely alone in this immense house, she wanted Jim's touch more than anything. She wanted the security of his warmth to help her go to sleep. She didn't want the tapping of the keyboard to be their only connection.

She could hear the wind outside. How many miles away from civilization were they?

We can call someone if something goes wrong. We're not that remote. Things are fine.

She closed her eyes. But all she could do was listen to Jim's tapping.

∽

SHE AWOKE WITH A shiver.

She looked up and could see her hands trembling in front of her face. She wore flannel pajamas. The wind whipped at them as she walked along the trail with only the small piercing blade of the flashlight to give her any sense of her surroundings.

Where am I?

The wind cut through her. The stars above looked more vibrant than she could ever remember seeing them. The moon was half full and lit some of the forest. The ground felt cold and wet on her bare feet.

This trail looked well used.

Who would use it and why?

She didn't know what time it was. Or where she was headed. Something simply told her to start walking alongside the mountain, to head into the woods.

The darkness smothered her, and she heard strange night noises. Everything felt so cold and remote.

Several hundred yards into the woods, with the outside lights of Edge Hill still casting a glow from its ominous hulking shape, Stephanie came upon what looked like the doors to a bomb shelter set into the ground.

She tried to open one of the wooden doors, but a heavy bolt kept it shut.

Why is there a bomb shelter out here?

She looked up, and the wind whipped her hair and she could feel her body shaking.

If this is a dream, it feels too real.

She jerked at the shelter's doors several more times.

A noise came from behind her. The cracking of a branch. She turned and looked, but couldn't see anything.

"Hello?"

Her flashlight shone into the black, but there was nothing to see.

She needed to go back to the house. Even if this was some dream, she would be better off going back to the house in her dream than staying outside in the cold.

You're far away, so far away, and what if—

Suddenly the lights of Edge Hill went off. She was bathed in complete blackness.

Another sound came from behind her. Again, she flashed the light as though it might ward someone off.

"Who's there?"

She heard faint breathing.

Or is that the wind?

She started back down the trail. The closer to the house she got, the faster she walked.

Halfway there, she started to sprint.

She sucked in air and felt sweat on her forehead and her feet were wet and numb and her body was frigid.

Finally she was at the front door.

It was still in the woods, watching her. She could hear faint whispers.

It's not the wind. The wind doesn't sound like voices saying your name, whispering evil things.

And then the night went black again, and she found herself asleep, and the voices and the shelter remained in the woods of her dream.

∽

"GOOD MORNING."

She slowly opened her eyes and saw Jim's smiling, gruff face. Her head lay on one of the pillows, perhaps the softest pillow she had ever slept against. She looked for the clock.

"It's okay. The kids are with Bob and Evelyn. Not only are we in a resort house, but we have nannies."

Jim's laugh soothed her. She couldn't believe she hadn't heard him get up.

"What time is it?"

"Nine thirty."

Stephanie sat up. "What?"

"Yeah. You were sleeping so nicely I didn't want to wake you."

"I'm so tired. I feel groggy."

"I brought you something."

Jim went over to the desk and returned with a tray holding a cup of coffee, some fruit, and an English muffin.

"Okay, so it's not a feast or anything, but I figured you might eat this. Bob was making pancakes."

"Thank you."

She leaned against the heavy walnut headboard and took a sip of the coffee. "It's good."

"I know." Jim walked over and peered out the window. "It seems like it's going to be a nice day."

"The kids . . ."

He came over and gave her a peck on the forehead. "They're fine. We're fine. Everything is going to be fine. Okay?"

She nodded and smiled. For the first time in a long time, they regarded one another with a slow tenderness. She could see the peace that had washed over his face.

Maybe things will be okay.

"I'm going back downstairs to the kitchen—if I can find it. This place is crazy."

"I'll be down in a few minutes."

Stephanie ate half of the English muffin and some fruit. Her head hurt and her whole body felt strange, almost sore. The strange dreams must've really done a number on her.

From where she lay, she could see through the window to the blue sky beyond the trees.

Maybe this is exactly what we need, God.

She moved the tray so she could get out of bed. Pushing back the large comforter, she caught a glimpse of something on her leg.

What is that?

Right below her knee, it looked like—

It was a gash. A gash covered with dried blood.

How did I get that?

She pulled off the sheets and checked her legs, her ankles, her feet.

Stephanie couldn't breathe. No air would come, and she wanted to call out but she couldn't.

Her feet were caked with mud, and her ankles and feet had scratches on them. As though she had been walking in the forest.

it was a dream it was just a dream it was only a dream

She stretched her legs over the bed and picked little bits of mud off the sheet, running it through her fingers.

I couldn't have. Jim would have known. He would have seen me go outside.

She studied the mud in her hands, the giant scratch on her arm.

"Hey, Steph?" Jim called.

She went to the door. "I'm going to take a shower," she called.

"You want any pancakes? There are a few left."

She was shaking and her heart raced and she called out "no thanks" and wondered if he could hear how panicky she was.

Studying her feet, Stephanie went into the bathroom to shower and change. *What is wrong with me?*

As she turned on the water, she knew one thing.

I'm not telling Jim. This is going to work. I'm going to make it work, and just because I'm having some issues doesn't mean anything.

She would deal with the dirty sheets—and her imagination—by herself.

14

The Clipping

It's time to go, time to get up, time to move.

Sometimes the voices were loud enough to be real people talking to him in person. He knew they were real whether they were loud or not, but sometimes they sounded as clear as someone standing in front of him screaming. They didn't always talk in screams, but now they did. They were signaling him to get going, to take action.

The wait is over. It is time.

He wasn't sure exactly what for. But he knew where his destination lay.

His fingers held the newspaper clipping. He carried it in his

wallet, folded in eighths. It was worn from opening and refold-
ing. He would need to be careful not to lose it.

Sitting in the chair in his hotel room ten minutes from the
border of Virginia and North Carolina, he looked at the article.
He had it memorized.

Reclusive Millionaire to Expand Smoky Mountain Retreat

Charles Wolfcott of the financial giant Edge Communications has
decided to add two more wings to his already impressive North
Carolina house. Built outside of Hartside in the Smoky Mountains,
Edge Hill was built in 1983 and rumored to be around 15,000
square feet. The additions will triple the size. The house is among a
dozen Wolfcott owns all over the world.

There was a photo of a large log cabin next to the article.

I've been there before.

Closing his eyes, he could see it. He could picture the drive
and the edge of the mountain and the tall ceiling inside and the
darkness of the night on the mountain.

*I've been there before and I'm coming back. I'm coming back, and
this time this is my time.*

He stared at the bloody scabs on his knuckles. Next time it
will be cleaner, easier. Next time he would use something other
than his hands. Next time—next time there would be more.

I'm getting stronger. I've never felt this strong. Ever.

He couldn't remember the last time he had slept. Really, truly
slept. Three days, maybe more. He didn't care.

The burn coursed through his body. His neck and back and
arms all stung, making him want to rip off his skin.

Soon enough. Soon enough this ache and burn would be quenched.

He finished reading the article.

The remote location is one of the reasons Wolfcott might have built
the mountain lodge. Located at an elevation of 3,800 feet, Edge

Hill rests on fifty acres of mountain Wolfcott purchased in 1981.
Further plans for the house remain up in the air, but it is specu-
lated this will be the last home Wolfcott will build and may serve as
a retirement home for the wealthy and reclusive businessman.

He looked at the picture again, touching it as though it had
texture, as though it were alive.

He would go back. It had been a few years, but he still knew
his way to the mountain lodge.

15

Strange Occurrences

Harry says you're a good guy."
Jim sat across from the tough, wrinkled man he had met
at the diner. Harry Wolfcott had encouraged him to hook up with
the man as soon as he got to Edge Hill. Three days had passed
since they arrived in North Carolina. He had finally reached Sheriff Nolan, and they had decided on a late lunch this afternoon.

"How you folks enjoying the castle?" Lou asked, his face never
losing the serious, stoic expression he had walked in with.

"It's actually very nice."

"I've only been inside a few times. Tell you the truth, the place
creeps me out."

Jim had finished his sandwich and was on his third Diet Coke.
Harry had suggested meeting the local sheriff just to make sure
Jim had a contact in the nearest town. "It would be good for a
few people to know you guys are up there," he'd said. In case
anything happened.

Jim wondered if much of anything happened in this town, much less on the mountain. The sheriff acted like he had nowhere to go and nothing much to do.

"I still find myself getting lost inside," Jim said.

"I was around when they built it years ago. It took them about two years. Wolfcott himself was only seen a couple times around these parts. Made people wonder, you know. Talk."

"About what?"

"About a lot of things. The guy was a recluse. Some thought he was crazy. *He* was hardly ever seen, but others were. And I'm telling you—there've been some strange things going on up at that house."

Nolan spoke in a matter-of-fact way, not trying to add drama to his words. He was the type who would tell you with a straight face that a Martian had landed on the roof and was about to come inside for dinner. His eyes were thin and steely, the eyes of a fifty-something man who had seen a lot in his time.

"Strange meaning what?"

They had been talking about their families and the town and the area, and up to now, everything had been nice and cordial.

Nolan looked like he was sizing Jim up. "I'm not trying to frighten you or anything."

"I don't get frightened very easily," Jim said. "It's fine."

Nolan nodded. "A few years ago, there were reports of people living in the lodge. No big deal—Wolfcott can do what he wants. But one night, there was a 911 call from someone who needed help. It got cut off. One of my boys went up to check things out and called me to come up. He was a nice kid but didn't know his left hand from his right. I got up there and saw some pretty freaky stuff."

"Freaky?"

Nolan nodded, his eyes looking more grim. "It was summertime. There was a woman found walking a mile or so away from the house, completely naked. Blood smeared all over her. She was hysterical. Saying strange things about what the people at the house had made her do." The sheriff cursed. "We brought her to the station. I had to go to the house to check things out."

"And?"

"And except for a couple who seemed to be in charge of the place, nobody else was there. We searched it, and I mean we searched it good. The woman made it sound like . . . She made it sound like there were some kinky things going on in the house, if you know what I mean. Lots of people. Weird stuff. But we got there, and there was nothing wrong. The woman stopped talking once she got to the station. We eventually had to let her go."

Jim waited.

Nolan took a sip of his coffee and looked out the window. "Not a lot of people in these parts talk about stuff like sacrificing altars and orgies and the like. I myself was a little . . . well, I was a bit taken aback."

"Did anything come from it?"

"Nothing. I went up to the house the next day, and everybody was gone. No cars. Nothing."

"Maybe it was just some people renting the place out. And things got out of hand."

Nolan studied Jim for a minute. "You obviously believe in God, don't you?"

The question brought a smile to Jim's lips. "Yes, I do."

"Here's the thing. I don't have much time for God and the devil and heaven and hell and all that stuff. Don't believe in it. If I can't see it, I don't believe it. That's my philosophy."

"I understand." *Maybe I can help in that area.*

"But I felt something the night I went up to the castle. I felt—I don't know—a presence. I'm not into the boogeyman or spirits or any of that. But I swear on my firstborn I felt something when I went into that house."

"What?"

"Something evil. Something that scared me. And like you, I don't scare easily."

Jim nodded. *I could tell you a few stories about evil spirits.* "I believe there are spirits you can feel," he said. "I've felt them myself."

"You're a missionary. You're supposed to say things like that."

"It's true."

"So have you felt anything up at the house so far? Any sign of anything strange or evil?"

Jim thought for a moment and shook his head. "No."

"Maybe it was just—maybe it was . . ."

"What?"

"I was going to say my imagination, but I don't have much of an imagination. My Linda says I was born without a creative bone in my body. If I don't see it, I don't get it. It's just—I know what I felt. What I sensed. And it was real."

Jim remembered the bloody blanket and the body convulsing and the hands reaching out to grab him and smother him.

He shoved the thought away. He knew evil existed, had seen enough of evil in his life, but he also believed God watched over and protected His flock.

"So far, the only sensation I've felt at Edge Hill is one of being overwhelmed by its size. I'm sure he spent millions on the place."

Nolan nodded, something obviously on his mind.

"What is it?"

"Harry didn't tell you, did he?"

Jim looked at Nolan and shook his head. He had only met Harry twice. The bulk of their communication had been by phone or e-mail. "Tell me what?"

"About a year or so ago—let me see, I think it was maybe last March, sometime around Easter—I had to go up to the lodge because of a missing person report."

"Someone disappeared?"

"Yeah, another young woman. What do they call that—irony? Coincidence? Whatever. Anyway, a handful of people—most in their twenties—were up there. Didn't tell me how in the world they knew Wolfcott. Pretty people, all of them. They reported a young woman, blonde—missing. She'd disappeared the night before. Several days later, she was still missing. We never found her. We contacted Wolfcott's people, but never the man himself. It was a big deal that got hushed over and eventually got put away. The thing is, someone *wanted* it to go away. And I know it was Wolfcott himself. When you have that much money, you can do anything you want."

"Are you saying Wolfcott paid to make the disappearance go away?"

"I know that's what happened. I had a bureau chief on the phone telling me it was an open-and-shut case and there was nothing left to do except move on. He kept saying, 'Move on. Move on, Lou.' I know my place in life—I know what I should and shouldn't do. So Lou moved on. But I'm telling you, that girl didn't just disappear. Something happened to her."

"Something like what?"

"I don't know," Nolan drawled. "But something happened. I know that."

Harry didn't tell me about this. But it was a missing person, that's all. It could happen anywhere. To anybody.

"Look, it was a long time ago, and Wolfcott's not even alive, so it's probably nothing. But I've never liked that house, and it's so remote. . . . You guys just make sure you keep in touch with me, okay?"

Jim nodded. "I appreciate your concern."

"I've seen too much ugliness in my fifty-eight years, and I don't want to see anything happen to a nice family like yours. Just be careful, okay? And if you see anything—anything strange—just let me know."

"Whatever the house might have been used for in the past is over with," Jim said. "I believe now all that space is going to be used in a lot of good ways."

"Sorta like painting over a room with a fresh coat of paint?" Lou asked.

"Yeah, sorta."

Lou nodded but looked skeptical. Jim wanted to bring up the subject of faith, but he didn't. He just couldn't try to convince someone of something he was having a hard time with himself.

16

Paul

She could remember a time in her life when she believed things worked out for the best and that life was safe. When the sun rose and set with her big brother, and he protected her even when her parents couldn't and wouldn't. And that was why she wanted to see him, why she wanted to talk to him. She was starting to remember more about her past and her childhood and her parents, and with those thoughts came questions. Lots of questions.

Jim hadn't come back from his afternoon visit to Hartside. The kids were with the Pattersons, who seemed to love their role as surrogate grandparents. Not only were they staying in an extravagant lodge with modern interiors and decorations, but she had built-in babysitters.

Stephanie took out her cell phone and tapped in Paul's number. For a few seconds the call stalled, the bars on her phone gone. Then it got through.

She couldn't help smiling when she heard him call out her name.

"Did you guys move yet?" an animated voice asked.

"I e-mailed you and told you we did. We've been here a few days."

"So? How is it?"

"It's . . . Paul, it's incredible. It's like we're on vacation."

"That great, huh?"

"You have to come see it."

"You know, some of us have responsibilities."

Paul was always joking, half cynical and half serious.

"You can take time off. When was the last time you saw us? And the kids?"

"I know. Guilt, guilt, guilt. I already told you I'd come up."

"When?"

"Sometime. Soon. Things have been crazy. I'm switching jobs again."

"You switch jobs every six months," Stephanie said.

"This one might be more permanent. It's in California."

"California? Seriously?"

"Yeah. I have a couple weeks left here and then a few weeks off. How about I make a trip to North Carolina before I head west?"

"We're not going anywhere."

"How are the kids?"

"Great. Zach's in heaven. He stays busy exploring the house. It's incredible—really. There are ten bedrooms you can pick from when you come, and that's in *this* wing. A workout room. A movie room. Bring some of your DVD collection."

"What? I only have about a thousand DVDs."

"Well, bring some family ones."

"Sorry, I don't know if I have any of those." He laughed.

I miss that spontaneous, free-spirited laugh. I need some of that in my life now.

"It'll be good to see you," she said.

"How's Preacher Jim?"

She laughed at the nickname and told him Jim was doing fine.

Paul understood their faith and their call to the mission field, but he liked to give them a hard time about it. From their very first meeting, he'd called his brother-in-law Preacher Jim.

Paul would probably say that he was a Christian, but he was very confused about the Christian faith in a lot of ways, and most of that had to do with their parents. Stephanie had always tried to come alongside Paul and encourage and support him, even though she knew some of the things he was doing were not right. He struggled. But from her perspective, everybody in this world struggled.

"Jim will enjoy having you up here," she said.

"Yeah, it'll be good to see everyone."

There was a pause.

"Hey—have you talked to Mom and Dad lately?"

The question surprised her. "Are you serious?"

"Yeah."

"Have you?"

"No. But I've been . . . I've been thinking of seeing them sometime."

"Really? Why?"

"I don't know. Maybe it's the thought of moving to the big CA. I figure if I go out there it's going to be a long time before I—if I ever . . ."

"It's been a few years."

"I know. And it might be—I don't know—it might be a lot longer if I don't try to at least make an attempt."

"An attempt at what, Paul?"

"Don't get all hostile with me, young lady." She could almost see the smirk on his lean face. "It's just," he continued, "I think it's time to deal with some of the past."

"They're never going to change."

"I know that. But I want them to know how much they affected me—us. How much they failed as parents."

"They won't care."

"I don't want them to care. I just want them to hear me out. I want to speak my piece and then move on. That's what my therapist tells me I should do."

"You're seeing a therapist?"

Paul laughed. "You always said I was a little crazy."

Do I tell him? Do I tell him now?

"Paul?"

"Yeah."

Tell him about the dreams and the nightmares and the fears and the hallucinations. He might not understand, but he'll listen. He won't judge. He won't act like you're crazy.

"It'll be good to see you," she finally said. "I'd like to talk about Mom and Dad."

"How come?"

"Just because—I don't know. I find myself thinking about Michigan a lot these days. Our old house and the old neighborhood."

"I try not to think about them."

"Let me know some dates, okay?"

"I will."

"Paul?"

"Yeah, what is it?"

"Just—please try to come. I know you'll enjoy it."

"Okay, I promise."

"I'm going to hold you to it."

"Great. Just another thing a woman in my life can hold over my head. Add it to the list."

They both laughed and said their good-byes. Stephanie clicked off the phone and sat there thinking. Her reverie was interrupted by a voice coming from one of the wall intercoms.

"Stephanie? Are you there?" It was Evelyn, and she sounded frantic.

"Yes, I'm here," Stephanie said, pressing the intercom.

"Is Ashley with you?"

Stephanie glanced around. She hadn't seen Ashley for the last hour. "No. Isn't she—"

"I can't find her, and Bob and Zach don't know where she is either."

Stephanie sucked in a breath. "Where are you?" she asked.

"I'm on the south side, in the family room. By the large kitchen."

"I'll be there in a minute. Don't worry, Evelyn. She can't have gone too far."

But in this house, she could have gone anywhere.

God, please don't let anything happen to Ashley.

17

The Secret Passageway

When was the last time you saw her?"

Zachary tried to remember but could only recall lunch in one of the kitchens a couple hours earlier. What sort of place had two kitchens? Actually, it probably had three, one in each wing. But they weren't allowed in the north wing, so he hadn't checked that out. Zach assumed his little sister had just wandered into one of the spare bedrooms.

"I've been playing by myself in the family room," he said. "I'll help you look for her."

They were in the south wing family room, its lofty ceiling showing pine logs in an intricate puzzle-like formation. There was a fireplace on one side, not as big as the one in the large room over in the west wing. Some of Zach's toys were on the rug, where he'd been playing and watching television on the large screen on the wall.

Mom continued to call out Ashley's name as she rushed down the hallway checking the rooms on the first floor. Zach decided to go upstairs and check out those rooms.

The south and the west wings each had a couple of staircases. The one he went up now was a spiraling staircase, probably made more for convenience than for looks. He didn't think Ashley would have gone up these; more likely she'd go up the main staircase that was spacious and led to a loft that overlooked the living room.

Two hallways jutted out from the top of the spiraling staircase. He chose the one on the left, recognizing the rooms down there. Each room in this house had a theme. Some had a color theme, like the blue room over in the west wing. Or a hunter's theme like the room he chose. There was one room that to Zach looked like a bunch of stuff from somebody's garage, but his parents said it was "a 1940s room."

The first room Zach searched was "the bear room," a small bedroom with a white cedar bed, a bear rug, bear-accented pillow shams, and pictures of bears on the walls. A couple windows leaked light into the room. It felt nice and cozy. Nothing too unusual, nothing too exciting.

"Ashley?" he called. Zach opened the closet door and looked inside. Just some empty hangers and a couple boxes marked "Bear Room."

Back out in the hallway, he could hear Mom calling for Ashley. She must have come upstairs to look in the bedrooms. This particular hallway was narrow with low ceilings and dim light. He went into the second bedroom. It was the same size as the bear room, but this one was very modern with furniture that seemed out of place in a log cabin, even one as big as Edge Hill. The bed was low to the ground, and everything in the room was black and white.

Zach stared at a strange black-and-white photograph on the wall of a couple, an older man and a younger woman. She was a fashion model, he supposed, with long dark hair and lots of makeup on her eyes. Zach wondered if the older man with her was her father, but the man had his arm around her in the way that Dad sometimes held Mom.

He walked over to the closet. Just some lone hangers on the bar. As he stepped into the closet, he felt cold. Very cold.

Zach rubbed his hands together. For a minute he listened, wondering where Mom was.

Why am I so cold?

Something round on the wall outside the closet got his attention. It looked like one of those things that set the temperature.

A thermostat. That's what it was. He was never supposed to touch the thermostat. Heating a house cost a lot of money, and Mom and Dad decided what the temperature should be.

Were there thermostats that worked just for single rooms?

If Mom and Dad were there, surely they would turn up the thermostat. It was freezing.

Zach reached for the thermostat and turned it. Nothing happened. He turned it left and right several times, wondering if it actually worked.

This time he heard a noise—softly—from the closet. It sounded like a patio door moving, sliding and shifting.

He looked inside the closet. Nothing.

Wait a minute.

On the right-hand side, in the bottom corner, a piece of the wall was missing. It was black and open, like a secret passageway.

Was that there last time?

It was a square hole, about three feet high and three feet wide.

Maybe Ashley went through here.

But he knew it hadn't been there before. He must have opened it by turning the thermostat.

Maybe that thermostat's a fake.

Zach knelt down and peered into the opening. The cold air came from the hole. He couldn't see anything.

His mother's voice called out again from farther away.

Tell Mom and Dad about it. Tell them before you go inside.

Zach knew he should. But something else told him to go inside, to check it out.

Maybe it's a secret passageway.

He got on his knees and began crawling inside.

His skin quickly froze in the musty air. The wood floor felt cold against his hands. He reached up to see if there was a ceiling, then felt the walls to his left and right. Then slowly, very slowly, Zach stood up.

He could stand upright in this hall. It was a secret passageway.

Maybe leading to the north wing.

And maybe there were lots more in the house.

A pulse of excitement rushed through him.

Zach felt for a light switch, but there was nothing. Light spilled in from the closet, but it only illuminated the first few feet of this small corridor.

For a minute he thought again about getting out of there and telling his parents. But he would do that later. For now, this was a secret hallway he needed to check out.

He walked carefully, his arm stretched out to make sure he didn't bump into anything. It was so cold, as if there was an opening to the outside letting in the winter air. He could hear the creaks in the wood as he walked, each step slow and deliberate. A few times he glanced back to make sure the closet door was still open.

Zach walked for a few minutes, maybe more. He couldn't tell. The passageway seemed to go on forever.

I need to come back here and bring a light.

He heard something in front of him.

Footsteps?

He stopped and tried to see into the darkness ahead.

"Ash?" he asked, knowing it wasn't his sister.

It sounded again—a footstep. It was so black in here, there could be someone right in front of him and he wouldn't know.

"Hello?"

He turned back to see the opening to the closet, so small now and so far away.

I gotta get out of here. I need to tell Mom and Dad.

As he was about to turn around, he smelled something strange. Something that reminded him of . . .

Who?

Papa Miller.

It smelled like old man's cologne.

Why do I smell Papa's cologne in this closet?

Zach was about to call out when something grabbed his ankle. Something warm, something that gripped his ankle hard and didn't let go.

A hand it's someone's hand someone's grabbing me someone's holding me back

He wanted to scream but couldn't. Instead he instinctively swung his hands, but they swiped only air. He could still feel the hand gripping his ankle.

Zach kicked out his other leg and again got nothing but air.

With everything in him, he pulled away from the warm grip and sprinted back toward the opening. He reached it and dove through, skinning his palm and elbows on the wood floor.

Without even looking back, he ran to the thermostat and turned it back and forth several times with his shaking hands.

The sliding sounded again. He looked inside the closet and saw the wall appear again. It was amazing. The dark wood gave no hint there was any doorway or sliding wall or panel.

He looked down at his ankle, then noticed his bleeding elbow. He couldn't catch his breath.

"Zach? Zach, where are you?"

His mother's voice startled him. Spotting the intercom near the light switch, he went over and pressed TALK ALL.

"I'm upstairs."

"Come back down. We found Ashley."

"Okay," he said, surprised his voice sounded so calm.

He looked back at the closet. Maybe he had just imagined something grabbing onto his ankle.

No. Walking down the stairs to the first floor, Zach knew something was in that passageway. It was there, and it was real.

18

The Box

Sometimes it was difficult for her to breathe. Because it was difficult for her to sleep. Because, ultimately, it was difficult for her to relax. Ever. The prescribed Xanax helped, as did the sleeping pills Stephanie sometimes took. But the sense of peace never came. It had not come for a long time.

The winds howled outside. It was late—past midnight. The rest of the house slept, but Stephanie was in the kitchen finishing off a glass of wine. She had never drunk any sort of alcohol until a few years ago, attending a dinner with fellow missionaries who drank wine like it was no big deal.

Tonight she wanted one more glass before going to bed. After the scare today with Ashley, she needed a good drink. Wine made her sleepy, and sleep was good.

They had found Ashley playing in one of the downstairs bedroom closets. There were so many rooms in this house, it was difficult keeping track of them all. She had talked seriously with Ashley about staying close to the rest of the family in this house. It wasn't good to roam because not only did they get worried, but she might hurt herself and they wouldn't even know it.

Ashley promised not to go off on her own again. Then she reached into her pocket. "Look what I found, Mommy," she said, holding out a key.

It wasn't just a key. It was one of those old-fashioned kind of keys, an antique of sorts that looked dark and rusty.

"Where did you find this?" Stephanie asked.

"In the room. In the closet."

Later that afternoon, after Jim returned from town, Stephanie had gone to the room to see if the key fit any of the locks, but it didn't. Maybe it was from some part of the house she hadn't seen yet.

Now, alone in the kitchen, she pulled the key out of her pocket and wondered again what it unlocked. She thought about the north wing.

I wonder what's inside that wing.

Probably just more rooms. There were already enough here. She didn't need to see more.

But why keep that wing locked? And why did this key come out of nowhere?

She would try it out in the coming days. Maybe it worked on some random door. Or maybe it was just one of the many strange artifacts that belonged to this house.

It feels cold in here. Even when the heat is on full blast and I'm wearing layers, this place feels cold.

Stephanie couldn't shake that ominous feeling. She didn't like this house—if she could even call it a house. It was like three lodges connected, with strange rooms and an even stranger floor plan. She always had trouble finding her way around big places, like malls and amusement parks. Jim teased her about having no sense of direction, but it wasn't funny, not here.

Maybe the rooms shift and change places when I'm not around, she thought with a tinge of humor.

The clock on the microwave said 12:47. She finished her glass of wine and headed toward her bedroom. This time she took the small, winding staircase from the kitchen.

There were timed night-lights in various areas of the house. But as she reached the top of the staircase, she noticed light coming from beneath the door of a bedroom down the hall to the left.

Maybe Zach is exploring.

Each room offered him a new adventure. Even though she felt the house was too big and too cold, and Jim was still finding it hard to relax and take a break from work, Zach seemed to have made an easy transition. He loved exploring the house, and she didn't mind, as long as he was careful. But he shouldn't be up at this hour.

Something seemed different with Zach at dinner.

She didn't know what it was. He was more quiet, more distant. He'd been like that ever since Ashley's disappearance. Jim thought perhaps he'd gotten scared and didn't want to admit it.

For a minute, Stephanie wondered if she should get her husband. This late at night, roaming around the house might not be a good idea, especially for her. Jim had endured enough of her sleepwalking and nightmares.

Don't bother him. He was really tired tonight.

She walked to the end of the hallway. When she reached the door with the light behind it, she felt a chill and stopped.

"Zach?" she called softly.

She knocked on the door. It certainly wasn't the Pattersons. Neither of them ever stayed up past ten o'clock. And they wouldn't be roaming the house anyway.

"Hello?" she said in a slightly louder voice, pushing the door gently.

The door screeched open, and she looked into a room she hadn't seen before.

It was a pirate-themed room. That was the easiest description. Perhaps the designer or decorator or maybe even Wolfcott himself had meant it to be Mediterranean, sophisticated instead of Halloweenesque. Dark reds and blacks complemented the old-fashioned furniture and nautical accents. A compass on the wall, several small miniatures of boats with their sails up, a sword hanging above the bed, a hat that Bluebeard might have worn.

The light emanated from a small lamp on the dresser. The dresser itself looked ancient. She walked over, no longer questioning that someone else might be there. A large mirror faced her above the dresser. Stephanie glanced at herself and thought she appeared tired and ugly. On top of the dresser was a large square box, dark wood with a flat top and a large opening for a key to fit inside. She tried to open the box, but it wouldn't budge.

For a moment, she felt light-headed. Maybe it was the wine or the late hour or a combination of both. Maybe it was entering this strange room and feeling like she was somewhere else, in an amusement park.

This is the fun house and the rooms move and trade places and to-morrow this room might not even be here.

She thought of the key and took it out of her pocket. Why not? With the way things had been happening, she wouldn't be surprised if it worked. And it did. She fit the heavy key into the large opening and turned it twice. Something clicked, and the top of the box moved.

Stephanie gasped. How could this be? Ashley went missing on the main floor and found a key and gave it to Stephanie, only for Steph to discover this box later in the only lit room in the house.

Maybe Ashley left the light on.

But she hadn't noticed any lights on earlier when she came downstairs.

Maybe I just missed it.

She studied the wooden box before opening the top. It looked aged and beat-up, like a world traveler with well-earned scars. Something inside told her not to open it, to leave this room and this box alone.

It's not your business so leave it alone.

But her hands set to work anyway, almost of their own accord.

She froze.

It can't be. It can't be. I'm dreaming this just like I'm always dreaming, and this is my nightmare because what I'm looking at can't exist. It can't be—not here, not now.

She exhaled, and for a second she could almost swear she saw her own breath, as though she were outside.

Inside the box lay a photo of her family. Her parents, smiling, looking so young, and her brother, Paul. And there she was, in her father's arms.

What is happening? God, what is happening to me? What is happening to my mind?

She wanted to reach out and touch the photograph, but she couldn't. Touching it would make her wake up in bed next to Jim. Touching it would make it go away, and she didn't want it to go away.

I don't think I've ever seen it before, and I want to touch it. I want to hold it. I want it to be mine.

For a second she could feel tears well in her eyes. Was fear or exhaustion causing this? She didn't know.

Her body shook.

God, what is this and how did it get here?

She heard something behind her and jerked, her eyes moving from the box and the mystery inside it to the mirror in front of her. She could see behind her, the bed and the chair next to it and

Dear God no no oh God no please God

the figure sitting in the chair.

A man sat in the chair next to the bed, a grin on his face, eyes that didn't blink, just staring at her, watching and staring.

She froze. She blinked, but he was still there, grinning.

"Hello, Stephanie."

The voice was heavy and sounded like it came from all around her. She wondered if she had heard anything at all.

Wake up wake up please God let me wake up

The man started to laugh. She could see black teeth that looked like they were rotting away. His face started turning red.

It's blood. He's bleeding. He's decomposing right in front of me.

The grin continued, and her body shook. She closed her eyes. Something in front of her slammed shut. It was the box.

Wait

She looked back at the mirror and saw the chair.

On it lay a Siamese cat, sitting upright and staring at her.

I'm losing my mind I've officially lost my mind and I have nobody to tell I'm scared I'm scared I'm so scared

The cat jumped off the chair onto the carpeted floor. Stephanie jumped herself, afraid it would come toward her, afraid it would attack.

But the cat moved toward the open door and went into the hallway.

Her heart raced, and she shook. She couldn't move.

Get out of here get out of this room

She briefly thought of the box that was now shut.

Tomorrow. I'll get it tomorrow.

She willed her legs to move, and she finally got out of the room, leaving the light on and the key in the box.

Outside in the hallway, she quickened her pace until she found herself half-sprinting toward her bedroom.

She slowed down as she passed the kids' rooms. As she entered her bedroom, she could feel her heart beating and her forehead sweating.

I didn't imagine this. I didn't dream this. I'm awake, and I saw what I saw.

Minutes later, in the comfort and safety of her bed, Jim's heavy breathing reassured her with his presence. She thought of what she had seen.

What terrified her the most wasn't what she saw in the chair.

It was what she saw in the box.

A photo she couldn't remember ever seeing before. She recognized all of them, but not where the photo was taken and when.

It can't be. Whatever else I might have seen, I couldn't have seen that. I imagined it. Something like that cannot be here in this house.

But it was.

And that terrified her.

19

Sacrifice

As soon as he walked into the smoky, noisy, crowded bar, he knew it was perfect. Perfect for his needs. Perfect for *their* needs. Fulfilling their needs would appease the voices, the endless voices that never shut up. They haunted him and made his back and his gut and his mind ache endlessly—and he needed to appease them to shut them up.

I'm going to find someone for you.

He ordered a drink and went through the motions. He was good at going through the motions, and nobody knew. Nobody really knew. But *they* knew, and they saw all. They gave him powers too. Sometimes he was able to see things that others didn't see.

There are so many of us and we're in control because God gave up a long time ago. He doesn't care anymore. His powers aren't what they used to be.

He sipped the drink and watched and waited.

Tonight there would be another sacrifice.

He couldn't help being excited. He couldn't help the smirk on his face, the anticipation. This felt better than anything else, and nothing could top it—nothing.

He took another drink and scanned the crowd and found her.

She was perfect. Dancing, moving, prancing around, showing off, making all the other men watch her.

Her eyes caught his. They lingered for a moment, then continued on.

There you go.

He knew it was her. She would be the one.

He kept staring, kept smiling, kept acting.

Just one more. Just one more tonight. Just one more for the road before the big one.

There was so much to do and little time to do it.

The dancing woman looked his way again.

Keep it up. That's right, keep it up.

He finished his drink and ordered another. All for show. He didn't need a tonic to soothe his nerves. He didn't need alcohol to make him feel better.

I know how to feel better and quench this thirst and give them what they need.

He made his move to the dance floor.

20

Ghosts

Bob Patterson's face looked weathered under the wrinkles and white hair, but his eyes were still calculating and crisp. They were slivers between wrinkles, becoming even smaller when he smiled, which he did frequently.

"Sure you don't want one?" Jim asked him, sipping a beer as he stood on the deck overlooking the valley below.

Bob shook his head. "Those just make me tired."

It was a sunny afternoon, and with the rays hitting them, it felt like a spring day. The wind was hushed and the clouds had vanished. Jim squinted his eyes as he leaned over the wood railing and peered through the bare trees at the ground below.

"Can I ask you a question?"

The older man was sitting on a patio chair. He didn't even bother looking Jim's way as he said a casual, "Sure."

"Have you ever gone into the north wing?"

Bob's eyes shifted, and he studied Jim for a minute. "No."

"You ever wonder what's over there?"

"I figure more of the same. More rooms. More of everything."

Jim thought of his conversation with Sheriff Nolan.

"Ever wonder why they don't want us to go over there?"

"I just figure there's still personal stuff over there that someone needs to go through. And they don't want strangers doing it. And it's not like we need more space."

Jim chuckled. "That's for sure. It's just—do you ever . . . ?"

"What's that?"

Tell him what you're thinking.

"Do you ever get spooked out by this place?"

"Sometimes the size is overwhelming. Yes, sure."

I'm not talking about the size.

"What about Evelyn?" Jim asked.

"Oh, she thinks there are ghosts. But she's wired that way. She sees things in her mind."

So does Stephanie. Maybe it's just a woman thing.

"But this place doesn't—you don't feel traces of . . . ?"

"Of what?" Bob said.

Jim wasn't sure exactly what he was thinking or feeling. Something had been nagging at him, and he wasn't sure how to describe it.

"I don't know. Of something."

"Nothing more than anywhere else."

What was that?

Jim stared into Bob's face, but it was gone. Whatever look had been there briefly, it was gone.

Fear? Nervousness? Secrets?

"Do you ever feel anything . . . ?"

"A dark presence?" Bob asked.

"Yes."

Again, a shadow crossed Bob's face. He wasn't telling Jim something. There was more to the look, to the conversation, to what Bob knew.

"I've always felt that Satan and his minions are out to get people like ourselves, people doing work for the kingdom. I've felt it a lot over the years. I try to keep my prayers plentiful and to arm myself with the Word."

"But when it was just the two of you here . . ."

"We've been fine," Bob said sharply.

Okay, old man. Don't want to go there—fine by me.

Jim took a sip of his beer and looked over the railing.

There's no such thing as ghosts. At least not the kind in movies.

But Jim knew there was such a thing as spirits. And he wondered if he was feeling the heavy presence of something dark, something evil, something that didn't want them in this house.

21

On the Stairs

It was evening, and everyone was downstairs in the media room except Stephanie. She walked down the hallway, carrying her latest devotional book. When she reached the head of the stairs, she looked down the hall.

For a moment, she thought of going back to the room. To see if she could open the box again.

To see if she would still find the photo.

Her entire body shuddered.

As she started down the stairs, she felt weighed down. Her chest tightened, and for a second, she couldn't breathe. She sat down on a step, setting the book down and wrapping her arms around her shoulders.

She couldn't stop shaking.

What's wrong with me?

Her body felt out of control, and she didn't know what to do.

I don't want them to see me like this. Especially not Jim.

She closed her eyes.

"God, help me. Please, God, help me. I know You can hear me, so why won't You help me?"

Finally the shivering eased and stopped.

She glanced at the book on the steps—a "devotional for busy moms."

How about a devotional for women losing their mind? How about one for moms who hallucinate? Who see pictures of their family in little boxes in strange rooms in mysterious houses?

She had never been scared of the dark or spooked out, and even after everything she'd seen in Dambi, Stephanie knew God was always with her. But God's comfort had been lacking recently, and her darkness had been evermore present.

"What do You want of us?" she asked Him, feeling cold and empty.

She feared for her family, and she knew she needed to tell Jim these thoughts. But she wasn't sure when. Or how.

22

The E-mail

TAWI PASSED AWAY LAST NIGHT.

Jim stared at the laptop screen in stunned silence as he had for the last half hour. As if looking at the words long enough might make them go away, might change their meaning. He had taken his morning cup of coffee into the library to check e-mail, a daily ritual. It was still black outside, and everybody in the house was sleeping. A small lamp lit the deep mahogany bookcases and desk. This room had become his designated office where he spent hours reading and writing. Or where he was supposed to be reading or writing, but instead he sometimes came and checked e-mail and surfed the Web and tried to focus but couldn't.

How would he tell Zachary this news? Stephanie already knew of Tawi's illness, and she had suspected that word might be coming any day. But Zach—he didn't know anything. Jim had hoped to keep Tawi's illness from Zach in the event that maybe, just maybe, his prayers would be answered.

Why? That's all I want to know. Why?

Tawi had been his closest friend in Dambi. In some ways, Jim felt closer to Tawi than he ever had to any of his brothers. The man had a heart for God and had wanted to help the Millers adjust to the village and their surroundings. He spoke decent

English and helped enormously with the language barrier. He had been a second father to Zach and had loved the children as if they were his own.

And now he's gone.

Jim read the message from Tawi's cousin detailing the last vicious bout of the mysterious illness that claimed the man's life. Tawi was the fifth person to die from it; it had already taken his wife months ago. Perhaps if they had lived in Wheaton, the illness wouldn't have been so mysterious. But out in the village in the jungle, there was only so much they could do. And the illness that started like a common cold morphed into something else, something deadly.

The silence of the room covered Jim like a shroud. He closed his eyes and tried to pray. Nothing came out.

He knew Tawi was in a better place, but that didn't make him feel any better. Tawi was only twenty-seven years old. He should have had a long life ahead of him. He had been a good man serving God and loving God. So why, then? Why did he have to die?

And what about the three children left behind? Three children left alone without parents?

Jim thought about his last conversation with Tawi before they left.

"A man from the woods—a sorcerer—he said he's doing this," Tawi had told him.

"Doing what?"

"Making us sick."

That was after three of them had died. Three, including Tawi's wife. And now five were gone, including Tawi.

Was the sorcerer really responsible? Where was God's hand in this? Where was His power over life and death?

I've been praying for Tawi daily ever since we left. For months. Several times a day. And nothing. Nothing.

Jim felt sick to his stomach. He wanted to be back in the village in their small house having dinner with Tawi and his family. He didn't care if they ate the same meal they had eaten five times in a row. He wanted to hear Tawi's laugh and see the way his nose and eyes crinkled when he smiled. He wanted to share the Bible with Tawi who listened like an enthusiastic child. He wanted to go scouting in the surrounding mountains and talk about God's creation and nature.

Why, God?

He wanted to pray, but why pray to a God who could've spared Tawi's life and instead let him die?

Everybody is going to see now. They're going to see and question where God was in all this. They were already questioning it, but now they're going to have unanswerable doubts and uncertainties. They're going to think the dark side is stronger.

And even though he knew the doubts and anger were wrong, Jim didn't let them go. He couldn't.

All he could think about now was the look he would see on Zachary's face when he told him the news.

~

THE DOOR OPENED, AND Stephanie saw Jim walking in.

"Where've you been?" she asked him as he took off his thick winter parka.

"Just outside. Walking."

"Are you crazy?" she said, taking his coat and hanging it in the nearby closet. "It's freezing outside."

"I just needed some air."

"Jim—is everything okay?"

He looked at her in silence for a moment, then nodded. "Yes, everything's fine."

"Did you have breakfast?"

"No, but I'm starving."

"I was thinking of making the kids French toast."

"I can be a kid."

They walked into the kitchen, and Jim poured himself a cup of coffee. He sat in a chair and played with Ashley, who had all her toys spread out on the floor underneath the table. The sun shone through the sliding glass doors that went out to the deck, filling the room with light.

"Paul called this morning," Stephanie said as she cracked eggs into a bowl on the granite counter.

"Yeah? What'd he say?"

"He's coming next week."

Jim continued to play with Ashley and didn't say anything. Stephanie knew something was wrong. Sometimes the best thing to do with her husband was to give him space and time. He would eventually come around and let her know what was going on. At least he always had in the past.

She looked for a whisk to beat the eggs—sometimes it was overwhelming using a kitchen this size with everything at her disposal. Just give her a microwave and a heating dish and she would be fine. She felt like she was looking for something half the time in this kitchen. And she always found it in the most unusual place, forgetting afterward and having to go through the same routine again.

"We haven't seen him in three years," Stephanie reminded her husband.

"Well, it's going to be a little tight," Jim said, waiting for her laugh.

That used to be their standard line when anybody came to visit: "It's going to be a little tight." It always was tight, from their small apartment to their little house in Dambi. Now their houseguest had thirty different rooms to choose from.

"How is he?" Jim asked.

"He's doing very well," Stephanie said, recounting their conversation.

She couldn't help but be excited about Paul's arrival. Zachary barely remembered him, and Ashley didn't know her uncle at all. He had only been around twice since her birth. But even more than for the kids' sake, Stephanie was eager to have some time to be around her brother herself.

There are things I want to ask him. Things I want to know about my childhood.

As she prepared breakfast and Evelyn Patterson strolled in asking to help, Stephanie wondered what was wrong with Jim. He seemed tired and overwhelmed. She started to say something, but he was busy making flying noises for Ashley.

It would have to wait until later. Just like it always did.

23

The Hidden Room

Even though it was bright outside without a cloud in the sky, Zachary knew he needed a flashlight. The passageway was black, and he needed as much light as he could get down there. He had been thinking about this for four days and nights, wondering if he could go back into the secret passageway. He'd asked Mr. Patterson for help and had been given a flashlight from a room that stored a variety of tools.

After lunch his dad went to town with Mr. Patterson. Mom was with Ashley, and he told her he would be upstairs in his room reading. She wouldn't worry about him. He stood outside the closet door, concentrating on the thermostat as he held the heavy flashlight.

I can do this. I can do this.

The other day had just been about nerves. There wasn't anybody in the closet. Nobody had grabbed his ankle. It had just been his mind making up crazy things.

His hand went to move the thermostat, and he was startled to see that it was shaking.

Stop that.

Zach moved the dial back and forth several times, as he had before. Just as he concluded that it wasn't going to work this time, he heard the sliding, swooshing of the closet wall moving.

He turned the flashlight—one of those big ones with lots of batteries—and aimed its beam at the opening. He could see nothing but the wood floor stretching out before him.

For a minute he just stood there, waiting, straining to hear or see anything unusual. He noticed nothing.

Go on, go inside.

He crawled through the small opening. Once inside, he shined the light on the floor, then around the walls. One side was slanted just like the roof of the house. The other side was straight and taller than his father. The walls were just drywall with paint or tape on them. Zachary shone the light down the corridor and in the distance could see another wall. He wondered if it had an opening in it.

Go. Check it out. Don't be a sissy.

He began walking down the passageway, feeling more confident now that he had the light. He walked slowly, listening for any movement. It took him a few minutes to reach the wall.

He spotted a small doorway just like the other one, but couldn't see any way to open it. He tapped the wall, trying to get it to slide, but nothing.

Then, in the corner of the passageway, tucked in the edge between the drywall and the wood floor, he spied a small black button. He hesitated for a moment, then pressed it.

The door opened, and light spilled out.

Something inside him tightened.

Don't go in there, Zach. Don't. Turn around and tell Mom and Dad about this.

He knelt and looked into the opening.

This time the hole led not to a closet but to an actual room. One he had not seen before.

I've seen every room in this house. Except in the north wing.

But he hadn't turned or gone far enough to be in the north wing of the house. This was still the south wing, right? It had to be a hidden corridor, a room that was somehow hidden from view.

For a moment he couldn't move. But he willed himself to go through the opening. As soon as he stepped inside, he felt cold and scared and knew he shouldn't be there.

The room was smaller than most of the bedrooms in the house. Two small windows let in light. The only things in the room were a dresser with a mirror on it and a large bed that took up most of the space. The walls were bare, and there was no other furniture.

What surprised him was that the bed was unmade. A comforter rested to one side, the covers and blankets crumpled in a big ball at the foot of the mattress. As though they had just been used. As though someone had just woken up.

The room felt musty. But more than that, there was a feeling of dread that Zachary couldn't shake. He remembered a time in Papua New Guinea with his father, going to a place that Dad said was full of spirits. Evil spirits. That's what Zachary felt. But why? This was just a drab old room with an unmade bed.

Then he saw the tripod in the corner. It was as tall as he was, and the top of it was flat and square. It looked like the kind his parents had for their video camera.

The tripod was facing the bed.

Why would someone have a tripod set up here?

Zachary wondered what had gone on in this room. He wondered if it was adult stuff, the kinds of things Mom and Dad tried to keep from him.

He felt enclosed, trapped, desperate to leave.

I need to tell Mom and Dad about this.

There was a door behind the tripod. Zachary walked over, moved the tripod, and tried the door handle.

It was locked.

He wondered where it led. Another secret passageway, or maybe a whole unexplored section of the house.

As he walked alongside the bed, a movement caught his eye. A blur of sorts, near the dresser. He checked, but there was nothing.

He could feel his heart pounding.

Don't be such a baby. Nobody's here.

As he looked down at the bed, he saw the jerking motion again in his peripheral vision. This time he knew where it was coming from.

The mirror.

Stepping closer to the mirror, he glimpsed his own reflection. He looked scared.

As he stared at the reflection, the room started to turn black. It was almost like a gray cloud was forming behind him. He turned to see if anything was there, but again, there was nothing.

He looked at the mirror.

And gasped.

The face looking back at him wasn't the face of an eight-year-old, but the face of a man, angry and intense. He had a bloody lip and a bruised cheek and was dripping with sweat. He stared at Zach without blinking, without saying a word.

Then he grinned.

No.

Zachary grabbed the tripod and rammed its legs into the mirror, shattering the glass all over the dresser and the carpet.

He stood there, holding the tripod, breathing in and out.

What did I just see?

A piece of the mirror revealed his terrified face, completely drained of color.

I shouldn't be in here.

Zach looked around the room to see if anybody was there. If anybody had heard him break the mirror. He set the tripod on the bed and got his flashlight, rushing down the black passageway until he climbed back through the opening to the closet and the room adorned in black and white décor.

He slammed the sliding door shut and tried to figure out where the other room had been. Now that he had escaped, he was starting to feel brave again.

He thought he understood why that particular room was a secret. With the bed and the tripod—things went on in that room, adult things. But what had he seen? Even if it wasn't real—like the hand grabbing him in the passageway—what had his mind imagined?

It was real. I know it.

He waited in the bedroom to see if anybody called his name. But for several minutes, he heard nothing.

I can't tell Mom and Dad about this, not now, not after breaking the mirror. What will I say? I saw an evil man looking at me?

He would keep exploring. There was a lot about the house that needed to be discovered, and he had plenty of time to do it. He might tell Mom and Dad about some of the other things he discovered, but not this room. They didn't need to know. They would just worry. They always worried, and they didn't have to.

They wouldn't know something was broken.

It wasn't his fault. He knew what he saw. What he felt.

He didn't ever want to go back to that room.

Or ever mention it to anybody.

24

Watcher

He saw them.

The woman and her two children.

Walking out of the huge house into the driveway toward their station wagon.

Acting as though they were the only ones here within miles.

Nobody else was around. Not the husband or the other couple who lived in the house.

He knew about all of them. He'd been watching them for some time now.

Secret, hidden, silent, he watched.

He waited.

The woman looked nice and sweet and likable. The daughter looked young and friendly. But the boy . . .

Something about that boy.

That was the one he was after. Ultimately, he was here for the boy.

The trees provided cover. He could blend into the countryside without any difficulty.

It was afternoon and the little family was going somewhere. He didn't know where. He didn't care. He was here, he had finally arrived, and now he was waiting, watching.

Awaiting further instructions.

They would come.

He knew they would come.

And when they did, he would act.

Nobody would know. Nobody would hear. And this nice little family that looked so sweet would suddenly be taken from this world without a care and without notice, and he would enjoy every second of it after waiting for something like this his whole life.

His mouth watered and he licked his lips in the frigid cold of the day.

Soon enough.

25

Dinner

"I'm full."

Jim and Stephanie stared at their son. Zachary was full? The boy was a bottomless pit when it came to food. But tonight at Colby's, a restaurant in Hartside that specialized in barbecue, he had actually accomplished the unthinkable. After a couple of plates of barbecued pork, along with fries and a salad, Zachary was stuffed.

"Oh, come on," Jim said to his son with a smile. "You can do better than that."

"I can't eat another bite."

"Sure about that?"

Jim himself was reaching stuffed status, rare for him as well. He had always been a big guy who could eat a lot, but tonight he had overdone it.

The waiter came by asking if they wanted dessert.

"Anybody? Zach?"

They all shook their heads.

"Come back in a few minutes, and we'll let you know," Jim told the waiter. Sipping a glass of sweet iced tea, he relaxed in his seat.

"So, what's the big news?" Stephanie asked.

He took in her girlish face with the round eyes and a splash of freckles across her nose that he loved and she hated and realized he hadn't really looked at his wife for some time. Between the move and the studying and the work he was trying his best to avoid, Jim had been too busy. And now with the news of Tawi's death—something he had yet to tell Stephanie and Zach—Jim felt weighed down.

Maybe he was overeating due to stress.

What he wanted to do was lose himself in his wife's arms. He wanted to crawl up and around her and get tangled inside of her and feel the freedom that came with that like he had in the old days. Before the two years in Dambi.

Before he grew up.

"No big news," he finally told her with a gentle smile. "I just wanted us to get off the mountain for once. They say there's a storm coming."

"Really? When?"

"This weekend. They're predicting a lot of snow. Maybe a foot up by us. Maybe more."

"I wonder if Paul has heard. He's supposed to be coming this weekend."

"You'd better tell him to hurry up."

"He's already booked his flight."

"It's supposed to start on Saturday."

"You think—will we be okay?"

Jim touched Stephanie's hand. "Of course we will. We just need to stock up on things—that's why Bob and I came to town today. Just in case—in case anything happens."

"What could happen?" Zach asked.

Jim hadn't been aware that Zach was listening to them. His son sometimes seemed lost in his own world, and it wasn't Jim's habit to press him. Jim liked people to leave him alone, and he figured Zach felt the same. The concern in the boy's voice surprised him.

"Nothing will happen," Jim said. "It's just—since we're so far from town, we need to make sure we have enough supplies in the house. In case the power goes off. Or we get snowed in."

"Can we get snowed in?"

Zach looked frightened.

"It would be okay if we did. It might take them a while to get to our house. The plows, I mean. But we'd be fine. We just need to make sure we have enough food and—"

"Could we starve to death?"

Jim laughed and glanced at his wife. "No, of course not. But that doesn't mean we shouldn't prepare. Nothing is going to happen, Zach—we'll be fine. It just helps to take precautions."

"What if we get snowed in and nobody knows about it?"

"Zach, we're not that far away from town. And people will be checking in on us. The sheriff, for one. He's a good guy. He'll make sure we're okay."

Zach nodded and looked at the table, becoming lost again in his own world.

"I guess I should make a run to the grocery store," Stephanie said.

"We can go together if you'd like," Jim said. "Leave the kids with the Pattersons."

"Sounds okay by me. You really think we'll get a lot of snow?"

"I'm kinda hoping we do," Jim said. "Wouldn't it be fun to make tunnels out of the snow?"

Zachary nodded, obviously unimpressed.

What's wrong with him?

"What if the power goes out?" Stephanie asked.

"There's a backup generator in the house. Bob knows how to work it. There's also all that firewood in the basement—the stove in the great room still works."

"I thought it was just for show."

"Bob said it's real. And there's enough wood for a couple winters."

The waiter came back and asked if they'd decided about dessert. Jim turned to his son.

"I'll have the brownie sundae," Zach said without further thought.

Jim laughed. "Why don't you bring a few forks with that?"

Tonight something felt different. Better, safer, warmer. He didn't know why. But midway through eating the warm brownie with the hot fudge and vanilla ice cream, Jim realized what it was.

He was off the mountain, away from Edge Hill.

It was being away from the house itself that made him feel better.

He tried to shake off the thought, but he couldn't. He knew it was the truth.

Maybe they all felt that way. But nobody wanted to admit it since they would be heading back there tonight. Heading back up to the house at the end of an unlit dirt road. The massive, lodge-like house that had not been lived in for years and that had secrets of its own.

Jim didn't want to go back there. Not tonight.

26

Blood

She found herself alone.

"Jim?"

He wasn't next to her. She was a light sleeper, and usually when he got up she woke up. Almost always. But maybe the stress and the cold

maybe the wine

contributed to her being out of it.

"Jim?" she called out again, the darkness of the large room thick and overwhelming.

She shoved the comforter down and sat on the edge of the bed, adjusting to the darkness and trying to figure out where he might have gone.

The clock radio showed 3:43 AM.

The carpet felt cold against her bare feet. She wondered where her slippers were.

"Jim?" she called out again, this time just to hear her own voice.

YES.

She stopped in the middle of the room. The voice was clear and audible, coming from somewhere close.

Her breathing stopped, and she wanted to move on and to call out but she couldn't.

I SEE YOU, YOUR SLENDER FRAME. COME HERE.

This is in my mind all in my mind

I SEE YOU THERE, SCARED, HALF NAKED. I SEE YOU.

She turned toward the bathroom. The door was closed, but a slit of light escaped under the door.

The sliver of light crept toward the wall next to her. It turned orange and spread, illuminating the entire wall. Then it suddenly started to turn red.

Lines of blood dripped down the wall.

I'm imagining this all of it I'm dreaming

YOU CAN SEE EXACTLY WHAT I'M SEEING—THE BLOOD, THE DESECRATION THAT YOU HAVE COME TO.

"Jim!" she cried, the blood on the glowing wall wet and flowing.

She still couldn't move.

YOU SHOULD NEVER HAVE COME HERE. YOU DON'T BELONG, BUT YOU ARE NOT A STRANGER. WE KNOW YOU. WE HAVE SEEN YOU BEFORE, AND YOU SHOULDN'T HAVE COME BACK.

Stephanie fell to her knees, tears running down her cheeks, her body paralyzed and her mind trapped. The low voice sounded like it was coming from underneath the bed.

She couldn't move, staring helplessly as the blood moved toward her, about to suffocate her.

"Steph?"

She jerked and put her hands over her face to shield herself.

"Steph, what are you doing?"

A light suddenly came on, and the blood on the walls vanished. Jim knelt next to her, holding her.

God thank You God thank You

"What happened?"

"I was just—I woke up and didn't see you there—I must have been—I must've been dreaming."

He nodded and looked disappointed, sad.

"I'm sorry. . . ."

"It's okay," Jim said. "I needed to go to the kitchen—this cough is getting pretty nasty. I'm sorry. I thought you knew I was leaving." He looked as if he wanted to say more.

He thinks I've lost my mind. And I don't blame him.

The wall was bare. There was no light in the bathroom.

I'm losing my mind, and this place is making me do it.

"Let's go back to bed."

She moved toward the bed uneasily, afraid a hand might reach out from the darkness and grab her ankle.

That's what they do in horror movies.

Quickly slipping underneath the covers, Stephanie wished Jim would wrap his body around her. But it had been a long time since he had done that without her asking. It had been a long time since intimacy had been something she could take for granted.

She stared sightlessly at the wall for a long time. Waiting to hear something, anything.

She knew she wasn't dreaming.

But she still wasn't sure if she was losing her mind.

27

The Key

Jim sat in an uncomfortable office chair checking out ESPN .com on his laptop. He was supposed to be researching his paper, but he suddenly felt too tired. He'd spent the last six months reading and studying, and sometimes he felt overstuffed with information. Information on everything from the Old Testament to Greek-English language studies to linguistic software. He checked his e-mail for progress on the translation work.

Sometimes he wondered why he poured so much of himself into his work. The studying and the analyzing and the reading. It used to be his endless fascination and his desire to get things right—really, truly *right*. But after everything that had happened, the last few months and especially the last few weeks in Papua New Guinea, nothing he read made anything seem right. What he wanted was some face time with God. He wanted some questions answered. He wanted to stop reading scholars' thoughts and formulating his own and start hearing from God.

I've heard nothing. Not even a dial tone.

It's not like these were new thoughts. But on the mountain, he had hoped to feel less overwhelmed, more in touch with God and his family. Neither was happening.

The kids were still adjusting. When were they *not* adjusting? He knew it was for a good cause, but still he sometimes felt guilty for moving them so much. The move from Illinois to North Carolina had not been absolutely necessary, in one sense. But he had thought it would be a great opportunity to relax and rebuild.

He ought to send his parents another e-mail and let them know how things were going. But the words wouldn't come. He didn't want to put a good spin on the last few weeks. Not after hearing about Tawi. Normally Jim would throw in a Bible passage and talk about God's providence and grace, but now he just couldn't. He wasn't so sure what he believed about providence and grace anymore.

I sat by his bed for hours on end, praying, asking God to heal him, asking God to save him.

It would have been one thing if this was a normal disease that spread through their village with explainable signs and symptoms. But this had been different. Three village members, including Tawi's wife, died—just like that.

Satan tightened his fingers over that village, and God didn't choose to stop him.

Jim closed the e-mail and felt his body shudder and his fists tighten.

I'm furious. Do You hear me? I'm angry, and this is Your fault. I asked for a miracle, for a sign, for anything, and this is what happens. I wasn't praying for me but for Tawi, for the village, for all those people who were scared and skeptical.

He wiped away a tear from his face. He hated being vulnerable, being sad. But at least those two things always turned into anger. Anger was better. He could handle that.

The worn Bible on the desk next to him had been unopened for some time now.

You know where you can find hope. Why don't you take your own medicine—the medicine you're so quick to tell others about?

Not here, not now. He didn't want to hear God talking to him. He didn't want to hear it.

Idly he opened a desk drawer. Inside lay an assortment of keys, all strewn about and unorganized. Most looked identical, either silver or gold—standard keys. Some had markings on them—little sticky notes or strings and tags saying Main Door or South Wing Bedroom #4.

For several minutes, Jim examined the mess of keys. Then one in particular caught his attention. It was wrapped in paper and labeled North Wing, West Entrance.

He unwrapped the paper to examine the key. It was just like the one he had for the front door to this wing.

But this one leads into the other section of the house.

He held the key for a moment, feeling like he was suddenly carrying a deep, dark secret.

It's just a key.

He slipped it into his pants pocket. Maybe he'd take a little walk some morning or afternoon. No harm in that. Nothing wrong with checking things out. It was his responsibility.

An e-mail popped up on his screen. It was from a missionary friend who was serving in Africa. He started reading the message that began with praise to God and a quote from Psalms, but clicked it off and deleted it before he finished.

If God is interested in me, then He knows I'm angry and why I'm angry, and if He doesn't want to talk with me, then I don't want to talk to Him.

He shut off his computer and walked out of the office. As he headed down the hallway toward the kitchen, he reached into his pocket and felt the key dig into his hand.

28

Flesh

He wanted to now, right now, right this very instant, but he couldn't. They forbade it.

I need to I need it I need

The room was small and bare, and he sat on the edge of the bed breathing in and out and listening and waiting. He could feel the presence of the one, and he knew what he needed to do.

Wait it's about waiting it's about being patient

He could feel the presence of past souls in this room. What had gone on. Unspeakable, unmentionable things left their memories in pain and fear and sin and misery like a coating of paint on the wall and the scent of sulfur in the air.

I can feel you in this room right here surrounding me and your presence is very real very present very here

The knife didn't waver as he pressed it against his skin. The blade felt good against his flesh. He punctured the skin and watched the blood flow down his arm. The sight aroused his senses.

He tightened his fist around the knife and dug into the flesh, so tender. He knew where to cut and how deep to go not to hurt himself permanently.

Just a taste just a small taste just a little taste of what's to come

His fist in a ball around the knife, his eyes closed, his mouth covered in a smile, he heard the noise.

Footsteps, then a key.

He sucked in a breath.

Not yet. It's too early. They're not all here yet, and it's not time.

He withdrew the knife and stood up, then went over to the closet.

The footsteps stopped outside the door.

I can't be here it's not time it's not time do not be seen.

He looked around the small room. The dim light from the lamp was surely visible under the door.

The footsteps resumed, going back the way they had come. Back to the door to the other wing. The door opened and closed, and the lock clicked.

Fear. Fear stopped him. Fear always stops them. So many are full of so much fear, but not him never him.

He listened for a few more minutes. But he knew the steps wouldn't come again for some time.

He was still safe on this side of the house. The key had been found and the door unlocked. But fear prevented him from being found. For now.

Blood dripped onto the carpet, and he wiped his arm with his fingers. He licked them, savoring the familiar taste.

Soon so very soon I've been promised my time is come and it is almost here

He laughed.

PART THREE

Seclusion

29

Big Brother

He'll get here," Jim told her as he opened the stainless steel refrigerator door and looked inside. "It'll be fine."

Stephanie was too busy to stop what she was doing and too busy to listen to what her husband was saying. She had been in the kitchen for the last couple hours preparing dinner. Snow had been falling all day. If Paul got delayed because of the bad weather, at least he would be able to eat leftovers when he arrived tomorrow and the entire week after that. She had enough food for twenty people.

"It smells good," Jim said, taking a Mountain Dew out of the refrigerator.

"Excuse me," Stephanie said, reaching around him for some Parmesan cheese.

"Have you tried calling him?"

"Several times, actually. He must be out of range."

She set aside the pan of garlic bread. It would be a while before she put it in the oven. As she went through her mental list of things to do—pasta with homemade sauce, one of the few recipes she carried from her childhood—she tried not to consider the possibility that Paul might not come. She had been looking forward to seeing him for, well, months actually. It had been so long. And recently, more than ever, she felt like he might be able to talk to her, really talk to her, to listen to what was going on inside her, and maybe have a few things to offer.

"I think Paul should come around more often," Jim said, snitching a cucumber from the salad bowl. "You need any help?"

"No, that's okay, thanks."

Evelyn had already offered half a dozen times, but Stephanie wanted to do this herself. She wanted to prove to her big brother that she could cook better than Mom.

And now all this work will be for nothing.

Jim leaned his big frame against the counter. He eyed the glass next to the stove. "You must *really* be stressed if you're drinking," he said.

"Don't start."

"I'm just saying—"

"Not now."

"It's going to be fine," Jim told her. "He'll call and let us know where he is. We'll just have to wait and be patient."

"I know. It's fine."

"It's *not* fine, and you know it. You're more stressed about this than you are about our big Christmas dinners."

"It's been a long time since I've seen him, that's all. I just want this to be . . . I want it to be special."

"It's going to be special, Steph. Just—don't be upset if he doesn't come."

"I'm getting a bad feeling. . . ."

"What?"

"I'm worried something happened to him."

"Steph . . ."

As Jim crossed the kitchen toward his wife, Zachary bolted into the room with wide eyes and a huge grin on his face.

"Uncle Paul is here!" he called, out of breath from running.

Jim looked at Stephanie and smiled, and a sense of relief washed over her. A small part of her wanted to cry.

"You stay in here," Jim told her, putting a hand behind her

neck in a gesture that said, *It's okay.* "I'll go get him. It'll take us half an hour to make it to the kitchen."

They both laughed, and Stephanie shifted into high gear. Dinner was going to be a home run.

❧

"A TOAST," SAID THE tall, lean figure at the dining room table. "To my baby sister, on seeing her again after a very long time, and on sharing my first glass of wine with her."

Stephanie laughed as she hoisted her glass and looked around the table. Even Ashley was holding up her plastic cup.

"Mom, can I try some wine?" Zachary asked.

"No sirree."

"Oh, come on, Steph," Paul said. "Mom and Dad let us try it when we were young."

"And look what it did to you," she joked.

Paul joined the conversation then, telling them the roads leading up to Edge Hill were very difficult to travel, even with four-wheel drive. He'd switched rental cars and gone with an SUV when he got to Asheville, having heard the ominous weather reports.

Seeing him again felt natural and right. He had come in and given her a big hug, and he seemed exactly the same as last time she saw him. He had a metabolism most women would kill for, and his face had only a few more wrinkles than it did ten years ago. His hair was still cut short, spiked like a teenager.

People often remarked that Steph and Paul didn't look anything like brother and sister, and Stephanie had always thought that was because Paul got most of the good genes. So she was delighted to hear Evelyn say she saw a close resemblance.

Paul quickly got to know the Pattersons. He was just one of those people. In a room full of a dozen strangers, he could make each and every one of them feel important and special. To Paul, they almost always were.

"So, Miss Stephanie, where did you learn to cook like this? Surely not in your little village overseas."

"You learn to be creative when you don't have everything at your disposal."

"Including food," Jim said.

"Yes, food helps." Stephanie laughed. "But I've always been a good cook, haven't I?"

Jim tapped his large belly as he worked on his second plate of pasta, meatballs, sausage, and bread. "Don't I look underfed?"

They all laughed, and Zachary asked again if he could try some wine.

"What grade are you in again, Zach?" Paul asked.

"Third."

"Yes, eight years old going on twenty," said Jim. "He's very bright for his age."

"So what do you think of being up here on the mountaintop?"

"It's cool."

"Do you like this house?"

Zach gave a shy, almost nervous yes. For a second, Stephanie wondered if he was hiding something. But he was probably just nervous because of Paul's arrival.

"Okay, so I just gotta say it," Paul said, his Midwestern accent coming out the more he spoke. "What's with this place? I mean, I'm going to stop sending you guys support checks. Maybe you should start sending *me* money. Look at this."

"Pretty incredible, isn't it?" Jim said, smiling.

"Yeah, you could say that. This is outlandish. Who built this and . . . and what was going through their minds?"

"A man named Charles Wolfcott," Bob said, his thick eyebrows looking scholarly as he spoke. "A multimillionaire who some say built this as a retirement home."

"And so . . . two missionary families are staying here now. Makes sense."

"Charles passed away less than a year ago. The only blood

relative he had anything to do with was a brother in Florida. Very different kind of man. It was his idea to open this up as a center to house missionaries on furlough."

"Wow. I might have to get into the missionary business." Paul looked around at the ornate dining room.

They spoke about the house, and Stephanie served dessert and coffee. The kids wanted to play, so Evelyn agreed to watch them. Stephanie was grateful for the offer—and she knew Evelyn was probably just as happy to turn on the television and watch one of the many satellite channels instead of chatting at the dinner table.

"So how have you guys been? I mean really been?" Paul asked.

Stephanie looked at her brother. She couldn't understand why this man wasn't married, why he didn't have at least five children. He had so much to offer; it was a shame someone didn't have his heart.

"We've been good," Jim said.

Putting on a good face, Stephanie thought. *As always.*

"But it's been a bit of an adjustment, coming back to the States. Being back in Wheaton."

"Pleasantville?" Paul asked with a chuckle. "Too bad I couldn't visit you up there."

Paul had never hidden his feelings about the town they lived in. He said it must be a residence requirement to be a member of a church and have at least four children. White, yuppie, preppy, self-righteous suburb.

Sometimes I agree with him.

"There were just a lot of things to do," Jim said.

"Too many things to do. Jim was going to school and trying to write a paper and dealing with his parents, and it ended up—"

"It's good to be here," Jim interrupted.

Paul looked at both of them, clearly waiting for one of them to say something. Even Bob Patterson seemed caught in the awkward silence.

Now is not the time, Steph. Just wait. Paul isn't going anywhere, and

it makes no sense to talk about serious issues with Bob and Jim here.
Wait until you're alone with him.

"We're very glad to be here," she finally said. "Can I get you guys some more coffee?"

"Stephanie, let me just say," Paul said, stretching out his arms and yawning, "that this is probably the best meal I've had in years."

"Well, you need to come around more often."

"I know. It's my own fault. By the way—I don't mean to put you guys on the spot, but do you have an extra bedroom you can spare?"

❧

PAUL STROLLED INTO THE family room in the south wing where the television hung on the wall and where the adults usually congregated. He had tucked Ashley and Zachary into bed at their request, and now he came downstairs with a grin on his face.

"Have I told you that you have amazing children?"

"Come to think of it, no," Stephanie said.

"You do. They're really great, Steph."

"Thank you."

"You have to be a good mother to have children like that."

"Well, Jim does his share too."

The Pattersons had already called it a night, and Jim was off somewhere, politely giving Stephanie some time with her brother.

Paul selected one of the three couches and sank into it.

"So tell me," he said, "are you happy?"

The question didn't surprise her. It was the timing that took her off guard.

"Sure, I'm happy."

"About half a dozen times tonight, I saw a look of sadness on your face. A heavy look, like you've got a lot on your mind."

Suddenly she wanted to break down and cry. Let it all out. She didn't know why she felt like doing this in front of Paul. Maybe it was because he was the only link she had to her past and her parents. Maybe it was because he knew her, and she felt she could tell him anything.

"There has been a lot on my mind," she said. "On both of our minds. Jim has been going through a lot."

"Like what?"

"Some stuff happening in the village, for one thing. I told you a little about it." She told him about the unexpected deaths that she and Jim attributed to spiritual warfare. And now the recent death of Tawi that Jim had just told her about.

"It's hit Jim especially hard, though I know he's putting on a good face about it. He tries to hide his emotions, but I'm his wife. He doesn't realize I can see through it."

"You can see through a lot of things in people," Paul said, his blue eyes unblinking. "It's a special gift you have."

"I don't know about that. I sometimes just think—I don't know. I think the devil is trying to discourage us in every way, and I take it as an attack against Jim and me. It's been hard."

Paul rubbed his chin and thought for a moment. "Steph, you know me, right? You know I love you."

"I do," she said.

"And I've always given you your space on things about faith and all that. You know where I stand. That doesn't mean I think you're crazy or Jim is crazy, and it doesn't mean I love you any less. But it's just—things happen—people die, for instance. People get sick. Or people go through busy times. Or depression. Or hard times in a marriage. Or a job that stinks. Or anything like that. You know—it doesn't have to be the devil doing it. Sometimes that's just the way life is. And you have to go through it. *You* have to deal with it. Prayers are fine and good, but sometimes the only thing you have on this earth, and the only—and I mean only—things you can control are your own actions and feelings."

"I know. It's just—there have been things you don't understand—"

"There are probably a lot of things that feel like spiritual attacks or the devil trying to put you down. But you guys—man, you guys were overseas in the jungle, talking and living with a bunch of natives."

"It's not like that," Stephanie said.

"Yeah, well, it's sorta like that. And Steph—I don't disrespect you for that. I love you for that passion and that belief. You've really got that faith thing going on. But it's not *all* about faith and God. Remember, you have yourself and your family to deal with. You have your own two hands and feet, and you have your mind and you can do a lot of things on your own, whether there is a God who loves you or not."

She nodded and came over to sit by her brother.

"You know—I'm supposed to be the one with the answers," she told him, holding his hand.

"No you're not. Look—who practically raised you? Did you forget about that?"

"Of course not."

"We both grew up pretty fast."

I don't want to ruin tonight by talking about Mom and Dad.

"I see it in your eyes," Paul said. "Don't worry. I'm not going there. We'll have time to talk about them later." He squeezed her hand and kissed her on the cheek. "It's good to see you, Steph."

"You too, big brother."

30

Pictures

The kids were in bed, and the Pattersons had retreated as well. Stephanie and Paul were talking on the other side of the house, giving Jim the opportunity he needed to slip away. It was the fourth time he had entered the north wing. He had only checked out a few rooms so far, but each time his disgust and dread grew.

He couldn't believe this place had so many ugly sides to it. The more he discovered, the more tainted it became.

I have to do something. I refuse to let my family be near such filth.

He quietly walked down the hallway. This was where he had gone last time, where he had lingered for a long time. Then left full of guilt and frustration. Left feeling dirty.

He pushed the door open, jumping a little at the slight squeak of the hinges, and looked around to see if anyone was there.

You're alone. Stop being so spooked.

The wind outside was loud and violent. He entered the library and locked the door behind him. Inside were a leather couch and love seat surrounded by bookshelves. The collection of books had been the first thing he noticed. Bizarre books and titles of all sorts. Books on religions and symbols and hunting and languages and art and photography and everything in between. There were books on sex, how-to guides and art books that might as well have been pornography. And then there was a large section of hardbound books—*Playboy* and *Penthouse* and other magazine collections displayed like literature.

This was where Jim had come the other night, first flipping through the books on the occult and Eastern religions and then coming across these magazines.

He had glanced. That was all.

But the images and the content stuck with him. It bothered him. It tugged at him and offered temptation. He hadn't said anything about it to Stephanie, simply because he didn't want her to worry. But even that made him feel guilty.

He took the folded garbage bag out of his pocket. He would get rid of this. He didn't want it here, whispering to him to look a little more, suggesting there was nothing wrong with sampling, with taking just a bite.

Jim shoved handfuls of the books into the bag, filling it with as many as he could. As he did, he resisted looking inside. He forced himself to think of his family, to think of them close by.

A verse stuck with him from his Bible reading that morning. "So obey my instructions, and do not defile yourselves by committing any of these detestable practices that were committed by the people who lived in the land before you." The verse had jumped out at him from nowhere, as they often did. It was from Leviticus, an often overlooked book.

These days Jim could relate a little more to Moses and the Israelites. After their experiences in Dambi, he understood the term "wilderness" in ways he couldn't before.

As he tied the top of the bag shut, he understood why this wing was locked up. Somebody didn't want this stuff seen.

What else lies hidden away in these dark, silent rooms? What sort of dark deeds were done in these spaces?

Jim walked back toward the great room in the house, carrying the heavy bag that was stretched to its limit. He would carry this to town and drop it off in the garbage there. It was a small step, but he knew he would feel better getting rid of this. For his family.

For myself.

Another passage of Scripture came to mind. A Psalm: "Do not hold us guilty for the sins of our ancestors! Let your compassion quickly meet our needs, for we are on the brink of despair."

Jim knew they weren't on the brink. They were stuck in the pit of despair, swallowed deep and covered over.

He wanted to believe God had a plan and purpose for all of this. But he didn't know.

He was afraid to find out.

31

The Campfire

The howling winds beat against the house. She pictured the massive structure, a fortress against the elements, standing there upright taking a beating from the snow and pounding ice. Tucked inside were seven of them—the Pattersons, Jim, her, the kids, and now Paul.

The news channels said it was going to storm all night and all weekend, and Hartside and its neighboring towns might get a foot of snow. Who knew how much Edge Hill would get?

Jim was resting after their long evening. Wine had that effect on her husband, putting him out like a light. She could tell she was buzzed, a little too much, but it didn't matter. As Paul said, who was there to judge? He was the last person on earth to judge her. *So drink up,* he had said with his playful laugh and mischievous eyes.

As she washed her face, the first signs of age showing underneath and around her eyes, she thought of their conversation about God. The subject didn't come up a lot, but tonight it had, and it brought back a flood of memories about her teen years and coming home and how everything had suddenly changed.

Stephanie often joked to friends that it was by accident that she became a believer. Of course, some people didn't like that joke. Some believed God chose His followers from the beginning of time. Others simply believed that salvation was the work of the Holy Spirit.

She knew these things, but she also knew that if it hadn't been for her tenth-grade friend Courtney, her road toward faith would have been very different—if it had even come at all. But Courtney hadn't known what they were in for. If either of them had known the camp set in the Michigan countryside was a Christian camp, they wouldn't have gone—Courtney because she would have thought it was boring and Stephanie because her parents wouldn't have allowed it.

"Don't get into trouble with any boys," her mother had said.

That was the only advice her parents had given her. Neither of them had told her to stay away from altar calls and late-night prayer vigils and pastors talking by the campfire. They hadn't told her not to listen to Bible readings, and they hadn't ordered her not to ask questions she had carried all her life.

The camp was run by Christians who were sincere and loving. They weren't like the televangelists her parents mocked or the pious churchgoers in her neighborhood who never even bothered to wave hello. They weren't like the preachy kids at school who made others feel bad for not believing. These were simply loving, fun men and women who wanted to befriend the campers.

It was during the second week, after a night of singing praise songs around the campfire, that Stephanie finally broke down and let go. She was sixteen years old and had lived her whole life believing there was something more, something else, something better, but she could never articulate what it was.

Her parents were distant and strange, and sometimes they frightened her. She didn't know necessarily why, but she knew they kept things from Paul and her. Her older brother knew more than she did, but he kept his information from her too. She was the baby and the younger sister, and he wanted to protect her and said things like, "It's just Mom and Dad. Don't worry, I'm here." And yes, Paul was there, but even that sometimes didn't feel like enough. So around a campfire in the middle of July under a star-filled sky and a moon so full and bright, singing about God's goodness and creation and listening to the pastor talk about the meaning of life, Stephanie finally prayed.

She didn't know exactly how to do it or what to say, but she knew her prayer was heard. Every word she uttered, every fear she expressed, every doubt that arose in her mind, every question and request—they were heard. She believed God was above and around her because she could *feel* Him. She could feel the goodness and the presence of something holy and powerful and mighty and good, and she prayed a simple wandering prayer, confessing that she didn't know who she was or where she was going but she didn't want to be on her own anymore.

Stephanie knew she was a sinner—admitting that wasn't a problem. She knew she failed time and time again. It was the thought that those failures and those sins could be taken from her, that this man who had supposedly died on a cross and then come back to life wasn't just a sweet Sunday school story or a wacky, made-up tale, but it was true and He had cried tears just as real as her own and had bled with the same flesh and bone as her own—and He had done it *for her.*

So she prayed as the fire crackled around her, surrounded by campers and loving, caring adults.

She prayed. And from that moment on, her life had completely changed. She felt different and knew that this had been her moment. Not just a fleeting summer moment in a teen's life, but a moment that would last for eternity.

Stephanie brushed her teeth and remembered that time with both fondness and fear. The bad part had been coming back home, telling her parents what had happened, seeing the stunned expressions on their faces, seeing their look of shame and betrayal. It would have been one thing if they had laughed at her or called her naïve or silly, but their reaction wasn't slight annoyance or skepticism—it was outright hatred.

For the next two years, Stephanie lived like a Christian in Communist Russia. She was an outcast, and she had to hide her beliefs, much to her shame and doubt. She couldn't even open up to Paul, who didn't understand why she was going through the pain of believing in something that had to be too good to be true.

"The only things I believe in are my own two hands and what I can do with them," he told her.

It was only when she left for Providence Christian College in Summit, Illinois, that she found peace. The same peace that had descended on her that summer night at the campfire. Throughout the next decade, there were many times when that peace rested with her, when she felt God's presence and knew things were okay.

She longed for that peace to return and believed that when she finally closed her eyes and took her last breath, an eternity of peace would await her. To be free of worry and doubt and anxiousness and, most of all, fear would be a wonderful thing. To close her eyes at night no longer wondering what she might dream about and why and what would happen and what Jim might think. To wake up in the morning and not feel the distance between herself and Jim and wonder what was happening to her and why she wasn't fulfilled, or wonder about her place as a mother and as a wife. To not worry all the time.

Rest in me.

She found nighttime tough because sleep sometimes didn't come, and when it did, it came at a cost. Jim and Paul and her children didn't understand what it was like to be a mother and a wife and to try to love God when she knew that so much in her had been programmed by her parents *not* to love and cherish God.

Being around Paul brought back memories of her youth. She was amazed that somehow through the pain and sadness, God had led her to Him. Perhaps He had chosen her before the beginning of time, or perhaps she had simply been in the right place at the right time to accept God's love and forgiveness and finally be able to see and smell and breathe in something that had been missing for sixteen long years.

Hope.

She shivered. Not at the cold, but at how life had worked out. Paul, her brave independent older brother, made no concessions about knowing or believing in God. Yet he was doing fine. He was happy and content and enjoying life. And then there she was, she and Jim. She was growing increasingly scared at Jim's distance and his anger. She wanted to talk to him, but she didn't know how. She was frightened of what he might say or, even more, at the possibility that he might not say anything. That he might turn his back, as he often did.

She didn't know how to turn to God anymore. She was losing her faith, and she was afraid of gaining it back. She was isolated and cut off from everybody, most of all from her heavenly Father.

She loved God. It was just . . . sometimes the stress of life overwhelmed her.

It's more than just stress. It's something more. Something deeper. Something darker.

But she refused to go there. She didn't want to spend another night having nightmares. Paul was here, and she would celebrate his arrival before the storm got too bad. They would have an enjoyable and memorable time together, and she would somehow dig herself out of this hole she had fallen into.

32

In the West Wing

Living at Edge Hill was like visiting another country. Every day there was something to discover about it, some new room Zach hadn't seen or some new hidden passageway. Each day he worked in secret on his map of Edge Hill. So far, he had most of the south and west wings finished.

That morning, as the grown-ups finished breakfast and talked about boring things like the president and politics, Zach checked out the west wing. This section of the house had been built first, according to his dad, and it differed slightly in style from the south wing. There was a kitchen, though it wasn't as large or as nice as the one in the south wing. The bedrooms were normal, and there was a game room that Zach spent a lot of time in, playing pool or foosball with his dad or with Mr. Patterson.

His parents thought he was just playing when he went off alone, making up imaginary scenarios in a large house. They just told him to be careful and to stay out of things. He wasn't bothering anything looking for secret passageways. Maybe one day, before they left, he would show his parents his map.

If only I could get inside the north wing, he thought as he walked down the hallway off the large room in the west wing. *There's got to be a secret passageway that leads over there.*

Since discovering the first secret passageway that led to the small room with the bed and the tripod, he had uncovered two more. One had been in his father's study, of all places, in a walk-in closet that had a door much like the first one.

Zach discovered it while using his father's laptop to surf the Internet (something else he didn't bother to mention to his dad). It led to another room, an office filled with files and folders and lots of papers. They looked important, with bank names on them and lots of numbers. There were a few filing cabinets that were locked too. Zach figured this must be where important (and top secret) files were kept.

The other passageway was a bigger discovery. Zach had been playing in the great room close to the fireplace—a huge one, big enough for his father to walk through. It looked clean, almost too clean. Zach got up close to examine the ornate cedar mantel and stone base. As he stared past the inner hearth at the firebrick back, he noticed a slight opening, as though something was lodged in the stone. Zach pushed against the back wall, but it wouldn't budge. *Maybe it's just a defect*, he thought. But maybe it was something else.

Another passageway.

So he looked around for a button or a switch.

After twenty minutes, he found it. On the right-hand side of the mantel, near the back wall, in the same color as the wood, with only a slight bump distinguishing it as a button. He pushed it and heard a slight movement inside the fireplace.

Nobody was around, so what could be the harm of exploring?

Zach climbed into the fireplace and found a short passageway that led to a ladder going down. This led to a closet in the back of the empty basement. He was slightly disappointed. The basement wasn't exactly exciting.

As he passed the west wing's master bedroom, Zach realized he had drunk too much orange juice for breakfast. He needed a bathroom fast. He hurried into the big bedroom and then into the master bath. The hickory cabinets and granite countertops seemed pretty fancy. There were two sinks and doors underneath. He glanced at them, wondering for a minute . . .

What if?

He caught himself just as his aim missed the toilet.

Oops.

This was why Mom told him to use just the one bathroom, off his own room.

He wiped up the mess with some toilet paper, then washed his hands and checked underneath the sink.

Nothing. Just an ordinary sink cabinet.

He tried the others. He was used to opening and closing every door he could find, pressing every button or switch or lever.

As he opened the cabinet door, he almost closed it automatically. But he realized something was different.

The plumbing for the sink looked different, more sparse. There was more space in this cabinet. And there was no back to it.

He climbed inside and reached toward the back of the cabinet. There was a panel there. And it was open.

Here's number four.

Zach looked behind him. Why not? He crawled through to the other side, into an opening that was three feet by three feet. When he could finally stand, he was in a narrow hallway sprinkled with light coming in through small holes in the ceiling. The hallway went for twenty feet, then turned right.

Without hesitation, Zach followed it.

33

Mom and Dad

When was the last time you spoke with them?"

Paul looked at his sister and smiled. He was sitting on a bar stool next to the kitchen island while Stephanie washed the dishes. "I wondered when you'd ask about them."

"I waited awhile."

"I'm stuffed and happy. Do I have to talk about them?"

"Of course not," Stephanie said, drying a frying pan.

"You know I'm just kidding."

Stephanie glanced out the window. The snow had stopped. Jim had been talking about making one more run to Hartside while he could. According to the TV reports, the storm was going to pick up again later.

"I saw them a month ago."

She stopped what she was doing and gaped at her brother, perched on the stool in his sweater and jeans, still looking twenty-five.

"Are you serious?"

He nodded. "Yeah. Figured I'd tell you in person."

"How are they?"

"Same as always. Sometimes I wonder if they'll ever change. Or—wait, I take that back. Sometimes I wonder why I expect them to ever change."

"And they—how is—"

"Mom is fine—health-wise. That's what you were wondering, right?"

She nodded and looked away, feeling the weight of her tears, not wanting Paul to see them.

"She's feeling better than she has in the past few years."

"That's good," Stephanie said.

"They asked about you. You don't write to them anymore?"

"Why should I? All they would do is throw my letters away."

"They didn't know you were overseas."

"You hadn't told them?"

Paul took a sip of his coffee. "I don't talk with them that much, you know."

"Yeah, well, they don't hate you."

"They don't hate you either."

"They hate my beliefs."

"Well, yeah . . ."

"And that's pretty much me. My life. Who I am."

"Yeah," Paul said.

"They haven't even seen Ashley, you know that? She's five years old. It's ridiculous."

Paul cursed. "No, that's what it is."

"What was it like, being back home?"

"Same as always. Nothing about that house or that neighborhood changes."

Stephanie put a plate away and leaned on the kitchen island, facing her brother. "Paul, can I ask you a question?"

"Of course."

"Do you remember when we were growing up, living at the house on Willoughby Drive. . . . Do you remember bad things happening there?"

His face tensed, and for a second she thought he might not answer.

"What do you mean?"

"I just . . . over the past few years, I've sometimes remembered things—weird things, things that don't make sense."

"Like what?"

"I don't know. Sometimes I—sometimes I dream. I have nightmares. Recently they've been worse. And sometimes I dream about that house. About things that happened there."

"What things?"

"Weird stuff. Not abuse—I'm not talking about anything like that. I just sometimes wonder . . . what Mom and Dad were into. There were a few times when I thought they might be into some strange stuff."

Paul shrugged. "They've always been a little different, you know. I think it's from the drugs they did in their college days." He smiled.

"I'm serious," she said.

"I am too. Look, at the core of it, they're both self-centered. Nothing more than that."

"But—there is more. I know there is."

"Like what?"

"Do you ever—did you ever see them—I don't know—practicing any sort of . . ."

"Any sort of what? Doing what? I don't get what you're talking about."

"Sometimes I wonder if they were into the occult."

Paul looked at his sister for a moment, stunned by her comment, then let out a big laugh.

"Dad? Into the occult? Steph—I think you've been out amongst the natives for too long."

"I'm being serious."

"You're crazy. Yeah, and Mom and Dad visit the Playboy Mansion on weekends, too."

"Paul—"

"Where in the world did you get that idea?"

"Remember all those books Dad had in his office? On magic and spirituality and things like that?"

"I don't recall books on devil worship."

"They had things all around the house. Ouija boards. Tarot

cards. Remember that psychic they had over for dinner one night?"

"That was just curiosity. Steph, come on. You can't be serious."

"I am. I'm just—there were other things."

He's not going to believe you. He's not going to understand.

"Like what?"

What about the party? What about the time Mom made you go to the séance? What about the time you were locked in your bedroom and felt the forces of Satan?

"Steph?" Paul said.

"Yeah."

"What's wrong? You're completely white."

"Nothing. I'm just tired. I just—it's exhausting thinking about Mom and Dad."

"So don't."

"But I—they're still my parents. Our parents. You've been able to keep an amicable relationship."

"It's all superficial," Paul said. "It doesn't really matter, you know. It doesn't change the fact that basically we didn't have parents growing up. Sharing a meal with them doesn't compensate for a lifetime of neglect and self-centeredness."

"Sometimes I wonder if I should call them."

"You know how that would go," Paul said. "You'd go into it with an expectation, thinking they might actually act like parents. Then they would disappoint you. You know?"

"That's why I don't call or write or do anything. Why I've chosen for them not to be a part of my life. My family's life."

"What does Jim say?"

"He leaves it up to me. He understands. He sees how much they've hurt me."

Paul tightened his lips and forced a concerned smile. "You don't need them, Stephanie. *We* don't need them. We've gone long enough without them."

"I know. It's just . . ."

She fought the tears again, this time unable to turn away before Paul saw them. It was okay. He was her big brother.

He stood and went to her, put his arms around her. "You've done fine without them. You don't need them. You'll never need them."

34

Visit

The noise jerked him awake.

The house didn't have a doorbell, but it did have a buzzer that registered on the intercoms throughout the house. It was late afternoon, and the ominous clouds outside looked like they might start dropping snow any moment. Jim wiggled out of his semisleep on the couch and sat up. He was alone in the media room.

"Steph?" he called as he got up and walked toward the living room. "Steph? You there?"

"In here," she answered.

She was working on a puzzle with Zachary while Ashley played with her toys nearby.

"You hear that?"

She nodded. "Were you sleeping? I'm sorry . . ."

"It's fine. Who do you think it is?"

"I don't know. I don't think it's Paul—he said he was going to take a nap. And I don't know why the Pattersons would have gone out."

"I'll go check."

Jim walked down the hall into the great room. Sometimes

the size of the room intimidated him. The high ceilings and windows normally would have been inviting, but now just revealed the blurry darkness of the storm outside. And it was colder in this room because of the huge windows. He glanced at the fireplace.

Maybe I'll have to get a fire going in that thing.

As he passed the door to the north wing, he thought about his last trip to that part of the house.

I can't get those images out of my head.

The buzzer went off again. Maybe Bob had gone out for some reason and was locked out.

He undid the two bolts of the large main door and opened it. Some of the caked-on snow surrounding the doorway dropped off onto the wood floor. For a second Jim didn't recognize the big figure at the door.

"I was beginnin' to think you guys weren't here after all," a southern voice said. The crusty face of the sheriff from Hartside grinned at him. "You gonna make me stand out here all day?"

"I'm sorry," Jim said, gesturing the man inside.

Lou Nolan wore jeans and a thick coat and carried several days' worth of beard on his face. He pulled back his hood and wiped down what little hair he had.

"Just thought I'd check up on you folks before the roads get worse."

"How are they? I haven't been out in a couple of days."

"They've plowed most of the way up here," Lou said. "It's just the last couple miles or so. You can drive on them fine now, but you might have some problems in the next day or two. The storm is doing a U-turn and heading back this way for another pounding. I figured I'd make the drive up here while I could."

"Well—here, let me take that coat," Jim said. "Why don't you make yourself at home?"

"Might be a little hard in this place."

"Too creeped out for a cup of coffee?"

"Nah. Never."

Jim led the way into the house and introduced Lou to Stepha-nie and the kids, then offered to give the sheriff a tour of the rest of the house.

When they reached the great room, Jim thought about tell-ing Lou what he had found in the north wing. He had already shown the sheriff most of the south and west wings.

"So what do you think?" Jim asked him.

"I think the guy who built this was off his rocker."

"Yeah, but it's a nice place to live."

"It's too big, if you ask me. What in the world did he build it this big for?"

"I have no idea. But my son sure likes it."

"Tell him to be careful."

"I do," Jim said.

Tell him what you found.

Lou looked around the room and finished his cup of coffee. "You guys stocked up on food and other supplies?"

"We are," Jim said. "But I was planning on going into town to get a few more things."

"It looks like it's already starting to snow a little more."

Tell him. Just tell him that you found some strange things, that you have some questions about what else might be over there.

"Jim? I added a few more things to your list," Stephanie said, walking into the room and handing him a piece of paper.

It can wait, Jim thought. *It can wait until the storm is over and I'm visiting Lou in town and I check out a little more of what's actually over there.*

Jim smiled at his wife as he looked over the list. The "few more things" had grown to a shopping cart's worth.

35

Car Problems

He watched the truck drive up to the lodge, saw the man climb out of it. There was a Madison County Sheriff's Department sign on the driver's door.

He could be a problem.

He waited, watching the house from the woods above. It started snowing lightly.

Take care of him. He might be a problem.

The last thing he wanted to do was draw attention to himself. Whatever he did needed to be quick and unseen.

He started walking away from Edge Hill, away from the stranger's truck and the family.

He might have a gun on him and that could be an even bigger problem.

He kept walking, listening for the sound of an engine.

After about half an hour, the sheriff approached him slowly from behind. He moved over to the side of the road while the truck slowed down and the driver rolled down his window.

"Hey, you lost there, buddy?" the sheriff asked in his annoying southern drawl.

No, but you are, and you're going to wish you'd never come down this road.

He made up a story about his car breaking down a mile down the road.

"You almost made it to the end of the road. I was just visiting a family there. What's wrong with the car?"

He mumbled something about the engine, maybe the battery.

"Well, let's go check it out. If it won't start, I can give you a ride down to Hartside."

He climbed into the truck, looking around, checking for a gun. He couldn't find anything.

"What's your name? I'm Lou."

He shook the man's hand and made up a name. It didn't matter what he said.

Lou drove slowly down the road, making small talk about the weather. He did his best to engage in this chitchat. As he did, he looked around the interior of the truck.

And then he found it.

That will be perfect.

It was a long, steel flashlight, one of those heavy-duty ones that probably weighed twenty pounds. It sat beneath his passenger's seat.

"I've lived around these parts all my life," Lou said. "I got a wife and a few kids and even a couple grandkids, though they don't live around here. . . ."

He reached down and grasped the flashlight in his hand as he stared at Lou and listened. He made sure he maintained eye contact, made sure he knew where Lou's eyes were.

wait just a minute just one more minute wait until he turns the corner

"So where'd you say you left the car?"

They had just made the turn and were heading on a straight path, Lou driving slowly, too slowly in fact.

He didn't reply. He just stared at the older man.

You need to shut up it's time for you to shut up

The flashlight felt light in his hand as he whipped it against the forehead of the driver. Lou's head jolted back, hitting the headrest as he let out a slight moan.

"What the—" Lou started to say.

But he didn't stop pounding the flashlight, continued until the car came to a dead stop just like the driver.

In the cold silence, he looked at Lou and then looked down at his hand, his clothes, the flashlight.

He needed to act quickly and clean this mess up.

36

Bite Marks

"You know what I forgot?"

"What?"

Stephanie's voice sounded distant on his cell phone, as though she were talking in a tunnel.

"Paper towels. We're almost out," Stephanie said.

"Guess we'll have to use regular towels. Or our shirts."

She said something, but he didn't hear it. "What?"

"—again and I'm thinking we might need more."

"I didn't hear what you said."

"I said we're already running low on milk again, and I'm thinking we might need more."

"I got some," Jim said.

"Where are you?"

"I'm near the turnoff. Have you looked outside? It's coming down hard. It's a good thing I decided not to go to Home Depot." He didn't hear anything. "Steph?"

It was dead. He must have lost her. Even without the storm, he could only get one bar at the house, and that sometimes faded in and out. He was only fifteen minutes away, so anything else could wait until he got back.

I might need to get new service.

It was good to get outside today, even with the threat of more snow, to get away from the house, see some other people. He had asked Paul if he wanted to go for the drive, but his brother-in-law had passed. Zach had wanted to stay in too.

I wonder what Zach is getting himself into.

Jim had enough on his mind for the moment. That key. The key that came out of nowhere.

Get rid of it. Give it to Bob. Or Stephanie.

But he knew the last thing his wife needed was more anxiety. He thanked God that Paul had made it to the house. His presence always seemed to make Stephanie lighter, happier. A couple years ago he might have been resentful of this, wondering why he didn't have the same effect on his wife. But it wasn't a competition. And maybe now some of her recent issues would ease up or even go away.

His mind drifted back to the key. And his journey into the office.

What else is over there? I only checked out a few rooms.

It fascinated him, but it scared him too. He needed to keep all of it away from Stephanie and the kids. From everyone, in fact. He just needed some time, time to meet with the sheriff, time to reevaluate if they should be up here.

"This place still gives me the creeps," Lou had told him.

He didn't admit that, yes, it still gave him the creeps too. He wondered what Paul thought and felt about the place. Jim's fears were just from what Lou had told him. Combined with Stephanie's nightmares.

The snow drifted sideways, and visibility became hazier. His windshield wipers weren't helping much. He drove the station wagon slowly, thankful for its European four-wheel drive.

Sometimes the surrounding woods looked like they could swallow him. The lack of human life around here was a stark contrast to the sprawling land of suburbia. Here, it was pitch-

black at night and the woods were thick and wild. It didn't help
they were on a large stretch of unoccupied land. Or that they
were in the middle of the worst storm North Carolina had seen
for a decade.

The wind whipped against the car, and he kept the radio volume down. He drove slowly, the tires spinning a little too much.
As he entered the straightaway that dropped steadily to reach the
driveway of Edge Hill, he noticed something dark at the edge
of the road.

What the . . .

At first he thought it was a dog, but as he slowed down and
squinted to see beyond the windshield littered with thick flakes,
he noticed it looked like a coyote, a wolf even. He drove a little
closer. It was a gray wolf, from what he could see, and he jumped
as it turned its head, its eyes glaring at him from the road. It
looked defiant, almost possessed, its eyes daring him onward.

He slowed the car almost to a halt.

The wolf continued staring at him, then went back to whatever it was sniffing . . . or eating.

That was blood on its mouth.

But he couldn't have seen that, not with this storm, not with
the blinding snow.

He kept driving, even slower now. The wolf looked up again,
then stared into the woods on the other side of the road, as
though something was coming. Suddenly it darted into the
woods below.

Jim kept driving until he was only a few feet away from where
the wolf had been.

Was that really a wolf? Do wolves even live up here?

He wondered what it had been eating.

And what scared it off?

Part of him said to just keep driving, stay in the car and keep
driving.

The wolf might come back.

Or worse than that, something might have scared the wolf off. Something in the woods. Something close by, watching him.

Stop it, Jim. You're acting like Steph.

He put the car in Park and got out, his coat unzipped and the wind blasting his face and neck. The snow didn't bother him. It really wasn't all that cold—not like Chicago. This wasn't bad at all.

The lights from his car illuminated the path in front of him. He could see the wolf's tracks. Something long and dark lay at the side of the road.

What is that?

He walked up closer, trying to make out what the oblong shape was. It didn't look like any animal. Instead, it looked

ragged?

like half a body, a torso without the rest of its body . . .

stop it

. . . a torso with its arm ripped off . . .

But as he examined it, he discovered it was a shredded coat. The arm had been torn off and the neck and edges looked wet and bloody.

If it was a coat, who did it belong to?

Get back in the car, Jim. That's not anything you want to be around. Get back in.

He stood next to the shape and tried to comprehend what he was seeing.

Drops of blood dotted the snow all around the dark coat.

Maybe it's just something the wolf found in the woods. No big deal, no reason to be alarmed.

He couldn't bring himself to touch the jacket. Snow was starting to cover it.

Where did all this blood come from? It's too wet to be some random coat found in the woods. The blood belonged to someone, and it sure wasn't that wolf.

As snow fell and he stared at the torn coat, the light from his car made an eerie glow on the bloody clump. Jim looked around, wondering if the wolf might come back. Then wondering if something else—something worse—was around.

Who does this belong to?

The snow howled against his ears and he stood, a silhouette against the car lights.

Get back in the car. Get back in now.

He felt like he was being watched.

Jim didn't just walk back to the car. He sprinted. As he neared the hood of the Volvo, he slipped on the snow and fell against the car. He bolted back up and got inside, to safety.

How safe is it really?

He locked the doors and just stared outside, the wipers not able to keep up with the fury of the snow.

Somewhere close by was the body that coat belonged to.

He knew he needed to call the sheriff. And he would once he got back to the house.

The car's wheels spun for a moment before gaining traction. Jim steered the car away from the ledge, and as he drove toward the lights of the immense lodge, he was surprised to be so happy to return to this place.

37

Slipping Away

Stephanie tried to imagine what might have happened. Ever since Jim had come back from shopping, something was visibly bothering him. He had tried calling the sheriff a dozen times, but the phone was either cutting out on him or there was no answer. Jim had told her he was just calling to follow up on their meeting, to schedule another, but his intensity was so strong. . . .

He's not telling me something, she thought as she walked into the kitchen to decide what to make for dinner.

Jim kept so much inside, so much from her. She didn't even know what it looked like to reach out to him anymore. It used to be easier. Before the kids came, before Dambi.

I know he's upset and hurt and angry about Tawi, but he never wants to talk about it with me.

She spotted the half-full bottle of red wine and decided to pour him a glass. Then she poured another for herself.

The winds still beat against the house. It was still snowing and didn't look like it was going to stop anytime soon.

Stephanie wore a thick turtleneck, jeans, and thick socks, but she was still cold. The howling storm outside just made her feel colder.

She brought the wine into the family room where Jim and Paul sat talking. The television that had been on was now black.

"I thought you might like this," Stephanie said to her husband.

He gave her a polite, though tired, smile and accepted the glass.

"Hey, wait, nothing for me?" Paul asked.

"Would you like some?"

"No, I'm fine. Seriously." He paused. "The television just went out."

"It's the satellite," Jim said. "It goes in and out during storms."

"It'll come back on," Stephanie said. "You can stop watching ESPN for a change."

One good thing about being in Dambi was not being addicted to television. Ever since coming back to the States, the television had been on all the time. Always in the background, always providing white noise.

"Everything okay?" she asked Jim.

"Yeah, sure."

"Did you get ahold of the sheriff?"

Jim shook his head.

"If I were him, I'd be heading down to Florida right about now," Paul said with a smile.

Jim didn't smile. Stephanie studied him, his tight jaw and unmoving brow.

It's not the kids. They're doing fine. So it must be something else.

"Any thoughts on dinner?" she asked, hoping food could brighten Jim's mood.

"Yeah, why don't you fix a real meal, not like those scraps you prepared last night," Paul joked.

"Maybe you're having leftovers."

"Leftovers would be fine with me. I'm low maintenance."

"Jim?"

He took a sip of his wine and looked at the black television screen. "I'm not that hungry. Just—you decide. Leftovers are fine with me."

She stared at him, but he wouldn't return her gaze.

Why won't you talk to me? Why won't you look at me and talk to me? Why can't you let me know what you're thinking?

"We're not having leftovers," she said to the men. "I see my brother how often? I think I need to fatten you up."

"Sounds good to me," Paul said with a smile.

Jim stared outside, as if he could see something out there in the darkness.

Or as if something out there could see him.

SLEEP DIDN'T COME EASY that night.

She had stayed up late, talking with Paul again. It was so relaxing, especially after a dinner of pork chops and lots of side dishes and several glasses of wine. Jim had gone to his office, as he often did at night, then came into the family room saying he had a headache and needed to go to bed. He helped tuck the kids in, then retired himself. Paul stayed up, telling her all about his recent job change. His life fascinated Stephanie—the business trips and the big cities and the prestige. It was truly a foreign life to her, one that sometimes she wished she had pursued.

Later, after saying good night and going to bed, she read a new novel from one of her favorite authors for an hour. When her eyes grew heavy, she turned off the light.

But she lay awake for another hour, listening to the wind outside, to Jim's heavy breathing, adjusting the covers again and again, feeling hot one minute then cold the next. The wine should have helped her go to sleep, but instead she felt dizzy, as though the world were spinning around her.

A part of her knew the problem.

You're afraid to fall asleep.

That's not true, she told herself. *I want to fall asleep. I'm tired. I'm exhausted, in fact. I could sleep for an entire week straight.*

You're afraid to sleep because you're afraid of what you might see.

But sleep eventually came.

And so did the memory.

THE LITTLE GIRL SHIVERS in her nakedness, clutching the towel around her. She shivers out of fear.

"It's okay," her mother tells her, stroking her hair, reassuring her.

She can't talk. The bathroom is bathed in darkness, and the only light comes from the cracked window. She can see the sky outside and the moon, a deep, glowing red.

"It's time to get in," her mother says.

She doesn't want to. She says she can't, but her mother tells her again that it's time. She doesn't understand, doesn't know what's happening. She's not supposed to be so afraid with Mommy right next to her. Mothers are supposed to protect their children, not scare them.

"Stephanie, get into the tub."

She looks at the tub, the dark liquid in it, the sheer gloss of its surface. She can't get in. Part of her knows what's in there, but another part of her says it can't be—that her mind is just making things up, that Mommy just wants her to take a bath.

"Go on, Stephanie. I'm not going to ask you again."

She cries and shakes, and her mother just looks at her.

It's so dark in here, so cold, so quiet.

She takes off the towel and takes one step.

The liquid is cold and thick.

"I can't!" she cries.

The uncaring glare of her mother weighs her down. She takes another step, climbing in and putting both feet into the tub.

"Now sit."

She sits, feeling unclean, feeling like this is some nightmare, like she'll never wake up, feeling trapped beneath a cold blanket, feeling like she won't ever breathe again.

Her body shakes.

And then her mother begins to speak some other language, some kind of chant, with a deeper, darker voice.

"Mommy, I'm scared."

For a moment she can't see her mother, can't see anything.

Her mother keeps talking, as if she's praying. Weird sounds in a language she's never heard before.

And then her mother takes some of the liquid and cups it in one hand to place it over her head.

It smells funny. It feels gross and dirty, and she shivers and continues crying. Her mother keeps praying and rubbing it over Stephanie's head and then her face.

"You belong to him now and will always belong to him. He will claim you as one of his children from here to eternity."

And the young girl, five years old, continues to cry, continues to shake, continues to try to take her mind and her heart and her soul away from this terror, this horror, this place she calls home.

～

STEPHANIE AWOKE AND SAT on the edge of the bed.

What is happening to me? What is wrong?

She could still see the image of the bath of blood and didn't know where it had come from or what had inspired it.

It was you, and it's a memory.

But she didn't believe it. Nothing like that ever happened. It was just a nightmare and that was it.

Her body shook, and she couldn't get rid of the images in her mind. She felt out of breath. A spiraling sensation circled inside her.

The young girl, the naked girl in the bathtub with her mother . . .

No stop it stop this it's just a nightmare it's just a continuation of everything that's been bothering you it's this place and this isolation

Four loud knocks sounded on the door to their bedroom. Stephanie jumped from the bed and landed awkwardly on the floor. The knocking was loud enough to awaken even Jim.

"Steph?" he asked.

The knocking continued. Stephanie ran to the door and opened it.

Outside in the lit hallway stood Bob Patterson in his pajamas, looking distressed. "Is Jim awake?" he asked.

"Yeah, I'm here," Jim said from behind Stephanie.

Stephanie turned on the bedroom light.

"We've got a problem," Bob said. "I went to the kitchen for some orange juice, and when I came back, Evelyn was gone. I can't find her anywhere."

38

In the Shadows

They were pathetic, all of them. The older couple and the husband and wife and even her brother. All pathetic and useless. They didn't get it and didn't understand and were too stupid to even figure it out.

I'm not here for any of you.

He could hear them downstairs talking, the older man talking to everyone else. Worried about his missing wife.

You shouldn't be worried about her. Not anymore.

He moved along the carpet without making a sound, without showing himself in the shadows.

He walked toward the boy's room.

They're too stupid to even check. They're assuming they're the only ones in the house. Assuming their precious children are safe and secure and asleep. Worried about the old couple who don't have many years left of their pathetic lives anyway. Oblivious and stupid. All of them.

He stopped outside the cracked door of the room.

He's the one I'm coming for. He's the one I've been coming for this whole time. The rest of them don't matter. It's him I'm here for, him I've been called to get, him who will be the sacrifice.

He knew—he could feel it. . . . A life and a spirit and a soul that made him worry, that give him trepidations, that made him summon powers to stop it.

This boy has a power, and he is meant to do something. He is meant for great deeds.

And that was why he stood outside the boy's room, in the darkness of the shadows, waiting and listening to hear if someone was coming.

But they were all downstairs.

They were all worried about the old woman.

It's time to do what I came here to do.

He nudged the door open and stepped inside the room.

PART FOUR

Isolation

39

Thirty Minutes Earlier

Zachary heard something coming down the hall as he read in bed by flashlight. He was reading *The Silver Chair*, number four in the Chronicles of Narnia. The noise was quick and sounded like a woman's scream—but not his mom's voice. This voice was different, older. He pushed back the covers and listened, holding his breath.

It's just the wind, he told himself.

There wasn't another sound. No scream, no voice, no movement.

But that didn't stop him from slipping out of bed and putting on a sweatshirt, then opening the door and quietly moving out into the hallway.

I heard something. I know I did.

He tiptoed on the carpet, his bare feet silently moving. He walked down the hall away from his parents' and Ashley's rooms toward the other rooms, the Bear Room and the Black-and-White Room, where he'd found one of the hidden passageways.

As he reached the end of the hallway, he stopped and peered around the corner, the night-lights illuminating the hall. He didn't see anything, but he waited and watched and listened. For one minute. Then another.

Just as he was about to move on, he heard something. Not a

voice or a scream, but movement. Footsteps. Faint and quiet, but footsteps nonetheless.

He froze, looking down each hallway. The one behind him, where he had come from, was dark and empty. The noise had come from the hall ahead. He couldn't see to the end of the hallway. But he could see light coming from beneath the closed door of the Black-and-White Room.

Someone's in there.

Zachary moved closer to the room.

Maybe it's Mom.

But it hadn't sounded like her. And the movement had sounded like two people, not one.

He was halfway down the hallway, walking delicately, not breathing, when the door cracked open.

No.

His only escape was to slip into the first bedroom, stumbling in the darkness and knocking his knees on the wooden bed frame. He swallowed a cry of pain as he knelt down and felt underneath the bed.

There's space, he thought. *Good.*

He slipped underneath and lay on his back, looking up at the bottom of the mattress. He could hear his heart beating in his ears, but he held his breath, his knee still aching.

He waited. And waited.

He heard faint steps, then silence.

Is someone there?

In the darkness, Zachary waited.

He wasn't about to go anywhere.

Half an hour later, he heard the footsteps in the hall, then on the stairs, then voices talking downstairs.

It was safe to go out.

Someone used the secret passageway, Zach thought to himself as he headed downstairs to see what was going on.

40

Beginning to Search

How long has the phone line been dead?"

Stephanie shook her head. She held the cordless phone in her hand.

"You sure it's not just that receiver?"

"I tried a couple phones upstairs," Bob said.

Jim let out a deep breath and thought for a minute.

"Steph, why don't you take the kids into the kitchen?"

"Is everything—?"

"Steph, please."

She nodded and took a half-asleep Ashley and Zachary into the kitchen.

The three men were left in the great room, looking at one another, each lost in his thoughts.

"Okay, we search the house."

"We've just searched most of it," Bob said, his voice frail and scared.

"We'll search again."

"What could've happened to her? I mean, I was just there—I just saw her—and then she . . . she just disappeared."

"She's somewhere in the house," Jim told the man. "We'll find her."

Paul stood next to Jim, his hair spiked and his eyes tired. He waited to hear Jim's game plan.

"Bob, why don't you go check through every room on this floor of the south wing?" Bob nodded. "Paul and I will go over to the west wing."

"What happens if we can't find her?"

"Let's just look, okay? I mean, maybe she just got a case of what Stephanie's had lately."

"What's that?" Paul asked, confused.

"Sleepwalking."

Paul nodded.

They watched Bob wander off toward the south wing.

"Want to start down here or upstairs?" Paul asked.

Jim gave him a look that made his brother-in-law stop and ask, "What's that look for?"

"I checked every room upstairs. I don't think she's in this wing."

"Then what?"

"I think she's in the north wing."

Paul obviously didn't understand the gravity of Jim's statement. How could he? He had just gotten there. He hadn't been there long enough to sense the presence of . . . others. Paul hadn't been inside the north wing and seen the strange, sick things Jim had seen.

"What is it? What's wrong?"

"Paul, look—I know you're not a religious man."

"Yeah. What does that have to do with anything?"

"Because I've felt—this house gives off—I don't know. Sometimes I can just feel it. The owner, the people who have been here—there were some pretty bizarre things going on here. And I've been over to the north wing."

"I thought it was locked."

"I found a key."

"A key? Where?"

"I just found it."

"Does Stephanie know?"

Jim shook his head. "And I don't want her to."

"Why?"

He rubbed the thick beard on his face. "I only went over there a few times. But I found some pretty disturbing stuff."

"Like what?"

"I found a room full of—full of photos depicting—well, depicting a lot of sordid things."

Paul let out a laugh. "What are you talking about?"

"Just really sick stuff. I got rid of all I could find."

"So the owners were into freaky stuff. So what? What does that have to do with Mrs. Patterson's disappearance?"

"I'm afraid of what else might be over there." He paused for a minute, producing the key. "And I'm afraid of what could happen if Mrs. Patterson gets lost over there."

"So we check it out and see if she's there. She was probably just sleepwalking, like you said."

"Yeah, sure. Probably."

"Come on, Jim. Don't get all spooked on me."

Jim looked at Paul and his friendly, rational face.

He doesn't understand the dark forces at work here.

"Let me get a flashlight," Jim said.

"They don't have power over there in the north wing?"

"Yeah, they do, but in case it goes out—just in case, you know."

I don't want to be stranded over there with no lights. God knows what we'll find.

He was worried about Mrs. Patterson.

Maybe the coat belonged to her.

But that was crazy. He'd had dinner with her since then and she hadn't gone outside. They would have heard her if she had.

Who did that coat belong to, then? Who, Jim? Why don't you answer that? Why don't you tell Paul? Because you're freaked out, that's why. Your wife has been seeing things, and you've been feeling things, and now that the storm has come, you're stuck here with a woman missing.

He walked away to try to regain his composure, to try to think a straight thought. Sometimes the anger that festered inside him turned to helplessness. And sometimes if he thought about it too much—his family and his faith and every single waking thing out of his control—his sense of hopelessness laced him with panic.

I can't tell Paul because I don't want Paul to think I'm losing my mind.

Another voice answered his own.

Are you, Jim? Are you losing it? It's easy to do, especially up here.

He stopped at the door to the kitchen. He stopped and turned around and suddenly felt the undeniable presence of evil.

God, help me. God, please help us. Protect us. Protect Mrs. Patterson and all of us. Please, God, hear me.

He went into the kitchen, and Stephanie rushed up to him with concerned eyes.

"Is everything okay?"

"Yeah. I'm just grabbing a flashlight. Where's the big stainless steel one?"

"Why do you need that?"

"I don't know," Jim said, catching Zachary's eye as the boy watched them from his seat at the table. "You okay, Zach?" he asked.

Zachary just nodded.

Jim found the flashlight on a shelf in the laundry room just off the kitchen. He checked to make sure it worked.

"We're going to start looking around," Jim said. "Just stay in here, okay? And if you see something or need me, call me over the intercom."

"Okay. Do you need me to—"

"Just stay here, okay?"

Jim kissed his wife's forehead, then walked back toward the great room where Paul awaited.

Where the north wing awaited.

With all its secrets and blackness.

41

The North Wing Again

Jim locked the door behind him.

"Why're you doing that?" Paul asked as they turned on a hallway light.

"I don't want anybody else coming over here."

"That bad, huh?"

"Yeah, that bad." *He'll see. No need to try to explain.*

"Maybe it's just that room."

Jim hoped he was right. But he had the feeling it was more, a lot more.

Sometimes he could feel dark forces, much the way he could feel the Spirit moving among Christian brothers and sisters. Sometimes the feeling he experienced during a church service was overwhelming, like being in the midst of a flood of joy and hope. Other times those floodwaters threatened to overwhelm everyone in their path. And he believed that was Satan at work.

Right now he could feel the presence of the dark one all around him. He couldn't shake the feeling that something bad was happening right now, that something bad had already happened. Had he really seen that bloody coat? And if so, who did it belong to? He wondered if he was losing his mind . . . if he had been on this mountain too long and had become too separated from God.

God doesn't listen to me, so why even bother?

But Jim needed Him now more than ever before. He knew he couldn't do this alone. He needed God in a mighty way.

I'm afraid for my family—for Stephanie, for Zach, for little Ash.

He muttered another prayer for God's protection.

Just like He protected Tawi, right? Just like He heard your prayers for your friend.

Were those thoughts brought on by Satan? Were doubts like that sin? Was it a sin to question God? To wonder where He was? To wonder why He hadn't answered so many prayers?

I believe in You, God, and I believe You made all of us and You control everything and You are almighty and powerful and loving. But, God, I just want to see Your hand. I want to know You really are listening . . . really are up there . . . really do love us.

"Hey, is that open?" Paul asked.

Jim turned to the door on his right. It was a side room he had passed many times before. But now the door was cracked open slightly.

The room was empty. Not even a stick of furniture.

"Nice color," Paul said.

The room was painted black. All of it. The walls, the ceiling, even the wood floor.

"I wonder what they were going for with this look," Paul said.

There was no overhead light in the room, so Jim used his flashlight. There was no closet, no windows, nothing.

Nothing except a design in the middle of the floor. Jim walked over and shined the light on it. It was a tile mosaic, and the colorful artwork looked like Egyptian hieroglyphics.

"What's that?"

Jim shook his head. "You wouldn't happen to know Egyptian, would you?"

"Sorry. I took Spanish."

The beam of light searched the black walls.

It feels cold in this room. Cold like death.

"Do you feel that?" Jim asked.

"Feel what?"

Jim walked toward the doorway and out of the room. He felt like he was falling, running and not able to turn around—afraid of what he would find if he did.

"Think we'll find her over here?" Paul asked.

"I have no idea. I have no idea what we'll find over here."

There was another half-open door down the hall to the left. The library.

"Let me see if there's anybody in here," Jim said. He went in and turned on the light. Layers of dust covered the shelves. Yet Jim had the sense someone had used this room recently.

A heaviness pressed against him.

God, help me.

He shut off the light. "Nothing in there."

Paul studied him but said nothing. They kept walking until the hallway ended, opening up to another great room. This one wasn't as big as the great room in the west wing, but it was far more ornate. A massive wrought iron chandelier illuminated the room with dim bulbs, a few of which were missing. It hung in the center of the room under an arched ceiling. A stone fireplace faced them as they followed the wood floor past an old baby grand piano. Above the mantel hung a painting of an elderly man with gray hair, very serious and stately.

"Think that's the owner?" Paul asked.

"Yeah, it's him. I've seen photos of him before. Strange, though. It's just—it looks recent."

They walked past four leather chairs arranged around a large ottoman.

Paul stared up at the painting. "Yeah, so?"

"The setting looks like this very room. See the piano?"

"Oh, yeah."

"From what I've heard, Charles Wolfcott hardly ever came to this house," Jim said.

"Think someone's going to build a lodge like this and *not* come here?"

"Someone like him, sure."

"Maybe the artist just added in the background."

Jim nodded. "Looks like Wolfcott didn't smile much."

"This place resembles him."

They looked around the room. Jim called out Evelyn's name, not expecting to hear anything back.

Two hallways jutted out from either side of the large fireplace. "Which way do you want to go?"

Jim looked back at the painting, then studied each hallway. A blurry shape darted past him on the floor, and he couldn't help but jump.

"What the—"

The animal, some furry creature, darted off down one of the darkened hallways.

"What was that?" Jim asked.

"I think it might have been a cat," Paul said.

"Really?"

"Yeah, or a really big rat."

"There aren't any rats up here."

"Better hope not."

Jim tried to slow down his pounding heart and pointed toward the hallway the creature hadn't taken. "Let's try that one," he said.

He flipped the light switch and saw the hallway went straight back with two doors on each side. Each one was shut.

Of course they're shut. Why not? Why would they be open?

He moved slowly toward the first door. The hallway was all red, a deep blood red. The walls, the floor, the ceiling.

Somebody had a fun time painting this wing.

On the wall were paintings featuring more Egyptian art and hieroglyphics. Jim wondered what they meant.

He opened the door. "Evelyn? Hello?"

Jim felt a pain in his stomach, a tightening that made him grimace.

"What's wrong?" Paul asked.

"Nothing," he said.

But Jim knew. It was this place, this hallway, this room they were entering.

He pointed the flashlight inside and saw strange glimmers of light. There was a whole wall full of ornate, exotic knives from floor to ceiling, probably fifty altogether.

The shuffling of Paul's feet behind him made him turn around.

"Look at that," Paul said.

A table stood in the center of the room with a long white sheet covering it. As Jim examined it, he noticed dark stains on its side. Something that had dripped. Or splattered.

"Is that—"

"I think so," Jim said of the blood splotches on the floor.

"At least it's not fresh."

"I want to know where it came from."

"Some animal, I'm sure."

"I'm not sure of anything," Jim said.

Jim felt a presence similar to what he had felt in the other room. Cold, empty, stifling, disturbing. He pointed the flashlight at another wall and drew back as he saw a face looking at him. Then he realized what he was looking at.

It was a goat head, a real goat head, mounted on the wall. Its hair still looked soft, its nose dark. Two long horns jutted out of its head, right above its glaring eyes. It had to be the largest goat Jim had ever seen.

"Think that thing is real?" Paul asked.

"Yeah. Wolfcott would want it real."

Paul was on the other side of the room, shrouded in darkness. He called out Jim's name.

"What?"

"Come over here."

That was when Jim noticed another table. This one held various instruments that at first looked like surgical tools. But as Jim examined them, he realized what they were.

First he saw a pair of needle-nose pliers, then a pruning knife, then a sickle.

What's that doing there?

There were a variety of knives on the table, some rope, a fishhook, a hatchet. One item looked like an elaborate wine opener with two clamps. Another was an exotic two-pronged fork. Next to it was a long rod with spikes on its edges.

I'm losing my mind.

"Tell me what I'm looking at," Jim said.

"Looks like something out of a torture chamber."

There were small instruments, like calipers and drills. The table was full of tools.

"Those are for show," Jim said.

"Yeah, I hope so. But I'm thinking some of them have been used."

"No."

"Look at that pointy thing there—you see that? It looks like—"

"Yeah, okay, let's go."

Paul picked something up.

"Look at this."

Jim shined the light on a leather mask with slits for eyes and a mouth.

"Can you imagine what went on in here?" Paul asked.

Jim shook his head. He wanted to find Stephanie and get out of this house, get far away from it.

"Check this out," Paul said.

The light illuminated Paul's tall form as he hunched over something in the corner.

"What's that?"

The flashlight's beam rested on a large chest.

"Want to open it?" Paul asked.

"I think I've seen enough of this room."

Paul looked at him, then back at the chest. "There could be a million different things in there."

"I don't want to know what's inside," Jim said. "I want to get out of here."

"Yeah."

Jim looked at the table in the middle of the room, the white sheet, the stains on the sheet, and the floor around it. He thought of what Paul had said.

What had gone on in this room?

He wondered if someone had taken photos of it. Probably, somewhere in that godforsaken study, there were pictures of what had gone on here.

"Look," Paul said, holding something up.

Jim pointed the light at him and noticed the shears in his hand. The edges looked darker, almost

wet

"Drop that and let's get going," Jim told him.

"This feels . . . I don't know. . . ."

"What?"

"It feels used. Like it was used tonight."

Dear Father dear God dear heavenly Father I need You we need You please hear me please protect my family from this madness

"Come on," Jim said. "Evelyn's not here."

"No." Paul looked at the table, then back at Jim with a grave face. "But she might've been."

42

Alone

Stephanie sat next to a sleeping Ashley on the couch in the family room when the intercom buzzed, startling her. She looked down and saw Zach staring at her with intense eyes. She got up and spoke into the box.

"Say that again."

"Are you still in the kitchen?"

It was Jim. Sometimes she could barely make out who was speaking because it was either too loud or too muffled.

"We're in the family room."

"Has Bob come back?"

"Not yet."

"Why don't you take the kids to our bedroom?" Jim asked.

"Is everything okay?"

"Sure, yeah. Everything is fine."

"Any trace of Evelyn?"

"Not yet, but she's around."

"Jim . . . ?"

"Everything's okay. Just—no need to stay up, okay? Everything's fine. We'll find her."

Jim sounded in no mood for debate or conversation. She told him to be careful, then picked up Ashley and told Zach to follow her upstairs.

As they walked up the stairs, images from her nightmare flashed through her mind.

Where did that come from?

She didn't know. The dreams and visions were getting scarier, darker. They felt so real. Things like that—where did they come from if they weren't real? Stephanie never watched horror movies or read scary novels. She tried to dwell on positive things, afraid of what disturbing images or distressing news might do to her dream life.

What about everything that happened in Dambi? You couldn't shut your eyes to that.

She held Ashley securely in her arms. She didn't want to let her go, nor let Zach out of her sight. The storm and the nightmare and Mrs. Patterson's disappearance had frightened her, but she needed to put on a good face for her children.

In the bedroom, the door closed and the lamp on next to the king-sized bed, she sat propped up on a pillow. Ashley lay next to her on her side sleeping, while Zachary lay on his back with his eyes wide open.

"You tired, Zach?"

"Not really."

"Everything okay?"

"Where do you think Mrs. Patterson went?"

"I'm not sure, sweetheart," she told her son. "Dad and Uncle Paul are looking for her."

"Do you think someone else is in the house?"

She looked at Zach, surprised at the earnestness of his question.

There's nobody in this house. Of course there's not. How could there be?

"I'm sure there is nobody else in this house."

"But how do you know?" Zach asked, his voice urgent. "How do we know? It's such a big house."

"Why would there be anybody else up here?"

"I don't know."

He didn't say anything more, but he kept his eyes open, staring at the ceiling. All she could see of him above the covers was his round little face and tousled brown hair.

"We're okay," she told him. "Daddy's going to be back in a few minutes."

"What if they don't find Mrs. Patterson?"

"I'm sure they will."

"But what if they don't?"

"Don't worry about that now, Zach. She'll be okay."

"But if she's not, what are we going to do about it?"

"Want me to read to you?"

"You always do that so I won't worry."

She smiled at him. "I don't want you to worry."

"But why are you so worried, Mom?"

"What do you mean?"

"I can tell."

"Then maybe you can read to me."

"I don't want to read," Zach said in his matter-of-fact way.

"Then maybe we can just go to sleep."

Zach didn't answer, and after a couple of minutes, she turned off the lamp.

For quite some time Stephanie lay there motionless, listening to the howling wind, wondering and hoping and praying that Jim and Paul were okay.

She was afraid that Zach was right. Maybe they weren't the only ones in the house.

43

The Video

He paused, taking a deep breath, meeting Paul's eye by the dim light of the hallway. Then Jim pushed open the door and shone his flashlight inside.

The last room at the end of the hall appeared to be another library. There were two couches arranged in a V facing a wall lined with dark wood bookshelves. Jim flipped the light switch, revealing walls that were a deep red. On each side of the ceiling were small stereo speakers.

Jim walked up to the bookshelves and was surprised to see there weren't books on the shelves but DVDs. "I think this is a movie room."

Paul nodded. "Interesting taste, huh?" he asked, pointing at one of the many adult videos resting on the shelf.

"Where do you think the screen is?"

"I bet it pops down," Paul said, looking around the room. "See where the video projector is?" Paul found the remote to control the drop-down screen. He pressed a button, and the screen slid slowly to an inch above the wooden floor.

"Great place to view a movie," Paul said, as if he'd already forgotten what they had found in the previous rooms.

"This place is abominable. I can't believe what's over here."

"I want to know what those are." Paul pointed to a stack of

unlabeled DVDs. He picked one up and read the inscription in black ink. "Halloween 2005."

There can't be anything good on that DVD.

"Think they filmed it here?" Paul asked.

"I don't know."

"Let's look."

"I don't think so."

"Come on. Maybe it'll show the house. Maybe we can find out what was going on here."

"I don't think I want to know what was going on."

Paul cursed. "It was something crazy, that's what I think."

"We need to keep looking for Mrs. Patterson."

"Aren't you at least curious? If it's freaky stuff, we'll turn it off. I just wonder—I wonder if it'll show Wolfcott. Or any of the house." Paul was already looking for the DVD player.

There is a reason this place gives me bad vibes.

"I found it," Paul said, bending over to put in the DVD while Jim just stared around the room.

The first thing I'm doing when the storm stops is getting my family off this mountain and away from this twisted place.

A logo appeared on the projection screen.

"I don't know if we should watch it," he said again.

"It'll give us some insight into this house. What used to go on here."

The opening shot showed the outside of Edge Hill, without the snow. Then the video cut to inside, in the great room. It was decorated in a Halloween motif, with candles burning and jack-o'-lanterns everywhere. The room was full of people dressed up in costumes. Elaborate, full-length costumes—the kind you find at an expensive costume ball.

"Wonder where all these people came from," Paul said.

Jim watched reluctantly, rubbing his arms to get warm. He didn't like this, any of this.

The video proceeded to take them through the house and

show the party, which was taking place in the west wing. There must have been a couple hundred people there in outfits ranging from mummies and vampires to Princess Leia and Darth Vader. Everybody laughed and carried drinks and chatted like they knew each other.

The film faded to black for a second, then opened in a dimly lit room that appeared to be empty. Jim looked at Paul, who was staring at the screen with fascination.

The darkness changed to an orange glow.

This isn't going to be good.

The camera moved, revealing a figure. It zoomed in on the face, a woman's face with a rag tied around her mouth.

Is that part of a costume?

Long, blonde hair flowed down to the woman's bare shoulders. She wore a cave woman outfit with ragged fringes on the edges of the costume. Her hands were bound behind her back. The camera moved down her legs until it came to the floor. She was standing on some kind of design, a picture on the floor.

"That's the room we passed, the all-black room. Recognize that tile?"

Jim nodded. He looked at the hazy lighting and the woman standing there, tears in her eyes.

"Turn it off."

"But what do you think—what do you think this is all about?"

"I don't want to see it," Jim said.

Paul continued watching, the woman's stifled cries echoing through the speakers. It felt like they were watching a snuff film.

That woman isn't acting. Those tears are real.

"Turn it off. Come on." Jim turned and walked out of the room just as the woman's cries turned to shrieks.

Don't turn around. Don't. Don't, Jim. Don't look.

She was howling, begging for someone to stop doing whatever they were doing.

"Paul, turn it off!" Jim commanded as he stepped into the

hallway. He heard silence and his brother-in-law coming up beside him.

"That couldn't be real," Paul said.

"Yeah, it could."

"No. Not that."

Jim looked at Paul. "We've gotta get out of this house."

"What? Right now?"

"When the snow stops. Do you have a cell phone on you?"

"In my room. It's not getting service though."

"We gotta call."

"Call who?" Paul asked.

"People have to know about this house, the things that have gone on here." Jim looked stern and tired. "This is an evil place."

"How can a place be evil?" Paul asked.

They started walking down the hallway.

"You can't feel it?"

"You're just freaking out because that woman's missing and because—because we've seen some weird stuff in here."

"It's not just weird. It's beyond that. This place—the things that went on here—"

"Jim?" Bob's voice came from the intercom at the end of the hallway.

Jim rushed to answer him. "Yeah, what is it?"

"You gotta come down here."

"Where are you?"

"*Now*," the frantic voice said.

"Where are you?" Jim repeated.

"In the basement. Take the stairs off the great room."

"Is everything okay?" Jim waited for an answer. "Bob?"

"No. Just come."

Bob sounded out of breath, panicked, afraid.

"Where are the kids? Stephanie?" Jim asked.

"They went upstairs, I think. They should be fine. Jim, just get down here."

44

Prayers in the Night

reat one, I pray to you. I pray on your name. I pray on your strength. I pray on your might. Give me your strength.

He knew everything going on in the house. Where they all were.

The boy with his mom and his sister in the upstairs bedroom.

The two men on the other side of the house.

The old man searching for his wife.

And the old woman. Yes, the old woman.

He could see all of them now in his mind. He could shut his eyes and see them.

The boy was safe for now. He needed to get him alone. It had to be alone. It had to be alone and in secret.

He would bring the boy to the north wing. That is what he had come here for.

Give me darkness give me power give me hunger give me might

He had never felt this strong before, this powerful.

None of them knew. But they would. They would know before this was all over.

Maybe even before this night was over.

45

Five Points

Wooden steps led to the massive open basement, bare except for a few tools and some building equipment. Since they were on the edge of a mountain, the west side of the house was still high above ground, with the east side buried in the mountain. Jim had been down to the basement a couple times, and light spilled through the windows in the daytime.

Now, in the middle of the night, the darkness in the basement felt suffocating. Only a faint light illuminated the stairs. Besides that there was nothing. The cold gripped Jim when he reached the bottom of the stairs, and he shivered. "Bob?"

A voice came from the far side of the room. "Over here."

A light cut the darkness, waving from fifty yards away. Jim turned on his own flashlight and started toward Bob, scanning the floor as he went.

"You okay?" Jim asked.

The older man looked deathly pale, the lines under his eyes thick and heavy.

"Where's Paul?" Bob asked.

"I asked him to go check on Stephanie and the kids. What'd you find?"

For a minute Bob didn't speak. The only sound was the howling wind, even more audible down here than upstairs.

"Bob?"

"Here. Look." Bob's flashlight moved toward the wall. At first Jim didn't know what he was looking at. He thought it was a blanket, then noticed something white.

Teeth?

He blinked and tried to discern what the crumpled mass on the floor really was.

"Is that an animal?"

"Yes," Bob said. "They're all around here."

"What is it?"

"A dog, I think. A German shepherd."

Jim thought of the wolf he had seen, the one gnawing on the jacket.

"It looks like it was drained of blood. Its throat was slit. And someone took out its guts. And its paws."

"And . . . there are more?" Jim asked, transfixed.

"There are a couple of groundhogs. And a cat. And some-thing—something I didn't even recognize. All with the same injuries."

"I don't get it," Jim said. He scanned the open area of the basement, as big as a hockey rink.

"The animals—these dead animals. They were placed in five different areas of the basement."

"And?"

"They didn't die here on their own, Jim. Somebody did this. And recently. I was just down here a few days ago."

Okay, Jim, just breathe. Just take in one breath after another. Don't freak out. Don't panic. You can't panic now.

"So what does it mean?"

"I think they were put here for—I think it was some sort of ritual. These animals—it was like they were sacrificed. And there's something else. . . ."

"What?" Jim asked, his voice shaking.

"I found this in the middle of the five dead animals." Bob

walked to the center of the basement and pointed his flashlight to something on the ground.

At first Jim thought it was another animal; then he recognized it as a sweater. "Bob—what—?"

"It's Evelyn's. She was wearing that sweater today."

"Did you—did you look to see if—?"

"I didn't pick it up. I just . . ."

"Yeah, okay. Look, Bob, we need to get out of this house."

The older man appeared not to have heard.

Jim tried again. "I say we go upstairs and all stay together."

"Jim, I . . . All I want . . ." He started to cry.

Jim didn't know what to do. He grabbed Bob's shoulders and held him as he coughed through his tears.

"She's the only thing—I don't know—I can't remember a life without her—I'm afraid, Jim. I'm afraid something awful has happened to her. What are we going to do?"

Jim held Bob in his arms and told him it was going to be okay, that God was going to protect them, that they needed to get upstairs and get through this night. He was worried about Stephanie and the kids.

"I looked through the entire house, Jim," Bob said, sniffling and wiping his face. "She's not here. All I found—that's all I found."

"Let's go upstairs."

"Where were you guys?"

Jim decided to tell him. "The north wing. I found a key to get over there."

"Did you find any sign of her?" Bob asked, still not wanting to leave.

Not now. Don't tell him now. It won't help.

"No. No sign of her."

"The five points. The dead animals," Bob said as they started for the stairs. "I think it's a pentagram. Someone did it on purpose. The sweater was in the middle. The animals looked like they were sacrifices. Maybe someone—maybe someone is playing around with us—"

"Come on, Bob. Let's go upstairs. Let's get out of here."

"I've been praying, Jim. I've been praying, but I'm scared it might be too late."

46

More Prayers in the Night

The wind wailed against the house, a monstrosity paying homage to one man's life and legacy. A tomb. And they were trapped inside it now, the snow continuing to beat against the walls and cocoon them inside. They were hunkered down with nowhere to go and no one to call and nothing to do but wait.

I'm waiting, God. Can You hear me?

Jim sat in the chair facing the bed where Stephanie and the kids slept. It was 4:36 AM, and with the bathroom light on and the door slightly open, he could see their sleeping faces.

He had been like this for the last half hour. He had tried calling off the mountain, but his cell phone wouldn't work. Stephanie woke up when he came in, but Jim didn't want to panic her, so he said everything was fine and encouraged her to go back to sleep. They would get off the mountain tomorrow and get help finding Evelyn.

He couldn't do anything more for Bob. Paul had produced a bottle of expensive gin—Jim didn't ask where he found it—and poured them all drinks. Jim didn't want any, but Bob polished off the first glass and had a couple more. They didn't talk much. All of them were tired and shocked and in disbelief.

Disbelief. There's a word for the day. For the year.

There were two beds in Ashley's room just down the hall, and Paul said he would stay there with Bob. He spoke to Jim in a whisper. "I'll watch over him. Tomorrow morning when the sun comes up, if the snow stops at all, I'll go get help."

"How will you get off the mountain?"

"We'll figure it out tomorrow," Paul said. "Just keep an eye on your family. We'll get help."

Jim and Paul shared a look, as soldiers might coming off a battleground full of atrocities. Sometimes words aren't necessary to know what someone else is thinking.

Now, sitting in the chair and drifting between sleep and fear, Jim watched over his family and prayed silently.

Where are You, God, and why are You so quiet? Why don't You help us? Why can't I sense You anymore?

He scratched his chin. Maybe this was his fault. His lack of faith. It was his anger at God that he was being punished for. Had God ever intended them to come to Edge Hill? Had he decided on his own, and now God was abandoning them because of his stubbornness?

God, protect us. Please, God, protect us.

Jim tightened his fists.

If You control the universe and everything works for the good of those who love You, why God, why do You let so many bad things happen and why does evil sometimes spit in Your face?

He didn't know if there was another person in the house. But he could feel the evil here. Of that he was sure.

Where is Your face? Where are You, God?

Next to the chair, tucked away so nobody could see, not even Stephanie if she were to wake up and join him, was a hunting knife. Bob had given it to him. He had brought it to the house in case he ever went hunting. Its foot-long blade rested in a leather sheath.

I'll use it. I have no problem using it.

Jim was tired. His eyes were heavy, drifting closed for a minute or two, then jerking open to see if Stephanie and Zachary and Ashley were okay.

They're all that matters to me, all that matters, all that I need to make it through.

Jim knew he would do anything to protect them. Anything.

The wind howled, and his family slept, and Jim remained in a half-awake/half-dreaming state of consciousness.

And as he continued to pray, he wondered if God could hear him above the screams of the storm. Or if He even cared.

47

Mother and Son

The wind made it look like it was still snowing, blowing snow off the tops of the high drifts that pressed against the front of the lodge. The windows downstairs were completely covered over, while upstairs they were plastered with chunks of ice and speckled with snow. From his parents' bedroom window, Zachary saw nothing but a world of white amidst the dark clouds. He looked in fascination at the fresh, untouched snow and the cold, frozen woods beyond.

"Can we go downstairs?" he asked his mother.

She looked tired and pale this morning. Something was wrong. All Zachary had to do was look into his mother's eyes to know that. Of course, he knew more. He knew that Mrs. Patterson was missing, that Mr. Patterson was upset and "getting a little irrational," as his father put it. Zach knew they couldn't call anyone because the phones weren't working. He also knew they were stuck here because of the snow. He had heard his father talking with Uncle Paul about options. Mom had told him to stay in this room—it was safer. Dad even brought their breakfast to them there.

She didn't hear the voice last night like I did, the voice that could've been Mrs. Patterson's, the footsteps into the Black-and-White Room. . . .

Maybe someone had gone into the secret passageway.

Maybe Mrs. Patterson is in there.

He remembered the yucky feeling he got the first time he went into that room. What if he found the older woman but something had happened to her? What would he do then? And what if—what if someone else was there?

You need to tell Dad.

But telling his parents meant they would know the truth—that he had seen ugly things, bad things. Things that someone his age shouldn't see. They would wonder how much he had looked at and why he hadn't told them right away.

But what about the sounds you heard?

Zach wasn't sure. Had he really heard that last night, or had he imagined it?

I didn't imagine these secret passageways. I didn't imagine those.

"You need to finish your breakfast," his mother told him.

Zach walked back toward the desk that held a plate and several glasses. He finished his orange juice and went over to sit on the bed. Mom sat in the same chair Dad had slept in last night.

"Are we going to be okay?" he asked.

Mom looked at him with tired eyes in a face that looked too thin. Had she lost weight since coming here? She didn't look healthy. She nodded and tightened her lips. Suddenly tears poured down her cheeks.

He walked over to her and gave her a hug, but this seemed to make it worse. "Mom?"

"It's okay, Zach. I'm sorry. I'm just tired. Really, I'm fine. We're going to be okay."

"Mom, God will take care of us. He will protect us."

She looked at Zach with red, wet eyes.

"What?"

"I love you. Do you know how much I love you and your sister?"

Zach nodded, embarrassed.

"You're growing up so fast it scares me sometimes. And sometimes it makes me so . . ." She started to cry again, and once again she held him close to her.

"So what, Mom? It makes you so what?" he asked.

"It makes me so proud, Zach. I'm so proud of you."

"We're going to be okay," he told her. And he believed they would. No matter what happened, God would protect them. God protected those who loved Him and put their trust in Him.

He looked at his mother and wondered when to tell her what he knew about the house.

48

Plans

Paul and Jim stood in the kitchen, all the lights on, the windows packed over with snow, discussing their options. They had managed to eat a little food and drink a lot of coffee as they tried to make sense of the night before.

Paul had just come downstairs after taking Mr. Patterson up to his room.

"How's Bob?" Jim asked.

"Not good. I don't know if it's this place or the panic or what. He keeps talking about demons and exorcisms."

"His wife is missing," Jim stated the obvious. "And after what we saw last night, I'd be the same." He set down his coffee cup and gripped his waist, stretching out his back and shoulders as far as they could go.

"I'd keep him away from the kids," Paul said, taking a sip of coffee. "He's beginning to scare me." He studied the snow against the windows. "I guess this means I can't use my car to get off the mountain," he said with a dark laugh. "Hope you guys are well stocked on food because I didn't bring any."

"We are." Jim rotated his head one direction, then the other, his neck cracking.

"What happens if the power goes out? We're already without phone service."

Jim stopped midstretch and stared at his brother-in-law.

That's a great thought. Stranded on this mountain without human contact, and the power goes out. Thanks, Paul.

"There's a generator for emergencies. Can't power the whole house, obviously, but it'll take care of the first floor."

"I don't think I've ever seen this much snow in my life. We had some bad storms in Michigan, but this—wow."

Jim was silent for a few minutes, looking at the wall and sipping his coffee.

"What are you thinking?"

"I'm thinking one of us needs to try to get help."

"You got a snowmobile handy?"

Jim smiled at Paul's upbeat tone. "No, but I saw some snowshoes in a room off the great room."

"The ones that look like tennis rackets?"

"These are elliptical snowshoes. A little more modern. Only the best for a place like Edge Hill."

Paul nodded. "So I bundle up and go in search of help."

"You want to?"

"Not really, but you need to stay here to keep an eye on the family."

"Mr. Patterson's here."

"Yeah, exactly," Paul said, his face suddenly grim. "I wouldn't trust him around them."

"What are you talking about?"

"I'm just saying he's not making any sense. I told him to rest."

"You don't think . . . ," Jim started.

"What? That he had something to do with his wife's disappearance? I don't know. I've seen a lot of crazy things in my life."

"Yeah, I know."

"You tell Steph what you found in the basement? Or over in the other wing?"

Jim shook his head. "No."

"Good. I think—you probably shouldn't."

"Don't worry about that. All I want is to get out of this place."

"Tell me something. . . ."

Jim nodded and waited to hear what Paul had to say.

"All this—this devil stuff—you know, devil worship, all that stuff. I know some people are into that, but do you really believe in it? I mean, really, truly believe in it?"

"Sure. It's as real as everything else I believe in. It's very present in this world. It's all around us."

"But can that really give someone powers? Can they really do things with that—with some kind of dark power?"

"I saw a lot of things in Papua New Guinea that I never in a million years would have believed if I'd just heard about them. I think because Satan has such a stronghold over there, his powers are even more on display."

"What sort of things?"

"I saw an exorcism while I was there. It was pretty—intense. It's real. All that stuff is real. And when you know that, even though I know God is all-powerful and I don't have to worry about any of those things because of Him—it's still scary when you see the face of Satan right there in front of you."

"But you believe that God protects you from all of those things?"

Jim hesitated, then nodded. "I do."

"Then what about your friend in the village who died? And the other deaths there?"

"Did Stephanie tell you about that?"

"She did. She said it's been hard."

"Yes, it has. Very."

"So what do you say about situations like that?"

"They're tough, obviously."

"That's the big hurdle for me. Christians have no answer for the pain and suffering that happens in this world. Unexpected tragedies. Where is God when those things happen?"

"He doesn't want those things to happen," Jim started, his instincts kicking in. "It's just that sin is prevalent, and humans—" He broke off.

"What?"

Jim shook his head. "I don't know. I'm too tired to talk theology."

"I don't want to talk theology. But some things make you doubt, right? I mean, you have to have doubts, Jim."

Jim wanted to go outside and dig through the snow. Do something, anything, instead of standing here talking about a God he didn't understand and maybe didn't know at all. This was one of those opportunities he used to pray for, a chance to share his faith and the almighty love of Christ with his un-believing brother-in-law. Stephanie and Jim prayed for Paul. And yet, here was his moment, and he didn't know what to say. He didn't want to lie to Paul. Paul would see through it. Most people would.

"Yes, I have doubts," Jim said. "I wish I didn't. But I do. And it's—it's been hard. When death happens to those you love, it's hard to understand why."

"When it happens to people you pray for, right?" Paul asked.

"Yeah, exactly. That doesn't mean that I don't believe God is in control or that I doubt His love for us, it's just—"

"But you doubt a little, right?"

"Yeah, sure, I said that. But that doesn't—I don't know. I'm too tired to think clearly this morning."

Paul finished his coffee and set down his cup. The moment had passed. "Okay, so here's the deal. I get ready to climb Mt. Everest. Then I go off. How long do you think before I'll find civilization?"

"Walk down the main road. Eventually you'll get to some houses."

"That could be a *long* way."

"You're in shape, right?"

Paul laughed.

Jim put their dishes in the sink and turned to go upstairs, but Paul stopped him.

"There's nothing wrong with having questions," his brother-in-law said. "Everybody has doubts. Even the apostles in the Bible. They had doubts. Didn't one of them deny Jesus?"

"Very good," Jim said. "I'm impressed."

"Come on. I know the stories just like everybody else. It's just—to me, they're just stories. Made up. Maybe some of those things really happened and some of them were exaggerated. Maybe there was a man named Jesus, and maybe he was able to turn water into wine, you know? And maybe he proceeded to get the entire crowd drunk, as far as we know. It's all in who tells the story."

"It's all in faith, Paul. You know, you should study the books of the Bible written by the man who has your name."

"The apostle Paul, huh?"

"That's the one. He was pretty vehement in his views before God humbled him. Ultimately, all of us—every one of us—will be humbled before God."

Paul chuckled, skepticism written across his face.

Or is it something else?

"What?"

"Nothing. I have to remind myself who I'm talking to," Paul said.

"And who is that?"

"You're a missionary. It's your job to talk like that."

"I have doubts and questions just like everyone. But that's what faith is all about. Believing and hoping *despite* those doubts. Don't you get that?"

Paul shook his head. "No. And trust me on this. I never will."

49

Outside

He waited.

One more day. That was all he needed.

The storm had been a surprise. Everything else was going as planned.

Soon, one by one, they would be gone.

And soon he would have his chance to be alone with the boy. Then he would bring him to the place where it would be done, where the sacrifice would be offered.

You won't grow up to be like your father, he thought. *You won't be able to infect others with that faith and that love and all those preposterous notions.*

He felt cold standing outside, waiting for his next victim. The old man, another stupid unwitting pawn in his plan.

He could still feel the old woman's tears caressing his hands as those very hands made her stop crying out. Made her quiet. Made her stop breathing. He took care of her just like he would take care of the rest of them.

But mostly, he would take care of the boy.

Zachary.

Already so full of lies and foolish notions.

You'll see that they mean nothing. That God has abandoned this world. That there is no hope except for what you make. That there is no sense in believing in anything.

He inhaled and felt the hairs in his nose freeze. The cold felt good. Deep inside, he burned and ached, and there was only one way to tame those feelings.

The day had just started, and he had a lot more work to do.

50

Helpless

"Bob, I want you to look at me."

The elderly man sat on the edge of the bed staring at the wall. He seemed to be in an almost catatonic state.

"Bob, come on. Snap out of it."

Bob's dark eyes moved slightly to look at Jim standing over him.

"Drink some of this." He had mixed a sleeping pill in with a cup of coffee. Maybe Bob didn't need the pill after all. He was doing a fine job of looking unconscious. "Bob, come on, just a sip."

Bob took the cup and drank obediently, as a child would. He handed the cup back to Jim.

"Paul went for help, okay? We're going to be fine."

"It's the devil, I tell you. It's Satan himself, and he's in this house and he wants us. He wants us all."

Jim sucked in a breath and nodded. He hoped Steph wasn't allowing Zachary to wander as he usually did.

"Another sip. Come on. Paul's going to get us some help, and we'll be off this mountain in no time."

"It's too late," Bob said, his voice deep and hollow. "It's too late. For all of us."

"Bob, come on. Another sip."

Jim proceeded to make the older man drink all the coffee, then helped him lie back in his bed.

"I'm going to find Evelyn, and everything's going to be okay. I promise you, Bob. Everything's going to be fine."

But Jim didn't believe it. And he wondered if his voice gave away his trepidation.

❧

BACK IN THE BEDROOM, Zachary was getting restless. "Why can't I go downstairs?"

"We're going to stay up here for now," Jim told him. "Do you want a puzzle to work on?"

"No thanks."

Jim spotted the half-eaten sandwich on the floor by Zach. He had gone to the kitchen and quickly made them some lunch, but none of them, including himself, was very hungry.

"Can't I go to my room?"

"What do you want in your room?"

Zachary shook his head and looked away. Jim stared at Stephanie for a moment, then walked over to his son.

"Are you okay, Zach?"

The boy nodded.

"You're pretty quiet."

"Is Mr. Patterson okay?"

"He's going to be fine. We're all going to be fine."

"Then why can't we leave this room?"

"For the time being, I think it might be best if we stay here."

"Is there someone else in the house?"

Jim put his hand on Zach's head. "Nobody else is in this house."

"What happened to Mrs. Patterson?"

"I'm not sure, Zach."

"Shouldn't we go looking for her?"

"No," Stephanie said sharply. "You're not to go anywhere in this house without us. Do you understand?"

Zachary's jaw stiffened.

"Do you understand?" she repeated.

He nodded, but unconvincingly.

"Zach, you gotta promise me you're going to stay put," Jim said. "This is a big house, and we don't know—"

"If someone else is in here?"

"Nobody else is here," Jim said.

"But how do you know?"

"I just know."

"Why did Uncle Paul leave?"

"To get us some—to go let people know the snow is bad and we don't have phone service."

"Is Mrs. Patterson hurt?"

"Zach, I don't know. I really don't know."

"But you think she is."

"No, I don't."

"Yes you do. I can tell."

"Zach, come on."

No one spoke for a few minutes.

"How long do we have to stay up here?"

Jim looked at Stephanie. He felt helpless and angry. *What am I doing here? What are we doing here?* "Not long. I promise you."

But he couldn't promise Zach anything.

It could be hours before they heard from Paul.

51

Drifting

Jim and Stephanie drift in similar waves of memory.

He remembers the small house with the hot, dim bedroom and the smell of vomit. He can see the figure writhing on the bed, the preacher next to him holding onto his arms and commanding the spirits to leave him. Jim remembers standing in the back of the room and watching with horror and fascination, praying for God to grant the man peace. The man buckles and pushes back on the bed. It takes four men including Jim to hold him down. This man is one of Jim's friends.

Stephanie remembers the morning afterward, her depleted husband sitting at the small table in their house, his face weary and without expression. She asks him what happened, but for the longest time he says nothing. He just sits there, lost in thought, lost in memory. Then he tells her the man is dead, that they lost him, that he just died.

They both remember the words.

Just died.

He feels anger at God and doesn't understand how it could have happened. The Maker of heaven and earth didn't listen to their prayers and allowed this to happen. All their efforts in the village would mean nothing. The villagers would see this as a sign. They would see that God wasn't truly in control, not when a possessed man couldn't be made whole.

Stephanie knows better than to offer false hope. She hugs him, but he doesn't hug her back. He feels cold and acts even colder. She withdraws, pulling away, going to another room and praying for him. She feels alone.

She feels very much like he does.

But he can't talk about it. He is afraid, afraid that God is not responding, that God isn't looking out for them anymore, that God might have some other plan. Jim wants to question God, but knows he can't do that except in private, in his heart. He needs to be strong for the rest of his family and for the village. So he doesn't say anything. He feels empty and wants—demands—an explanation, but the explanation doesn't come.

Does he have any right to wonder? To ask? To want to know?

He is serving God, and God is failing him.

And she senses his emptiness but she puts it on herself, on her own inability to be there for him. If only she could have done this or that, things would have been better. But she doesn't know where to begin or how to start over or how to break through.

They feel empty and lost and need God, but neither one speaks.

And a year later, drifting in slumber as the snow starts up again outside, Jim and Stephanie Miller still feel the same.

52

The Closest Thing

THE WILL OF GOD WILL NEVER LEAD YOU WHERE THE GRACE OF GOD CANNOT KEEP YOU.

For some reason, that refrain kept running through Jim's

mind. The words were inscribed on a plaque that hung in the hallway of his parents' house. He had walked past it a thousand times in his youth, mindlessly looking at it but never truly thinking about it. It was a saying, a Christian saying at that, a cliché. But now he examined the words. Was the saying true?

Maybe it is true, Jim thought as he stretched and glanced at the bed where Stephanie lay asleep next to Ashley. *Maybe God's will doesn't lead you to dark evil places where His grace can't keep you. But what happens if you're not following God's will and you end up in one of those places anyway?*

He stood and looked around the room for Zachary. He found his son in the walk-in closet stretched out on the floor, reading.

"You okay?"

Zach didn't look up, just nodded. A good sign. When Zachary was immersed in a good book, he didn't like to be bothered. It didn't matter if the interruption was for dinner or dessert or a television show coming on. He was like Jim that way.

"Stay put, okay?" Jim told him.

Zach just nodded.

Jim walked by the bed and looked down at his wife and daughter. They were beautiful. He couldn't remember the last time he had simply looked at both of them and remarked to himself how precious they were.

I'm a lucky man. He paused for a moment and couldn't help adding, *And a foolish one too.*

What had he been thinking, bringing his family here? His father had been right. His father was *always* right. What was he thinking? Getting away for some family time. Things felt worse here than they had in Wheaton. And that was before—before everything started happening.

Before this house turned into The Amityville Horror, he thought. *Or* The Shining. *All I need to do is get an ax and start wielding it around like Jack Nicholson.* The image wasn't amusing. He felt cold and scared. He didn't want his family hurt. And the absolute last thing he could imagine doing was hurting them himself. It wasn't right. It wasn't natural.

He decided to check on Bob. It had been an hour since he'd seen him.

I wonder how Paul's doing.

Before leaving the room, Jim looked out the window. It was snowing again, an apocalyptic storm, as though the world were ending, but in snow and ice instead of fire and brimstone.

I want to go somewhere warm. I want to go to a beach and get sunburned and drink piña coladas and taste the salt of the ocean water, and I never want to see snow in my life ever again.

He unlocked the door and opened it slowly. He still wasn't sure what exactly to make of Mrs. Patterson's disappearance. Did he believe someone was in the house?

Yes.

No, another voice said. *Not necessarily.*

Why are you moving so slowly, bracing for someone to come out of the shadows?

But he wasn't. He was just walking down the hallway slowly. He was a little jittery, sure, but that was because Bob was so agitated about his wife's disappearance.

How would you react if Stephanie just disappeared?

He knew he'd be worried sick. But he wouldn't spout off about Satan being in the house.

Does Bob know what you know? Has Bob seen what you've seen? Jim wondered. Maybe Bob knew more than he was telling. Maybe that was why he was so nervous.

Jim reached the door to Bob's room and listened. No sound within. The sleeping pill must be doing its job. But when he carefully opened the door and peered inside, he could see the bed was empty.

"Bob?" he asked, scanning the room.

The man was too big to be hiding under the bed. He knew that.

"Bob?" he asked again, looking in the closet.

Maybe he's just searching the house again.

For a second Jim thought about calling Bob over the intercom.

If you do that, they'll know you're looking for him.

Now it's "they," another voice said. "They" will know?

Jim stepped out into the hallway and looked each way.

Surely Bob had just woken up and gone looking for his wife.

But what about the sleeping pill?

Paul will be back soon, and he can help me look. Or stay with the kids.

There was no way Jim would leave the house without Steph and the kids, regardless of who was missing, and he didn't want to leave their room either. He wanted to stay in the room and hold out, but the thought of someone in this house made him unable to do so. Evelyn missing and now Paul gone . . .

Someone needed to go look for Bob, make sure he was okay, see if he had found any trace of his wife.

He walked back into his bedroom and locked the door behind him. There was something about having his back to the doorway. Something that scared him. Something that made him want to lock the door. Just in case.

In case the grace of God couldn't keep them right now.

53

The Same Dark Plague

won't do it."

"You don't have a choice."

"Jim, I'm not going to stay put with the children while you go wandering around this house only to find God knows what—"

"Please lower your voice."

"I'm not going to let you go."

"Paul might be—"

"Paul might be what?" Steph asked sharply. "He might be in trouble? He might be hurt?"

"I don't know."

"Yeah, and I don't want to be wondering the same thing about you."

Jim stared at Stephanie who sat on the edge of the bathtub. They had shut the door so they could talk alone.

"Steph—"

"What?"

"I'm worried."

"And you think I'm not?"

"I'm not saying that."

"I just—I want to get out of this house, Jim. Out of this place."

"I know."

"No, you don't. I've felt it ever since we got here. I've seen things."

"What things?"

"Just—things. I don't know. I've felt things. Dark things. I can't explain it."

"I know," he said again.

Stephanie studied her husband. For once she felt like he wasn't thinking of her as a crazy person. "You do? You know what I'm talking about?"

He nodded.

That's good enough for me, she thought. *A nod's good enough for me.*

"Then, what are we—what are you—"

"I have to go find Bob. I don't think he's well. He's not thinking right."

"His wife is missing."

"I know. And I don't want him missing too."

"Wait till Paul comes back."

"That might be a while."

"Jim?"

"Yeah."

"Did you go over to the north wing?"

He didn't answer her.

"You did, didn't you? What'd you find?"

"Nothing."

"Don't lie to me."

"It's nothing."

Her glance didn't waver. She knew he wasn't telling her everything. "Jim."

"Just—nothing. I want to get out of this place as much as you do."

"Should I be worried?"

"No," Jim said without hesitation. Then he looked at her, really looked at her, and they both knew he was lying.

"What is happening to us? Why? Why is God doing this to us?"

"Don't do that."

"Do what?" she asked.

"That. Don't say that."

"You know exactly what I mean. And don't tell me you haven't thought it too."

"Steph—"

"No! You're thinking it just like I am. That the same dark plague that was hanging over our heads in Dambi followed us here."

"That's not true."

"And part of me thinks maybe it's me."

Jim's face wrinkled in confusion. "What are you talking about?"

"I just—sometimes—I don't know."

I want to tell him about the dreams, about my childhood, about my worries.

"Sometimes what?" Jim asked.

She could only look down at the floor. She was surprised to feel Jim move toward her, embrace her, hold her close.

"This is not your fault, not even a little," he said. "I'm the one who brought us here. And I swear on everything I am that I'm going to get all of us off this mountain safely. Okay?"

She buried her face in his chest and started to cry. "I just want out of here."

"I know you do."

"And I don't want to be worried about our children."

"Don't be."

"But you know why—you know what I'm talking about. You feel what I feel."

"Listen to me. I don't know if there's someone or something else in this house, and I don't know where Evelyn disappeared to or where Bob is or whether or not Paul's going to get help. But what I do know is that—that nothing's going to happen to you and the kids. Nothing."

"And what about you? Who's going to protect you?"

"I'll be fine."

She looked up at his face, his heavy eyes, his thick beard.

"We're all going to be fine," Jim said. "Just—you have to trust me on this. You have to listen to me now and let me go." He was on the verge of tears.

"I will."

"I'm going to go out and look for Bob. If I don't find him soon, I'll come back. But I want you to stay put, and I want this door locked, and I don't want you letting *anybody* in if it's not me. Okay?"

"How long will you be gone?"

"Not long, I swear. Half an hour, an hour at the most. Okay?" He kissed her forehead. "We're going to get out of this place."

She nodded.

"And one more thing," he told her.

"What's that?"

"Pray."

54

Master Bedroom

The house was silent as a tomb, immense as a cave. The hidden sun and the blustery snow made it seem like evening.

Jim stepped off the stairs in the great room. He felt like he was abandoning his family, even though the door was locked and Stephanie was there with the kids. He carried the large hunting knife.

I can take care of myself if I have to.

He knew where he needed to go. It was inevitable. Bob hadn't found his wife in the south or west wing or the basement. The only place left to look was the north wing.

Don't go back there.

But he didn't have a choice. If somebody really was in the house, maybe he was over in the north wing hiding out.

Someone could've been here the whole time as far as we know.

A board creaked, followed by the sound of something scuttling across the wood floor.

Is that my imagination? Is it just the wind?

He stared in the direction the sound had come from but didn't see anything. He walked over to the doorway that led to the north wing. It was open.

I locked that door. I know I locked it.

What was it about doors that brought out his fears? A closed door in a cabin late at night. A closet door. The door to a base-ment. A trapdoor. Doors held secrets behind them.

I swear I locked that door.

He looked at the open door. He stepped through it.

The hall light was on. He walked carefully, always checking to make sure nothing was behind him. He passed the library and entered the large room with the fireplace and piano. A couple lights were on, but nobody could be seen.

It felt so quiet, so lonely.

The hallways on either side of the fireplace were dark.

"Bob?" he called, remembering how he'd called out for Evelyn hours earlier.

He couldn't stop thinking of the footage of the Halloween party. Did evil linger in a place, like a scent or a stain? Was it that powerful?

It was one thing to see Satan's power over a small village in the middle of Papua New Guinea, but this was a hilltop in North Carolina, a state where churches were plentiful and people didn't hesitate to say they believed in God.

Jim walked up to the piano. He stood looking at it, lost in thought, when the lights went out. He jerked his head and looked around. Nothing but black. For a moment he just stood, silent, not breathing, waiting to see if anyone was around. But he heard nothing.

As he moved toward the nearest wall, his legs banged into a love seat. The darkness was stifling.

He was in the north wing, and the lights had gone out.

Is it the whole house? Did the power go off completely?

Please, God, don't let it be the power. Please.

He felt along the wall for a switch and bumped a painting, dropping it to the floor with a crack. He fumbled through the darkness, searching desperately for light.

I've gotta get out of here.

He thought of Stephanie and the kids. If they were in the dark now . . .

They're fine. She's fine. The door is locked and she is okay and things are fine.

He wanted to believe God would protect them. That God watched over them now and was keeping them safe. But he wasn't sure. He had preached to hundreds and shared God's love and grace and power, and yet here he was, in a house on a mountain, wondering if God even saw them, if He was concerned in the least about them.

What's happening to me?

The wall finally ended, and he stepped into the space near the fireplace. A hall he had not been down before.

Through the dark, a flickering orange glow could be seen. It was at the end of the hallway, spilling out of one of the rooms.

Don't go down there. Don't, Jim. Don't do it.

But he felt like he needed to. He had to. God would protect him, right? What could it be anyway?

It's not Bob. It's something else. Don't go down there.

But he could feel his legs already starting to move, heading in that direction. At least the orange luminance was better than the pitch black. He passed a doorway and wondered what was behind it. He could only imagine. The depravity of what happened in this house, in these rooms.

Jim kept walking, the orange glow intensifying as he approached the end of the hall.

There was no noise, no movement, nothing as he arrived at the door. Inside was a large bedroom with a four-poster king-sized bed surrounded by gauzy drapes. The glow came from the dresser next to the bed where three candles burned in thick wooden holders.

His heart dropped, and his skin chilled. Everything in him wanted to run, but he couldn't. He needed to find out what this was. Who had lit these, and where was the person now? Was it Bob?

The walls were deep burgundy, and the armoire indicated this was a stately and ornate master bedroom.

Is it Wolfcott's room?

Jim had pictured something creepier, more evil.

He approached the bed. At first he thought it looked normal enough, but as he approached it, he could make out a shape underneath the covers.

Don't, Jim. Go away. It's enough. It's enough.

Nothing was going to harm him. A monster wasn't going to jump out and kill him and he was too tired and too frustrated to keep getting creeped out by little things like power outages and strange noises.

He hesitated for a second, then he pulled back the heavy comforter to see what was underneath.

Blank, lifeless eyes stared back at him.

He jumped back and let go of the comforter.

The eyes belonged to Bob.

Jim looked around the room. He stared at the darkness leading into a bathroom, maybe, another leading into a closet. The hallway.

Nobody was here. His chest pounded. He wouldn't be surprised to have a heart attack right now.

He stared at the figure on the bed. He could see Bob's face, pale as a ghost, staring at him with unmoving eyes. With eyes that asked, *Why?*

Pulling the comforter back farther, Jim choked and stumbled back, almost falling. His mind flailed as he closed his eyes against the horror. He couldn't believe what he'd seen, what had happened to Bob, what somebody had actually done.

Who could do something like that?

The warm glow of the candlelight must have been playing tricks on his mind, making him imagine things that weren't real.

Get out get out get out run Jim run

He needed to breathe, to run, to get away from there.

His mind pictured Bob and his damaged body.

An accident didn't do this somebody did somebody in this house somebody in here

Jim had seen enough to know someone or something had killed Bob in a vicious, horrendous way.

It was this house the spirits in this place the demons dwelling in here

He knelt on the ground and tried to breathe in and gain composure.

Something moved in the room. It was almost like a gust of wind that passed by him, through him. The candles went out and left him in darkness.

For a second he expected someone to attack him. But there was nothing. No noise, no wind, nothing. Just the unmoving figure of the old man in the bed next to him.

Get out of here go to the family stay with them wait for Paul to get help.

He spun around.

It was right there right behind you right over there

Jim staggered and hit his knee on the armoire. He winced and dropped the knife and groped to find it on the dark floor beneath him.

Get out of here get out run go!

He noticed faint light spilling from the curtains. He jerked them open and saw a sliding glass door. Snow covered half of it, but he could see it led out to the deck.

Get outside get out of here get away from this place

He unlocked the door and pulled at it. On the third try, he managed to open it. A blast of cold air brought in snow and made him shiver. It didn't matter.

Where are you going to go from here?

He wasn't sure, but he would go somewhere. The doors to the deck on the west and south wings were never locked. He would find his way to them and let himself in over there.

I'm getting us off this mountain away from this house if I have to carry my family on my back.

He stepped outside into two feet of snow and didn't look back.

He wasn't sure exactly what he had seen. Was Bob really in that bed with part of his chest missing?

He didn't care if he lost his mind. As long as he could do it far away from here.

55

Lights Out

Stephanie pictured the family snapshot she had found in the last room down the hall. She could see her hands opening the box, the photo inside, the image she couldn't get out of her mind.

Did I really see that? Or was it a trick? Another trick my mind's playing on me.

I've been here before.

That's what her eyes told her and what her mind suggested.

We've been here before.

But when? How? How could they have come here? And more importantly, why?

You know why. You know exactly why. You're just not admitting it to yourself.

She thought about her parents.

How could they have—what would have made them come to a place like this?

But she knew. She knew exactly.

The nightmares and premonitions were not coming because of what had happened in Papua New Guinea. Those spirits were tame compared to these. They were distant cousins, sure. But these were more violent, more hungry, more dangerous.

And they want you.

She had been in this house before. Both Paul and she had. When they were young.

The photo you saw didn't lie. It didn't lie the way your mind can lie, the way you can bury the past and bury memories.

She couldn't believe it, but she knew it was true.

How could we have—

The lights went out.

She froze on the edge of the bed, then called out for the children.

"Yeah?" Zachary asked.

"Are you okay?"

"Yeah."

"Is Ashley by you?"

"What happened to the lights?"

"I don't know. Is Ashley by you?"

"I'm here," her daughter said, tugging at her.

"Zachary, come over here."

"Why?"

"Zach, just come."

She held them next to her and thought for a moment. She couldn't call for Jim. But if the power had gone off in the whole house, he'd come back up here.

"Where did the lights go?" Ashley asked.

"They just went off."

"Why?"

"Maybe because of the storm."

"I have a flashlight," Zach said.

"You do?"

He went to the closet and came back shining a light at them.

"Don't keep it on too long," she said to him. "We might need the batteries."

"Is Dad coming back?" Zach asked.

"Yes. Any minute now." She could hear her voice wavering.

Stay strong. You have to stay strong for them, have to try to be strong.

Zach was by the door, checking the light switch.

"Zach, come over here."

"I can just check—"

A violent knocking silenced them. Zach darted back to the bed. "Mom, I didn't—"

"Shh," she said, holding both of them in her arms.

The banging continued, half a dozen knocks, then a pause.

It's not Jim.

She knew it wasn't Jim. He would call out her name and wouldn't scare them, especially with the lights off.

Zachary was trembling.

"It's going to be okay," she told him.

They waited in silence.

Then the hammering started again. She clutched her children even tighter.

Please God help us please God hear us please God help us protect us protect all of us with Your hand with Your protection please God be there hold us in Your hand

She waited, silent, wondering who was on the other side of the door, wondering if the door was strong enough to keep somebody out. The knocks were getting louder and more violent.

God bring Jim back bring him back quick

Zach took her hand. "Mom."

"It's okay," she said again.

"Mom, I want to show you something."

"Not now, just stay—"

"Mom, it's the closet."

The door rattled as though someone was ramming against it.

Dear God it's going to be ripped open dear God help!

"Mom. We need to go into the closet."

A heavy thud shook the door.

"Zach, you have to—"

"Mom, I know a way out of here."

She looked down at him, the luminance from the flashlight framing his small face.

"What are you—"

"There are secret passageways in this house," Zach said. "And I just found one in your closet."

Holding a crying Ashley in her arms, Stephanie didn't ask anything else. She followed her son into the closet as the sound of splintering wood filled the room.

56

On the Deck

He stepped carefully, trudging across the deck the vicious wind had piled deep with snow in some places and swept bare in others. There was a low railing on this deck, too low to be of any real use. The ground was several stories down, surrounded by trees and stumps and branches, all adorned with caps of snow.

God, where are You?

Nobody could hear him ask this question. Nobody would hear the answer either. Because the answer wasn't coming, and it hadn't come in a long time.

Where are You, and why won't You show me a sign?

Jim had spent his whole life trying to figure out what God wanted for him and his family. He tried to do the right thing. He prayed and he gave and he guided his family in the direction he thought they should go. But he was beginning to lose hope.

I'm supposed to show others hope, but how can I when I don't have it myself?

It had been building for some time, but it had overcome him on this mountain.

He had heard the whispering doubts as he'd sat on the couch trying to read, but instead he'd just closed his eyes, absorbed by the ache and the loneliness. He couldn't tell his wife, who was growing more distant as time passed. He couldn't show his two children, who were supposed to believe Dad had the answers and knew what he was doing. He couldn't share it with family or friends. His supporters and prayer warriors. How could he tell them he was crumbling with fear and doubt and that it had started on the mission field and was growing and festering even here in the middle of the wilderness?

It was your idea to come up here.

He had hoped that somehow this time away would lead him closer to the answers. Somehow it would lead him closer to God.

I just want to see You—Your face, Your hand, Your power.

Jim was afraid. Everything he used to believe in had become a question mark. Everything he spent so long leaning toward and learning about and trying to live out was lost in the darkness. He couldn't find anything to truly claim as his own.

I don't know anything anymore. I'm alone here, and I'm supposed to rely on God, but I'm afraid because I'm wondering if God even cares.

Another part of him said, *Of course God cares.*

It's not about us. It's about Him, it's about serving Him, it's about grace and love and mercy.

A curse rose on his lips, and he squelched it.

The wind howled, and he wondered if it was about to start snowing again. He stepped carefully over the snow and ice on the deck, trying not to slip, trying not to drop the knife in his hand.

Sometimes he felt so young and immature. He wondered if he was equipped to help anybody at all. Sometimes he felt like he was wandering just as aimlessly as the people he tried to help.

This was the life he had chosen and yet sometimes he wanted out of it. Sometimes he wanted away from this family and this wife and this religion and faith and all of it. Sometimes he wanted to do it on his own and that was it.

You can't and you know it.

Maybe he just wasn't strong enough. Maybe he couldn't actually admit that God didn't care. No matter what he had seen, he couldn't admit that maybe

there's no God at all

everything he believed in wasn't true, that maybe some things weren't able to be explained.

Someone is putting doubt in me. Someone is waging war on me, and it's not God. God has nothing to do with these doubts and insecurities.

It had been a while since he had prayed fervently. He couldn't bring himself to do it. He felt like a distant stranger from God, and he knew better. Some people didn't know any better, but Jim did. He knew God had every right to judge him and squeeze him and not put up with him.

God doesn't work like that. I can come to Him anytime.

God was calling out. He was asking Jim to come. But Jim couldn't. He didn't know why. But he couldn't. Something was stopping him.

Maybe it was the memory. The memory of the exorcism that had gone wrong, the memory of the man dying in his own vomit while all the Christians there stood back and watched and did nothing. They were powerless.

That was what he wanted explained.

He *demanded* that God explain it to him.

He made it over to the south wing and approached the door to the sunroom, a door he knew was open. Then he noticed the tracks on the deck.

There were footprints as big as his in the snow. Someone had come out on the deck, stopping as though they knew he was coming.

He still had the hunting knife in his hand, careful not to slip and land on the blade. He wasn't wearing a coat and was already frigid from being outside. His head and beard were coated with flakes.

He turned the corner of the deck, expecting to see someone. But nobody was there. The footprints continued on toward the door. When he reached it, he tried the handle. The door wouldn't budge.

He tried it several times, but it was locked. He fought letting go with an angry curse. All he could think about was being locked out of the lodge while Stephanie and the kids were in there.

In there with—someone.

The tracks.

He tried another door a dozen yards down, but it was locked too.

Panic began to rise in him.

He gripped the sliding glass door again and yanked at it. Nothing.

Maybe I can break the glass.

Jim studied the tracks leading toward and away from the glass door. He moved to the edge of the railing, leaning over to look down the mountain, trying to think of what to do.

I don't have the keys. I need to go back to the north wing, to the door I left unlocked.

But what if that door was locked too?

He shivered in the cold and set the knife on the edge of the wood railing so he could rub his hands together. His breath sent clouds of warmth into the air.

A clicking lock made him jerk and instinctively turn around.

For a second his heart raced and everything in him tightened up.

Then he saw the face at the door as it slid open.

The face smiled, and so did he.

Thank You, God.

57

Terror

There was a hidden door in their walk-in closet. It blended into the wall so well that it was no wonder she'd missed it. Zach opened it and crawled through first, telling her to send Ashley next. Once inside, they shut the door and Zach led them down a narrow hallway that opened up to another room.

They could still hear the pounding on the bedroom door as they moved down the hallway. Just as they entered the hidden room, Stephanie heard a loud crash from the bedroom behind them.

It's inside.

She hurried the children to the door and closed it, locking it, knowing that couldn't stop someone from kicking it in.

The small room had a couple of couches and a table. There was a television on the wall. Zach shined the flashlight beam along the wall, working his way around the room. The cold air smelled musty. Stephanie strained to hear something, anything.

In the darkness of the room, the flashlight off, Stephanie sat on the couch, Zachary in one arm, Ashley in the other. Her body shook, and she knew by her kids' stillness that they were scared too. As the minutes passed, the silence grew unnerving. She didn't know how long they should wait in this secret room.

Where's Jim? What happened to him?

As the doubts and fears started to grow, forming questions too horrible to ask and answers she didn't want to hear, Zach flipped the flashlight on and off.

"Mommy, I'm scared," Ashley said.

Stephanie held her daughter closer and told her everything would be okay. Her voice trembled. She didn't know what to do. So she did what she always did when her kids were troubled or worried or scared. She began to sing, slowly, softly, gently, the first song that popped into her mind.

"Blessed assurance, Jesus is mine! O what a foretaste of glory divine. . . ."

She snuggled closer to her children, fighting the chill.

❦

OUT ON THE DECK, Jim waited for the door to open. "Man, am I glad to see you," he told a grinning Paul. "When'd you get back?"

Paul raised an eyebrow. "Where's your coat?"

"Oh, it's—it's a long story. Did you get help? Did you get far?"

Paul shook his head. "That's a long story too."

Jim nodded, moving to the door.

"Wait, you don't want to do that," Paul said.

"What are you talking about?"

Paul stared at him without blinking, without saying a word, without moving.

❦

"THIS IS MY STORY, this is my song, praising my Savior, all the day long. . . ."

❦

"WHAT IS IT?"

Paul didn't say anything.

"It's kinda cold out here, you know? I need to get back in and check on—"

"You can't," Paul said sharply.

"What?" Jim rubbed his hands together, staring at his brother-in-law in confusion. "Is everything okay? I found Bob—it's bad. I mean it's—look, let's go in."

"No."

"Paul, what's going on?"

"You need to know something."

❧

"PERFECT SUBMISSION, PERFECT DELIGHT, visions of rapture now burst on my sight. . . ."

❧

JIM MOVED TOWARD THE door.

"Paul, please, let's go in—"

Paul didn't move. Instead, he reached up and grabbed Jim's neck. Jim fell back and lost his footing

my God what is he doing what is Paul doing he's out of his mind

and he couldn't breathe and gasped and choked and then realized that his back and thigh were pressed against the deck railing.

He tried to scream but couldn't.

All he could feel was Paul shoving him back, back, farther back, against the rail, over the rail—

"No!" he shouted.

And then Paul let go.

Jim felt himself falling, falling to the forest floor several stories below.

And everything he wanted to say and wanted to feel and wanted to think was swallowed up in terror.

∽

AND IN THE HIDDEN bedroom off the secret passageway, Stephanie clutched their children close and continued to sing. "Angels descending bring from above, echoes of mercy, whispers of love."

58

Falling

Everything he had ever wanted or needed or hoped for gripped his body and mind and soul, and for a moment he embraced it all and thought of all of those things he would never have a chance to experience.

Zachary's first high school football game and Ashley's first date and prom and graduation and college and marriage and grandchildren

And then he thought of Stephanie.

I can't leave her behind I can't leave her alone she needs me she needs me with her

And it seemed like the weightlessness and horror of his fall went on and on.

He saw Zachary's face, then Ashley's, then Stephanie's.

I love you I love you all I haven't been the father I needed to be the man I'm supposed to be the husband God wants me to be forgive me please forgive me please . . .

And then he saw something bright, something awful, something beautiful, surrounding him

embracing me

and then he landed, not with the vicious thud he had expected, but with a soft delicate bounce as though he had been dropped onto sheets of silk and satin.

I'm imagining this all of this I'm already gone already dead the bright light is heaven I'm floating away good-bye

He felt something against his face.

The sweet stroke of a gentle hand on his cheek.

Then his eyes closed, and he was out.

59

His Only Chance

He started up the stairs, taking his time. He knew they were upstairs, hiding somewhere. He had broken down the door and the room was empty, but they were up there. He felt it.

A lock meant nothing and neither did a door. If he had to, he would break down every single door in this house.

She'll open up, he thought. *She will if she hears me.*

If she hears her sweet brother calling her name.

All he needed to do was speak and she would open up and think there was still hope.

The old couple were disposed of and so was the man. He wasn't interested in any of them. It was the boy he was here for.

The boy named Zachary.

All this way for a boy.

The rest of them didn't matter.

He was here for the boy and knew what he needed to do.

To watch and wait and feel the pulse and know for sure.

He had to make sure.

And he knew that this was the only chance, now, tonight, right now.

60

Opening the Door

A deep pain swept through Stephanie, almost taking her breath away. She felt cold and empty—and very afraid.

Where is Jim? Why hasn't he come back?

There had only been silence for, what—fifteen minutes? Half an hour? She couldn't tell. Ashley was sitting next to her as Zachary stood and listened by the door. Stephanie had asked him to come back and sit on the couch, but he had said, "It's okay," in a whisper that almost made her believe it was.

The flashlight remained by her side. She wondered when the lights would come back on, when the heat would return. She was almost afraid of using the flashlight at all, afraid that whoever was out there would see it. It wasn't the darkness she feared. It was waiting. Every moment that passed and every sound she thought she heard and every time she asked Zach to come by her side . . . it all made things worse. Something was very wrong.

When is Jim coming back? When is Paul coming back? What if something happened to them?

"Can we go back out?" Zach asked for the third time.

"Please, Zachary, just sit down."

"I think he's gone."

"We don't know that for sure," she said in a whisper.

"But what if Dad comes back and doesn't find us? All we need to do is—"

"Zach, no."

"It's okay. I can run fast."

"You're not running anywhere."

She heard Zach drop into the couch across from her chair. She couldn't believe how calm he was. Ashley had already cried a few times, and each time Zach was right there offering more comfort than she did. How could her eight-year-old be stronger than she was?

But there he was, calm and ready to face anything.

"Zach?"

"Yeah," his voice replied in the darkness.

"What are you thinking about?" There was a pause. "Zach?"

"I was praying for Daddy."

"He's okay," she told him.

"Uh-huh."

"He'll be okay."

She turned the flashlight on and pointed it across from her to glimpse Zach's eyes, his face looking at hers, questioning.

He can see right through me. He knows I'm not sure. I'm not sure about anything, and I'm more scared than he is.

She was about to say something when they heard a voice. It came from close by. She instinctively shut off the flashlight, a slight gasp escaping her lips. She could feel Zach suddenly nudging up beside her with his shoulder. "It's okay," she said.

The voice continued shouting. For a second she didn't believe what she heard, but then she got up and went to the door.

The words were muffled, but she could still make them out.

"Steph, it's me. Steph, where are you?"

Paul! He made it back!

"It's your uncle! Here, give me your flashlight."

"Mom?"

"What?"

She turned the light on and saw Zachary's face. His eyes were huge, and he gazed at her, unblinking. "What if it's not really him?"

The voice sounded again. "Steph?"

"It's him," she said. "Come on, both of you. Zach, get your sister."

But when she opened the door and climbed through the passageway, calling out Paul's name, Zachary wasn't behind her. She continued on, knowing Paul was here, knowing they were safe with him. She quickly opened the small door in the closet and saw the beam of a flashlight coming from their bedroom. She made out Paul's frame.

"You made it back," she said, flashing the light just below his face.

He smiled and nodded. "Have you been in there the whole time?"

"Zach found a secret passageway. There was someone pounding on the door. Someone—"

"Yeah—they broke down the door. What happened?"

"We don't know. We heard it and then hid in here. Zach? Ash? Come on out here. Did you see Jim?"

"Yeah. He's downstairs."

She let out a long exhale.

Thank You, God. Thank You.

"Is everything okay?"

Paul shook his head. "It's not—we probably shouldn't talk about it here."

"What happened?"

"The roads were awful. I made it just a few miles and couldn't go any farther. We need to wait it out."

"The Pattersons—" she started.

"Jim told me."

She could feel Zachary next to her. Ashley asked where Daddy was.

"You okay, Zach?" Paul asked.

"Uh-huh."

"Paul, I'm not sure if the power is going to come back on. Jim went to find—"

"I know. Jim's working on it. He wants you to come downstairs."

"Maybe we should stay up here."

"It's fine. We should go downstairs and see him."

"Mom?" Zach asked.

"What about Mr. Patterson? Did Jim find him?"

"He's with him now. Why?"

"Really? Jim was looking for him when the power went off. He was afraid. And then someone was banging on my door. Someone wanted to—"

"That must have been Bob. Evelyn's disappearance has really gotten to him. He's acting a little irrational."

Bob didn't do this, she thought, examining the ruined lock from the wooden door.

"Mom?" Zach asked again.

"What is it?"

"Can I go to my room?"

"We need to go downstairs."

"It's okay," Paul said, putting a warm hand on her arm. "I'll stay up here with him." His face looked calm and he nodded, reassuring her that it was the right thing to do. "We need to find some more flashlights. And batteries. Jim's looking for some downstairs. Are there any others?"

"I have one in my room," Zach offered.

"See? I have one, and Zach has another. We'll be fine."

"Are you sure?" Stephanie asked.

"Jim's in the great room. Go on down, and we'll follow in a few minutes. Don't worry, Steph. Zach's in good hands."

She stared into the shadows, then took Ashley's hand and started down the hallway. She looked back and watched the two shapes in the darkness behind her.

She looked at the smaller figure and felt afraid for him. She didn't understand why.

61

Faith

*J*im.

He felt warm, secure, comfortable.

Jim.

It was bright, and he could feel himself flying, floating, dreaming, escaping.

Jim, wake up.

He didn't want to. He wanted to leave, to be free, to go away, to be far away from this pain, this darkness, this evil life and world and the suffering and the bitterness, all of life's troubles and woes. All of it *to be gone, to be gone.*

Wake up, Jim.

It wasn't a request. It was an order.

He sucked in a gasp of air and opened his eyes. Cold air filled his mouth and throat and lungs.

Get up, Jim.

At first he couldn't make out what he saw, but then he recognized the deck. High above him, stories above him.

I'm alive, he thought. *I'm alive. I fell several stories and I'm alive. But how . . .*

He looked down at his shoulders and arms and legs covered in snow. For a moment he wasn't sure he could move, but he flailed and thrashed and the snow parted easily.

He had landed in a snowdrift. An immense snowdrift. One

that had formed alongside the house. He had fallen in exactly the right spot to cushion his blow.

Jim, find your family. Now.

He didn't know if it was his own voice or if it was the voice of God or an angel. It didn't matter. He brushed himself off and tried to stand, but he couldn't get his footing. It was snowing again, of course, and the skies above still looked dark and heavy. He climbed to one side and eventually rolled over and out of the bank.

Find your family now. Find them, protect them, go to them.

He looked up but couldn't see anybody on the deck.

Then he remembered.

Paul.

It didn't make sense. But it didn't matter. Nothing had made sense for some time.

The fall and the snowdrift. The hands on him during the fall—the light and the voices and the feeling of protection. The darkest dark and the lightest light.

He rushed up the side of the hill toward the south wing of the house. It was getting dark, but he could still make out his surroundings. It would be even darker inside.

After climbing up the snowy embankment, he looked back on the drift he had fallen onto. It looked impossible the higher up he got. How could he have survived? How could he have walked away without any injury? But those thoughts were quickly buried in the terror of what had happened, the nightmare of what existed in the lodge.

As he climbed the thick snow along the house, trying to make his way up the steep hill, Jim prayed.

I need You now more than ever, God. Now more than ever, and I feel like my sins and shortcomings have doomed me and my family. Please, God, please hear me out. Please, God, help me. Help me. I cry out to You to help me.

His hands shook. His body shook. His eyes burned, and his

heart and soul and spirit ached. A deep ache that filled every ounce of him.

God, help me. I'm sorry for doubting You. I'm sorry for abandoning You. Please, God, spare my family. Spare them. I'll give my life for all of them. Please, God, just spare them.

The wind howled, and he waited for a word. A sign. Anything at all.

Faith was believing in something he couldn't see or feel, and he was trying. Jim was trying. But he had failed at that for so long. He didn't know what to do.

You're the only One I can turn to.

He closed his eyes and stopped to catch his breath.

Please, God, help me. Help me, please. Rescue me and my family. Please, God.

"I need You."

Help me and my family and shield us from the enemy.

"Protect them."

We're surrounded and we've allowed ourselves to be open to attack and, God, I need You. I need You more than ever. God, listen to me, hear me. I'm crying, and I'm crying out.

The wind screamed and the snow continued to fall.

Night would soon be upon them.

Jim shook.

His only hope was that God would be merciful. He had to believe his prayers had been heard. And he had to believe they would be answered.

He was frightened, but he knew he needed to be strong for Stephanie and the kids.

First, he needed to find them.

62

Uncle Paul

Something was bothering Zachary. He couldn't really say what it was, but something made him want to stay away from Uncle Paul.

His uncle sat on his bed waiting for him as Zach rummaged through his duffle bag, searching for a flashlight. Even though he had his back turned toward Uncle Paul, Zach could *feel* Uncle Paul staring at him. Suddenly his uncle spoke.

"Why do you believe the things your parents teach?"

Zach looked up. Uncle Paul was shining his flashlight in his eyes.

"I don't know. Why don't you believe?"

"What if you found out it was nothing but lies?"

Something in Uncle Paul's tone made him uneasy.

Maybe it's time to go downstairs.

"Mom and Dad would never lie to me."

"Do you know that?" Paul asked, his voice deepening. "How do you know that? Adults lie every day. It's very easy."

Zach put a hand in front of his face to protect his eyes from the beam. "My mom and dad don't lie."

"But what if everything they believe isn't true?"

Zach shook his head. "I know it's true."

"How can an eight-year-old be so sure?"

"Because I believe it. I just know it in my heart."

Uncle Paul laughed. The laugh was scary.

Something isn't right. I need to get out of here.

"You know it 'in your heart.' " Uncle Paul's voice mocked him. "What exactly do you know about your heart?"

Zach closed the bag. "Doesn't look like I have a flashlight after all." He stood up slowly and then glanced at Uncle Paul. He wasn't moving.

"How can a young boy know about things in his heart?"

"I just—I just feel them."

"You do. Just like that?"

Zachary nodded. He rubbed the side of his jeans and waited to see if Uncle Paul would move.

"There are things you don't understand about this world, Zachary. Things you're too young and naïve to see. But they exist. They're real. Not some notion of God and angels in the sky protecting you. That's not real. But some things are very, very real."

Zach shivered. He just wanted to go. "Let's go downstairs."

"Let's stay here for a while," Uncle Paul told him.

"I'd like to see my dad."

"No."

Zach froze.

Get out of here now, Zach. Now.

But he couldn't get past Paul. His uncle blocked him from the door.

"You're not going to see your father again."

Zach waited, his eyes focused on the man on the bed. Uncle Paul continued shining the flashlight into his eyes, blinding him with its powerful beam.

It's this house and this snow and all of this that's making Uncle Paul talk like that.

But something told him that was wrong, that it was something else. Something told him exactly what it was. And it told him to be very careful.

"Uncle Paul—"

"Your father had a little accident."

"What?"

"Yes. He's lying somewhere halfway down the mountain. Maybe lying right on a tree stump. He took a little fall."

"No," Zach said, shaking his head, edging toward the door.

"You're not going to leave."

"Uncle Paul—"

"Don't 'Uncle Paul' me. Your uncle is long dead."

Zach looked at Paul's face and then at the door.

I can make it. I can make it. Just run out. Something's not right with Uncle Paul. He needs help.

He thought about what Uncle Paul had said about his father. It couldn't be true. Of course not. Dad was fine.

He has to be fine.

Something inside him told him that Dad was okay. The same thing that told him Uncle Paul was not okay and that he, Zachary, was in a lot of danger.

"For some reason it's you they want," Uncle Paul said, his voice suddenly lower and deeper. "I don't understand it, but I will suffer the children, as they say. Or make them suffer."

Zach was only a few feet away now.

He needs help. He needs love. That's what will make it better.

"Uncle Paul," he said, "it's going to be okay. I know that everything will be—"

Out of nowhere a hand swung around and slapped Zach hard, so hard it blinded him for a minute, knocking him down.

"You miserable little ant," Paul continued in a voice Zach didn't recognize. "So insignificant. So weak. What is it about you that they want? What is it about you that they see? I don't get it."

Zach opened his eyes and saw the figure on the bed suddenly stand.

It's not Uncle Paul. I see him there, but it's not. It can't be. Why did he slap me?

"I was the one who called you that day," the figure told him. "The one who told you he was coming for you. You had to be all brave and holy and spiritual and not tell anybody, right? You needed to be filled with the Spirit. Let me tell you something, I'm full of the spirit too. But not every spirit is sweet and nice like yours."

Zach heard a laugh, and he was scared and shut his teary eyes and prayed a quick prayer.

God, help me. Please, God, help me. Help Mom and Dad find me and help Uncle Paul.

"Your prayers aren't going to do you any good, little boy. Not now. Your God has turned His back on you and your family. He's ignoring you, and He's not taking your calls. Got it? It's over. It's done." He swore as Zach got to his feet again.

"You're coming with me," said the man who looked like Uncle Paul.

"Where are we going?"

"To the fun side of the house."

A hand grasped his shoulder. He suddenly felt Uncle Paul's breath in his ear.

"You try to run and I will run faster and come up beside you and kill you. I swear on your God and every god out there I will, so don't even try."

Zach stood there, his body shaking, tears running down his cheeks.

Then the hand jerked him forward, toward the door.

63

In the Great Room

The echoes of the great room sounded eerie in the darkness. Snow still stuck to the windows, and whatever light might be left outside wasn't coming in. Stephanie sat on the couch brushing Ashley's dark hair with her hand and waiting. In another minute she would go back upstairs and find Paul to see what was wrong.

She shivered from the cold and pulled her sweater tighter to her.

"Where's Daddy?" Ashley asked.

"I'm not sure."

She wondered what Ashley was thinking. A five-year-old in a large house like this with a snowstorm and the power off. Ashley loved snow, that was for sure. She didn't realize how cold it was and kept asking to go outside and play.

Stephanie wondered how much life the batteries in her flashlight had. Looking around the large room that she had not spent a lot of time in, she noticed the open door to the north wing.

That's odd. Maybe Jim left it open, she thought. *Maybe he's over there now.*

She wasn't going to go anywhere. With the intercoms not working and the house so dark, she wanted to stay somewhere central.

Where are Paul and Zach?

The darkness began to make her feel claustrophobic, even in this massive room. The beam of light made her feel miniscule compared to the overwhelming dread all around her. She wanted to call out for Paul and Zach, but felt like she couldn't. Someone else might hear her. Someone who shouldn't hear.

Why isn't Jim down here like Paul said?

She wanted to get out of this house and off this mountain. Everything felt out of control. She felt like she was underwater trying to come up for air, but the surface was too high above her. As hard as she tried to swim, it didn't get any nearer.

She clutched Ashley close to her.

Please, God, help us. Help us.

She was afraid, but wasn't quite sure of what.

After another five minutes of waiting, she stood, pausing before going upstairs to find Zach and Paul. That was when she heard the pounding on the front door.

She grabbed Ashley and held her in her arms. Then she heard a muffled voice.

Calling her name.

"Stephanie!"

It was barely audible because of the thickness of the door, but she could still make it out. She knew the voice belonged to Jim.

What is he doing outside?

"Who's that?" Ashley asked.

"I think it's your father."

Stephanie walked over to the door and heard the voice again. It shouted her name.

"I'm here; hold on. I'm right here," she called, still clutching Ashley and trying to unlock the door.

"Open this up!"

"Okay, okay, hold on."

She opened the door to see Jim standing there in jeans and a shirt, with no jacket, pale and covered in snow, his eyes stretched wide and sweat on his forehead.

"Sweetie, what are you—"

"Where's Zach?" Jim said, his eyes intense, his jaw clenched.

"What?"

"Where is Zach?" he asked her again.

"He's upstairs, with Paul."

Jim looked at her with a face she recognized. She had seen that face once before, on the mission field after the exorcism.

After the failed exorcism.

It was a look of anger and intensity and confusion, but most of all it was a look of deep fear.

"You're positive?" he yelled, quickly stepping inside and shutting the door.

"About what?"

"About Zach. That he's with Paul."

"Yes. He just—he was looking for us and he said you—"

He grabbed her arms. "Stephanie, listen to me right now. I want you to take Ashley to the media room and lock the door and don't open it for anyone except me."

"What are you say—"

"Look at me."

"What?" She still held Ashley and stared him full in the face.

He looked at their daughter and then back at her, as if to say, *I can't talk about it now.* "Just do that for me, and I'll be back."

"Jim—is—should I—"

"Steph. Now. Right now. Go."

"And Zach?"

"Don't worry. I'm going to get him."

She knew better than to say anything else. The fear and concern and apprehension were all lost with the adrenaline, and she knew she needed to do what Jim said. She trusted her husband.

But what about Paul? What about my brother?

She couldn't feel her legs as they carried her through the

house, Ashley still in her arms, her mind racing, her heart hurting, her deepest fears suddenly exposed.

God, help us.

She kept praying it over and over. As if the more times she asked for God's help, the more chance He would hear them.

64

Jim

He watched Stephanie walk off with Ashley and felt a wave of relief and regret wash over him. He breathed carefully, trying to control the mounting panic. He couldn't tell Stephanie about Paul because he still didn't truly believe it and couldn't make sense of it. The only thing he wanted to do was get Zach and Steph and Ashley in a room and hold out until

until what?

the snow stopped and they got help.

Nobody's coming for you. You're stuck and this is all your fault.

He knew those were demons of doubt plaguing him, and that was okay. He could get through it. He had to think now. He wasn't sure what he was going to say or do when he found Paul. And he wasn't sure what he would do if Paul tried to hurt Zach.

He went to the fireplace and stopped there, feeling around for something. His hand touched the heavy black poker. It wasn't an ax or a knife or a gun, but it was something.

Do you really need that? Where's your faith, Jim? Where's your faith? You're armed with the Holy Spirit—isn't that what they tell you? Isn't that the big fat lie they tell in Sunday school?

Jim climbed the stairs, the poker in his hands, carefully making his way through the darkness.

It would only be darker upstairs.

God, I need some assistance.

But another voice answered. *What do you think that was back there? The fall?*

He didn't understand. He was moving on pure instinct. He needed to make sure his son was okay. He needed to get Zach back.

Why, Paul? It made no sense. No sense whatsoever. It was just Paul. Why would Stephanie's brother want to hurt anyone, especially any of them?

But Jim knew it was Paul who had shoved him off the deck. He hadn't imagined that. He knew that for a fact.

God, be with me. God, be with me.

He reached the top of the stairs. The poker was in his hand, ready to swing out if necessary.

He would do anything to get Zach back.

65

Not Alone

In the 40,000-plus square feet of the mountain lodge built by eccentric millionaire Charles Wolfcott, five hearts beat fast as they cry out to the God or gods they serve.

Stephanie sits on the couch, tears streaming down her face. She is terrified that something has happened to Zachary, that something is wrong with Paul, that Jim knows something he can't tell her. She hates being locked in this room with only two windows, the cold seeping in and clinging to her body and soul. Clutching Ashley doesn't help her feel better. Praying doesn't make her feel better. She's thirsty, but more than that, she's scared.

I've been scared so long, so long. God, I need You.

But she feels like this house. Like she's covered in a blanket of snow that's preventing her from being seen or heard.

Please, God, help us.

She prays for her husband, who is upstairs now, searching.

Jim still carries the poker and is going through room after room. He feels the broken handle to the door of their bedroom, but finds no one inside.

He moves quickly, the fear growing inside him with each step, each passing minute. The longer time goes by, the more he comes to the realization of where Paul and Zach must be.

You know it, so why even bother searching up here?

He knows they're in the north wing somewhere.

He knows what might be happening.

And he doesn't give up because he knows there still might be time, God might spare Zach's life just like He had spared his own.

Was that God or was that luck, because everything in me is wondering where God's hand is in all of this. If He was really up there, none of this would be happening.

He enters another empty room and knows where he has to go.

The north wing.

He knows Paul is there and so is Zach.

He doesn't know what he'll do when he finds them, but he won't think about that now. He goes back downstairs to the main room. Maybe there's another way to the north wing, but he only knows of one way and he will go through that door.

Inside the north wing, in the empty black room, stand the man and the boy. He tells the boy to go to the center of the room. The room is bathed in darkness, and the boy does as he is told.

The man is just a shell now of what he once was, of the human that used to be inside him. Now he is full of voices and anger and instruction. He does exactly what he is told without feeling fear or remorse. He knows this is why he is here. He can see the boy in the darkness and knows the boy can't see him. The boy is weak. He doesn't understand why they want the boy so badly, but he will obey anyway.

He studies the boy and sees the lack of fear on his face. Maybe that is why they want the boy. He is bold in his faith and fearless. He still has boyish fears just like any might, but there is something else. Something different. Something the man hates and desperately wants at the same time.

I'm not afraid, he says, but deep inside, he knows better.

But he also knows God is far from this mountain and far from this house and far from this room.

This is a special room.

It doesn't have to be anything special. The way he kills the boy. It can be done however he chooses. It just needs to be in this place, in this long-forgotten den.

So the man goes toward the boy who is in the middle of the room, the sacrifice room, and his hands stretch out, ready to grasp hold of the little neck.

He will squeeze until he feels and hears and sees the boy's last breath. Until the boy's little heart stops pumping.

The boy will die in his hands as it has been commanded.

And the boy named Zachary Miller, who is eight years old and alone in the middle of a pitch-black room, stands with his eyes closed and prays. He prays to the one God he knows is up there and who he knows is listening. Everything is in God's hands and everything is in His control and he prays in his mind knowing God hears him.

He thinks of the story of Daniel and the lions' den. It is a particular favorite of his, since he loves animals and loves the story of Daniel and his faith. He longs to have that sort of faith.

"Not a scratch was found on him, for he had trusted in his God."

And he knows that he can be like Daniel and that he can be untouched and unscratched because he trusts in God.

God, I trust You. I know You're there. Please, God. Help me. Please, God, protect me.

Zachary feels hands on his shoulders.

But he is not afraid.

He knows he is not alone.

He knows for a fact he is not alone.

66

Heartbeats

Jim walked into the large open room, the beam from his flashlight covering as much ground as possible. So far he hadn't heard or seen anything, but he knew Paul was here. He still carried the poker, ready to swing.

He hurried down one of the hallways, flinching at the faint creak of the floor with each of his steps. The darkness coated him, the faint light outside now finally gone. He felt heavy, as though forces were pushing him down.

God, please be with Zach.

That was his only prayer.

He looked inside the room with the torture tools and the white table. He scanned the room and saw the foul goat head and quickly moved on.

A noise from behind him made him stop.

He turned around and shone the light back into the cavern-ous room. The faint glow from the flashlight made everything look ominous, creepy. A figure could be standing right next to him and he might not see it. The darkness was consuming.

Jim walked back into the room and looked around again.

He heard another noise. Footsteps. And something dropping. Something heavy.

He ran past the fireplace to the other hallway, the one where the master bedroom lay.

Where Bob Patterson lies.

He stopped and pointed his light down the hallway. It looked longer than he remembered.

Pictures covered the walls.

Were those there before?

Pictures of men and women—vile, disgusting pictures posing as art.

I hate this place.

The beam of light found the doorway to the master bedroom.

Unblinking, cold, deathly eyes stared back at him.

Paul.

Jim dropped the flashlight with a gasp. He held firm to the poker and looked ahead as he picked up the light.

The face was gone.

Did I imagine it?

He ran down the hallway to the master bedroom, afraid of what he would find.

God, please. Please be with Zach.

He stood at the doorway and shone the light inside.

At the foot of the bed, Paul stood, looking at him.

Jim pointed the light first at Paul, his empty hands, his body, then at the bed.

hair brown hair his hair I see it

And he saw the form of a child stretched out on the bed.

No no no no no

He saw the hair, and he knew it was Zach.

Paul didn't appear surprised or defensive. He didn't react in any way.

Jim ran toward the man, brought the poker around, and swung it with his right hand, striking Paul at the base of the neck. His brother-in-law—the man standing there, this—this person, whoever he was—let out a sickening cough but just stood there, unmoving.

Jim struck him again, the heavy rod suddenly light in his hand, the metal striking the side of Paul's jaw. He heard the sound of bone cracking, then a deep gasp as Paul fell to his knees.

As he was about to go to the figure on the bed, his son lying stretched out, motionless and silent, Jim heard a sound that would linger with him till his dying day.

A laugh. An out-of-breath, wheezing, sick laugh.

Paul's face leered at him.

He lifted up the poker and brought it down squarely against Paul's head and his smirk and his evil and his depravity. The metal rod sunk deep into Paul's skull and stayed there. Both the man and the poker fell to the floor.

Jim went to the bed and dropped the flashlight and felt for Zach. His hands were shaking as he first felt his son's face

so cold so cold God so cold

then his forehead, then his neck. Then he picked him up and got the flashlight and stormed out of the room. His son felt so limp, so cold, so lifeless.

No no please God no not my son

He wanted to get out of this place. If he could he would run and keep running until they were far off this mountain and someplace warm and bright. Instead, he passed the large room in the north wing and ran down the hall to the great room. He locked the door to the north wing and then rushed to a couch and put his son down.

"Zach?" he called, trying to feel for a pulse, his own body shaking, his own heart racing. "Zach, can you hear me?"

Nothing.

"Zach?"

He felt along Zach's neck. By the light of the flashlight, Jim could see the marks there. Bruises.

"God, please! Please, God, hear me! God, please, please, God, help me! Oh God, help me! Help me!"

He burst into tears and his body shook and he couldn't control his quivering hands, and he wanted to close his eyes but he couldn't because he couldn't feel a thing. He couldn't feel a thing, not a thing. Not a breath, not a life, not a pulse, nothing—nothing at all.

Jim squeezed his hands together and swallowed and closed his eyes.

"God, I only ask one thing—that's all. Please, God, please let him be alive! Please, God, please hear me—God, please!"

His crying became wailing, intense and uncontrollable. He kept waiting to feel something, to hear something, to see something, to see Zach wake up and take a deep breath like they always did in the movies, but nothing was coming. Nothing at all.

Nothing.

67

Family

The father, a big man with a thick beard and a balding head, carries his son through the house without a care. He is not worried about the boogeyman coming out from behind a wall, or an intruder suddenly stopping him, or the vile disgusting figure that did this coming back to hurt him. The father brings his child to the mother who carried it for nine months, to the woman who cried during hours of labor, to the person who probably loves the child the most.

He is empty. He does not know what else to do.

He knocks on the door and tells her it's him.

And she opens the door and shines the light on him.

She is shocked and she screams and bursts into tears and grabs the son from the father, and he just stands and feels helpless.

He doesn't bother to close the door.

He wants to hold her, but he can't.

He wants to say something, but he can't.

He knows there is an anger deep and violent and raging and overflowing, and that anger is directed solely toward the one who did all of this—every bit of it.

And as his wife asks what happened over and over again and who did it and where is Paul, he says one thing.

"God."

God did this. He caused it. He allowed it. He turned His back on it. He turned His back on all of them, not just up here but starting in Dambi, where His powers were deemed insufficient.

God either doesn't exist or doesn't care.

And he can't decide which option is worse. Because the worst option he can think of is now in his wife's arms.

He goes over and holds his daughter, who is crying and scared.

He should be stronger, but he is not.

God should be stronger, but He is not.

He suddenly thinks that maybe this, all of this, every bit of it, has been nothing but proof that God is not there and never has been and all the teaching and preaching in the world has not mattered one bit. Those feelings from his childhood and those beliefs and those sensations were all medicine and placebos and mind-game shrink talk. Nothing but talk.

His wife screams, and he stands there holding his daughter, unable to talk, unable to think.

He might as well be dead too.

Zachary is dead.

Yes.

Zachary is dead.

And so is God.

And so is he.

He is a shell of a man and will always be, and they will always be trapped here in the darkness up on the mountain in this house.

He curses out loud and hopes, begs, pleads for God to hear him.

But nothing happens.

Of course it doesn't.

How could it? How could anything happen?

They are alone. All they have is themselves, and that's just not enough.

68

Flesh and Blood

Jim, tell me what happened." She had never seen her husband like this.

Zach is . . .

It was impossible. This was truly a living hell. This was hell and this was horror, and she didn't know what was happening.

Zachary's body lay in her arms, and she didn't want to let him go. As if her touch might revive him.

Prayers didn't work, but maybe this will.

"Jim, answer me."

He was on the couch in the media room, one arm around Ashley. It was cold, and the light in the room came from the flashlight propped on an end table, shining at the wall.

"Jim, answer me!"

He turned to her with swollen eyes that leaked despair.

"What happened? Who did this?"

"Paul," he said.

"What?"

"Paul. Your brother."

"What—where is he?"

"I hope he's in hell, that's where."

"Jim—"

"You want to know the truth? Bob Patterson is dead and his wife is probably somewhere in this house dead and now our son—"

"Stop yelling at me."

"It was Paul."

"But how—what—"

"I don't know. I don't get it. I don't know. He pushed me over the deck railing."

"What?"

"Yeah, and then I—I don't know. All I know is that something—he's not there. He's not right. I don't know. I don't know anything anymore. Nothing."

Ashley started crying again, and he held her tight and told her everything was okay.

But everything wasn't okay.

How can it be—Paul? . . . No, it can't. It makes no sense.

"Where is he?"

"Paul?"

"Yes."

He looked at her, then shook his head.

"I need to know."

"What?" he asked. "If he's alive?"

"Yes."

"I hope to God he's not."

"Jim."

"No. That man—how he could have—I don't know—he was standing there—I just—I had to."

"You had to what?"

"What did you expect me to do?"

"You're scaring Ashley," she said.

"Yeah, well, I'm scaring myself. Everything is scaring me. Aren't you scared?"

"Jim."

"I left Paul on the floor in the north wing, unconscious. Or more. I don't know."

"I don't understand—"

"Yeah, well, I didn't stick around long enough to ask."

She started to cry again and held Zachary in her arms.

Why, Paul? How could it be her brother? It was her brother. Not some stranger but her brother. Her own flesh and blood, just like Zach.

69

Burn

You still have work to do. Your time is not yet done. You need to get moving.

He felt the aching pain and tried to discern where he was, but could see nothing in the darkness.

The words whispered in his ears as they always did.

Go ahead go ahead Paul you have power I have given you power you can get up you still have work to do.

The pain was excruciating. His neck throbbed and his back felt like little pins were stuck in every vertebrae. But his head—

his skull, his cheek, his jaw—pulsed with agonizing hurt. He could feel and taste blood from the deep gash in his skull.

Get up it's time to work there is still work to do there are still the three of them left

But another voice in him, a part he hadn't seen or heard from in a long time

Paul yes that's right

said that he had already done what he was here for. That he had fulfilled his promise.

Doesn't matter. There are three of them left—take care of them, take care of them all.

He felt a surge of strength. He knew he should be unconscious or even dead, but this power was undeniable.

I've given you this now go get them go hunt them down and kill all of them each one of them

He thought of the kerosene canisters in the basement.

That's right if you can't kill them then you burn it you burn this house and the rest and you can burn yourself it doesn't matter it's good to feel something and you can burn it all you can burn all of this to the ground

He smiled again, and the last remnant of the man named Paul whom they had taken over years ago was dead and gone. Now it was just them, an army, and they knew what they needed to do.

He stood and felt strong and knew God wasn't here, that He wasn't anywhere, and now they had a mission to fulfill.

And if not with my hands then with the flames of hell.

70

Warmth

Everything he did was out of pure instinct, pure need. Jim started down the stairs to the basement. He needed to get the kerosene heater and bring it up to the bedroom where he had brought the family. They had switched rooms, moving to a master suite in the west wing.

The generator was not working, even though he had already checked twice. He wasn't going to try again. He needed to think of Stephanie and Ashley. He still had two people in his family alive. He still had two people to protect.

He had awakened to find Ashley shivering. He needed to get up and get the heater going and get some warmth. He wasn't afraid of Paul or anyone else coming to get him. There was fury in him unlike anything he had ever experienced before. He *wanted* someone to come out of the darkness and try to lay a hand on him. He dared them.

He dared God to let them.

Jim had found a heavy flashlight when the small one started dimming. This one was made of stainless steel, the kind that had eight large batteries in it. It shone a wide beam of light on the steps and the empty basement.

He glanced around for the dead animals. They were still there, bodies decomposing and stiff from the cold.

Just like Zachary is going to be.

He scanned the basement, the wide open area surrounded by white walls. Nothing else could be seen.

There were several kerosene heaters in one corner. He selected one and made sure it had fuel in it, then lifted the bulky contraption in both hands. He held the flashlight as well and walked quickly but carefully up the stairs.

Jim entered the great room and started toward the hallway to the west wing. Lost in silence, the light of the flashlight pointing to one side, he didn't see the figure until it burst out of the darkness and jumped him.

Something struck him in the side, and he fell, the flashlight and heater clattering to the floor. He landed on his side, dinging his elbow and his head. He protected his face, unsure where the next blow would come from.

The beam of the flashlight shone on the wall next to him. He could make out a tall, lean figure.

Paul.

The figure moved slowly toward him, something in its hand.

That blow didn't kill him? Jim thought in the second it took him to stand. *It should've killed him.*

He quickly went for the flashlight, rushing over to clutch it in his hand.

Something swung out toward him. He ducked, and it passed over his head.

Poker? Bat?

These were the thoughts running through his mind as he blindly reached out with his heavy flashlight. He swung it once, then again, then a third time.

The third time, he hit something.

Maybe a shoulder, or an arm.

There you are.

He swung again, this time higher. It reached its mark, hitting what Jim guessed was Paul's head.

The figure went down.

Jim jumped on it and began beating the attacker with his flashlight

no

and he swung, hitting him in the mouth, the face, the shoulder, the chest

stop it Jim stop it stop it you're not like him

and he thought of Zachary's face and he wanted to kill this man, to kill him, to maim and hurt him the same way he had hurt Zach, to take away something precious

Jim

and then he stopped, realizing he was crying, realizing the figure beneath him was panting and moaning.

Jim backed away, shining the flashlight in the man's face.

Paul's bloody face looked back at him. He was still alive; his eyes blinked, a smirk still on his lips. Blood gushed from cuts on his forehead and below his nose. One eye was swollen shut. His lip bled. And there was a deep red gash on his neck. He coughed up blood even as his lips formed a sick smile.

He should be dead. I know he should be dead.

"You can't hurt me." The words were garbled.

Jim didn't want to just stay there, waiting. He knew what he needed to do.

This time he's not going to get away. This time he's going to stay put. The tape in the kitchen. The electrical tape. Use that.

"You can't stop me," the man said with a laugh.

Jim grabbed Paul's hair and jerked him toward the kitchen and didn't listen to a thing he had to say.

71

Upstairs

Flicks of snow and ice tapped the window. Stephanie couldn't help shivering under the comforter as she cuddled Ashley. She wasn't sure if it was the cold or the fact that Jim wasn't back from getting the heater. Or the reality that her son—her dead son—was in the bathroom.

Should he be there or should he be here under the covers with us?

So many thoughts ran through her mind, they threatened to strangle her. She didn't want to leave Ashley and didn't want to leave Zachary and couldn't get over the fact that he was gone—really gone, really truly gone. It was just a body, but it was *his* body and she didn't want anything to be done with it.

God, where is Jim? Where is he?

A horrible thought kept coming back to her.

Paul.

Her brother had done this. Her own brother. How could he have hurt Zachary? Why would he want to? Why would he do such a thing?

It's this house. This wretched house that I came to once. That we came to.

She could remember now for some reason. She could remember being in this house, tucked under blankets, listening to the storm outside, the endless pitter-patter of rain. She tried to drown out the rest of the noise from her memories—the cries and the laughter and the voices and the whispers. They all came to her in the darkness, in the silence. She heard them whispering, paralyzing her, pinning her down.

You belong to us you belong to all of us let us come in let us join you don't be afraid

Stephanie wondered where that memory came from. She knew it was real. She knew it was real and that she had been in this house. Her parents had brought her here—both of them—for some reason. She didn't know why.

Is that what's wrong with Paul?

She needed to find Jim. She had to find him. She couldn't stand waiting, wondering.

I can't leave Ashley.

But she was afraid. She felt alone and afraid, and she needed to find out. She needed to be sure something else hadn't happened.

I can just peek. I can just run down a few steps to see if I hear anything.

She remembered being young and stepping out of her room to go down the hall. She remembered hearing strange noises from the bedroom her parents stayed in. But she had found others in that room, others doing strange things

stop it don't go there don't think back

and she knew she needed to stop these thoughts, to get up and find Jim.

"Ashley?"

Her daughter was asleep, worn out from crying and confusion.

"Ashley, I'm going to leave the room for just a minute. Just to see if Daddy is on his way." Ashley didn't respond. She lay motionless except for the rhythmic rise and fall of her chest as she slept.

Stephanie didn't bother trying to find a flashlight. She didn't want to be seen or heard. She unlocked the door and stepped out into the black hallway. She closed the door and stayed there for a minute, listening. She thought she could hear sounds coming from the bedroom she had just left. Strange sounds. Adult sounds.

I'm hearing things.

She opened the door and made sure Ashley was okay. Her little angel still slept in a strange, peaceful sleep. The irony was almost unbearable.

She shivered and walked toward the stairs. Ashley was fine. She would simply go a little farther to see if she heard anything. That's it. She wouldn't be gone for even five minutes. She had to make sure Jim was coming back.

She needed to know for sure.

72

The Truth

You don't frighten me."

Jim was using tape to tie Paul's hands to the wooden post in the center of the great room. His flashlight was propped on the couch, lighting them like actors on a stage. Jim yanked Paul's hands behind him.

"You're alone, and you and your family will end up just like your boy."

"Shut up."

Paul cursed at him and cursed at God.

"I said shut up," Jim told him.

"You're so afraid."

Jim rolled the ream of electrical tape around Paul's hands, using his teeth to cut it.

"I feel your fear," Paul said.

"Tell me your name."

"You tell me yours."

"Tell me."

Paul just looked at him.

I want to know the name of the demon who did this to my child. I want to know his name.

"This is dangerous territory for you," Paul said. "*Especially* for a man like you."

"What is your name?"

"You know my name, and you feel it right now."

"Tell me."

"No."

Jim felt a fury and knew he should just leave. He worked on Paul's feet next. Paul wasn't going to go anywhere. If he did, Jim would be there to stop him. He knew that. He also knew he had no business talking to the demon, that far stronger men and women had fallen short in attempts at exorcism.

I'm not trying to exorcise. I'm just trying to know who he is.

"Your God has abandoned you," Paul said.

"Shut up."

"You know it's true. He abandoned you in Dambi, and He's done the same on this mountain."

"Shut up."

Paul laughed at him and cursed again.

Jim didn't know what to say. He couldn't refute the man's words because he wondered if they were true.

God, where are You? How can I tell him he's a liar when I half believe the words he's saying?

"Your son died because God is dead and because the only power is the power you know to be true. Your own power."

Jim cut the tape around Paul's legs. He thought of using some of the tape on Paul's mouth.

"That wife of yours knows the truth. Ask her about this house."

"What?"

"Ask her. She knows. She's been here before. She and her brother have been here before."

"And who are you?"

"I am many."

"Who are you?"

There was silence. Jim asked again.

"Who are you?"

"I am hate and I am power and I am jealousy and I am lust."

"Those are your names?"

Paul stared, then spit at him.

"I am control."

The voice sounded deeper, almost like a different person. Jim had seen such things before. He knew of Satan's power to invade and terrorize people.

Remember how that turned out? You remember, right? You remember how that one time didn't turn out so well? How that affected everybody including you, right?

He reached for the flashlight. He wasn't here to save Paul. He just wanted to save his family. His remaining family.

"You can't stop me," Paul said.

"I will kill you if you even try to touch me," Jim told him.

A high-pitched scream rose out of the darkness, then a voice yelling his name.

"Jim!"

He swung the light toward the stairs and saw Stephanie.

"Get out of here, Steph."

But he could hear her footsteps touching the wooden floor and rushing toward them.

"Jim, what did you do?"

"Steph, no—"

He reached toward her as she rushed toward Paul. "Steph, stay away from him."

"The loving sister returns," Paul said.

"He's not himself."

"What are you doing? Jim, he's hurt. He's bleeding."

"And *he* did this to me, the sadistic pig," Paul said.

"He's possessed, Steph. He's possessed, and we need to get out of here."

"Paul!"

Jim held his wife back. The flashlight beam was aimed at the floor, sparing them the sight of Paul's face.

"Have you talked to Mom and Dad?" the voice in the darkness asked.

"Steph, come with me!"

"Have you, sister, dear sweet sister?"

"Jim, let me go!"

"Do you want to know what their last words were?"

"Jim—"

He held her in both of his arms and pulled her away from Paul. It was madness, pure madness, and Jim could feel the hate, the evil coming from the man. It wasn't Paul and hadn't been Paul for a long time.

"They said to kill them, to kill them both. They welcomed it with open arms. Can you believe it?"

"Stephanie, don't listen," Jim said, trying to get her to move. "Steph, please."

"What did you do to them?"

"Are we caring for them now, after leaving them at such a young age?"

"Shut your mouth," Jim said.

"Tell me something."

Jim held her and aimed the flashlight at Paul's face. The blood was wet and sticky as he leered at them.

"Did you know I tasted my first blood the summer we went camping with Mom and Dad? Remember that, sister? *Sister?* Remember? The man they found dead in the woods by the lake? The same lake we went swimming in? Remember the talk of the town?"

"Steph, please, let's go. Let's go back to Ashley."

"That was me," Paul said, laughing, cursing. "That was me. And I'm going to do it again, and again, and again."

Stephanie burst into tears and started running back up the steps. Jim followed her, leaving the laughing figure tied to the wooden post downstairs.

It was nearly ten o'clock, and the snow was still falling and the temperature still dropping. Jim and Stephanie got to the bedroom and unlocked the door and found Ashley still sleeping.

Jim looked at his wife and couldn't say anything as she sobbed. She needed him by her side, but he couldn't offer anything. He was as afraid and shocked and horrified as she was, and he couldn't feign love or empathy because he was depleted. He had nothing left to give.

73

Questions

The bedroom door was locked. Jim had gone back and gotten the kerosene heater, which now warmed the room enough to sleep without the comforter. He had gone into the adjoining bathroom and shut the door.

Stephanie lay with Ashley on the bed, looking at the wall and the ceiling, the faint light from the heater providing an eerie glow. She couldn't sleep and felt the pounding of fear and anger against her chest.

She prayed.

I know You're there, and I know You can hear me. So why won't You help me? Why, God? Why won't You help us? Why won't You show

Your power and might? Why won't You do something so easy, so simple, to just help us? God, why? Why did Zachary have to die, and why did Paul have to be—

Her prayers stopped as she started crying again. She knew there would be more tears and more sobbing and more pleading and wrestling.

It was not right. This was not right.

I should've known not to come here. I was being warned, but I didn't know, didn't understand. This is my fault.

How long had it been since she had felt peace? It had been long, so long. And everything that happened on the field

we opened ourselves up left our defenses down

and everything that ended up happening here was a result of a lack of faith.

That's nothing but Christian double-talk. It's not your fault. You can have a lack of faith. Missionaries can fail and have crises of faith just like everybody else.

And she knew Satan wanted exactly that. He wanted everything to happen just like this.

So why, God? Why would You allow this to happen? Why couldn't You have stopped this? Why couldn't You have been there before Zachary was killed?

She waited for word—any word—but none came.

It had been like this for a long time. Praying with no answers. Waiting. Wondering what God was doing and waiting to hear from Him.

Perhaps it was her own lack of faith.

But there was no reason for this. None.

I have always believed God, have always obeyed, have always tried to do what was right. And all I've asked is that He protect my children and my family.

"God, tell me why. Please, God, tell me why," she spoke out loud, amidst tears, amidst a broken heart, amidst pain she couldn't endure.

She would not be able to get out of this bed and walk tomorrow. She was done.

74

Anger

He stared at his hand, the fingers so familiar. He could see it even in the muted darkness of the bathroom.

He waited, the light of the clear night coming in.

I'm waiting on You, and I don't hear a thing, he thought. *I don't hear a thing or feel a thing. What is it going to take to get You to listen to me, God?*

He clenched his fist together, wishing he could strike out.

God, You know this. You see this. You did this. Why?

The pain in his hand felt good.

God, You did this. You do it all. I trusted You in my youth. I trusted You with my family. I trusted You in Dambi. But not here, not now, not like this, God.

Jim let out a sigh as hot tears streamed down his face. God could see that he was weak, that he was simple, that he was ordinary.

He touched Zachary's cold hand. His own body seized up, and he felt very afraid.

I would have given my own life, my own blood. A child should not die that way. God, tell me why.

A long sigh left his lips, and he tasted his tears. He once again touched Zachary's arm, then his hand. He wrapped his own hands around Zach's.

"I'm sorry, son. I'm so sorry. I'm sorry there wasn't more I could have done."

Jim didn't expect a miracle because miracles didn't happen in this life. You could read about them in the Bible and tell them to others and preach about them and translate them, but they didn't happen, didn't *really* happen because, of course, God would have to be up there present and watching in order for that to work. Maybe God was too tired of being overlooked or was simply too busy or just didn't care anymore.

God, I try. I want to know. I want to hear, but I don't hear or know or see You anymore.

"You can't help me," he said out loud.

Just in case God needed him to speak in order to hear him.

He stood up and left his son in the darkness of the room.

There was nothing more he could do.

75

Shudder

Something pushed him.

He could hear a rustling, a trembling, a deep resonating sound.

THERE IS GOOD WORK FOR YOU TO DO.

He could hear the voice in his ear, whispering, all around him, nudging him.

IT IS NOT TIME YET. NOT QUITE TIME YET.

But he didn't want to go back. He could feel them all and see them in his mind, but he didn't want to go back.

IT IS OKAY. YOU WILL BE CARED FOR AND WATCHED OVER, BELOVED.

The voice sounded like his mother and father and sister

all combined, soothing and hopeful. It sounded powerful and
peaceful at the same time. He felt like he was wading through
shallow water, drifting, so secure, so relaxed.

He felt free and loved.

I LOVE YOU.

He didn't want to go. He wanted to stay. He wanted to be
here forever.

*YOU WILL BLESS AND BE BLESSED AND LIVE A LONG LIFE, AND
IT IS TIME TO ARISE, ZACHARY. TIME TO BREATHE AGAIN.*

He breathed in a gulp of air, and it felt strangely confining
and almost suffocating. He didn't want to leave this place or this
feeling.

THEY NEED YOU.

But he didn't want to be needed.

GO AND BE USED IN A MIGHTY WAY.

He breathed in again. And again. His body shuddered. His
small, limiting, confining body.

FOR MY GLORY.

And he shuddered in fear, but also trembled with joy.

He breathed again, the breath of life, the breath of hope.

And he knew his place in the world. It was a limiting world
with a limiting body and his time was short, but he had been
given a little more. He vowed he would use that time for God's
glory.

Zachary sat up and opened his eyes. He found himself lying
in the bathtub, a blanket over his body and a pillow under his
head.

Even in his death, they had tried to make him comfortable.

He looked through the window and saw the cool blue glow
of the full moon. The door to the bathroom was half open. He
stood up and went toward the door.

76

Mother and Son

The bed didn't comfort her, nor did the small form of her daughter. She didn't know where Jim was, and she longed to feel his body against her own. To feel warmth and security and to know that she could suffer together with him. That she could grieve alongside him.

All she could do was clutch Ashley like a toy.

Her mind drifted in and out of some distant place. Memories fell all around her, and all she could see was her son's smile.

It was unbearable.

Her body shook.

Where is Jim?

She felt cold under the covers.

Stephanie wondered how long this cold, empty feeling would consume her. She thought of her parents, her brother, her son, her own childhood. Wave after wave of sadness hit her.

She clutched Ashley tighter, not caring if tears still leaked out of her eyes.

The bed squeaked and for a second she thought it was Jim. But the movement was too delicate. A small arm wrapped itself around her arm.

"I'm okay, Mom."

The tears fell, and she couldn't move.

It cannot be another dream. God wouldn't be so cruel.

She didn't want to imagine this. Zachary's voice sounded so real. But so many things in her life had seemed real and felt real until she no longer knew what the word *real* meant.

God, please.

"I'm right here, Mom," Zachary said.

She continued to cry as she turned around.

"Mom?"

She didn't know what to say or do. She was so scared she would reach out and he would be gone.

"It's okay, Mom."

And then she touched him, his hair—that sweet, thick hair and those cheekbones and the small chin and shoulders that were already getting so broad.

He's there he's there my son my son you're there

She reached out to hold him, and he was still there. As she wept into his neck, he was still there. And when the light came on behind the chair in the corner of the room, as it shone on her son in her arms, he was still there.

Zachary was there.

That was all she needed to know.

77

Father and Son

His hand shook.

It couldn't be. What he was seeing—it was the house, it was the nightmare, another image that wasn't real, another demon trying to terrorize his soul.

Zachary.

He saw his wife embracing their son and heard her sobs of joy. This was real. It was happening. But how?

He had just left Zach's side a little while ago. Had he slept? Jim wasn't sure. All he knew was that he had felt his son's cold hand and empty pulse and had known that God had let him die.

Such little faith.

He stood up and started to walk toward the bed. He prayed he wasn't imagining this.

He got to the edge of the bed and looked at Zachary as he spoke to his mother.

Do not doubt Me. Do not doubt My love.

Jim looked down at the miracle and couldn't believe his eyes or his ears.

"Zach?" he said.

And even as his son called him Dad, he still didn't believe.

It cannot happen this cannot be it cannot be.

He wanted to touch his son but couldn't. He trembled and was afraid—afraid of the hatred and anger in his heart toward the One and only One who could do something like this.

Put your finger here, a voice told him.

So he put his fingers on Zach's face, then touched his hand, the same cold hand he had clutched moments earlier.

Don't be faithless any longer.

I'm sorry, God. I'm so sorry. I'm sorry for my hatred and my doubt.

Believe.

He knelt down and embraced his son and wept tears of joy and knew God had done the miracle he had been asking for. He didn't understand God's timing and didn't understand why and felt ashamed at his thoughts. God could grant miracles or God could withhold them. He didn't know when or why, but he wasn't sure that mattered anymore. He knew God was good. That was what mattered.

Forgive me, God. Please forgive me.

He wept gently against the soft skin of his son's cheek.

78

Last Stand

The pounding started after midnight.

Jim jerked up from the bed where he lay next to Zachary.
He was exhausted, both physically and emotionally. But not enough
to keep from jumping to his feet when the heavy thud sounded
again. The door shook, and the floor around him moved.

He's at the door.

They had deliberately changed rooms for this very reason, in
case someone came up to try to get them.

In case he came back.

But Jim second-guessed himself now as the door rattled and
the frame shook.

It's not going to hold.

Jim didn't understand how Paul could be at the door doing
anything. He had tied the man up. He'd left the man downstairs,
in the dark, electrical tape around his hands and feet, blood still
draining from several wounds.

Maybe there's someone else in the house.

But Jim knew it was Paul.

And maybe—

No, he thought. *No more doubts. No more fear. No more questions.*

He knew God was with them and had listened to them. And
regardless of what happened now, Jim knew his family would
be protected.

My lack of faith didn't kill Zach. And I know the truth now. I know who brought Zach back, who controls all of this.

Jim stood there, the glow of the heater still going, the door shuddering with each thud.

Whoever was out there was pounding it with something heavy. The door vibrated and cracked.

"Jim?"

"It's okay," he told his wife. "Take the kids and get in the closet."

"Is it Paul?"

"Yes."

Stephanie gathered up the children and did as he said.

Don't be foolish. Don't be naïve. Be careful, Jim. Be very careful.

He had failed God too long and allowed this to happen. His lack of faith had made his family susceptible to attacks from the dark one. But God shone mightily tonight. Not because of anything Jim had done, but *despite* the things he had done.

Now Jim would stand up to whoever was behind the door.

God was watching and would take care of him.

The lock and frame finally gave way, and the door swung open.

79

Spirit

He had chewed through the tape without a problem. Even though he had tasted blood it was okay. He knew he was losing blood quickly, and he needed to take action before it was too late. Something unseen propelled him forward.

He had found a large block of wood and brought it upstairs to slam against the locked door. He would use the wood against the door first, then against the faces and heads of those inside. He would make them pay for taunting him, for tying him up, for testing him this way.

He would hurt them and laugh at their pain.

The door complied with his wishes more quickly than he expected.

When he walked into the room, he saw the man standing there, prepared to fight. The stupid man and his stupid faith and his stupid confidence.

The man called him Paul, but he no longer answered to that name. He was desire and want and need, and he needed and wanted and desired to kill the stupid man in front of him. He wanted to take the block of wood and jam it against the man's head.

"You have no power here," the man told him.

But he did. He could feel his power. It was overflowing. There was no stopping it.

"In the name of Jesus Christ the Son of God, you have no power here," the bearded fool in front of him said.

He cursed at the man and laughed. He started to walk toward him.

"The blood of Christ is washed over me and my family, and the blood of Christ saves me."

He backed up and watched for a minute. He felt something he didn't like. Something small.

But he felt the man's faith waning. With each step, he felt the man's doubts and fears.

He continued forward.

∿

JIM STOOD THERE, HIS family behind him in the closed closet.

He saw the bloody figure of Paul, the crimson stains streaming down his forehead and his lips and his neck. He also saw the block of wood in Paul's hands.

And Paul mocked and cursed him.

"Jesus Christ, the Son of God who died and rose again, saved me and will save me." Jim didn't know what else to say. "Jesus Christ is my God and Savior, and He will protect me."

But the figure continued to walk toward him. And with each step, Jim grew more afraid.

God, please! God, please help me! Protect me!

He stood his ground. "You have no power here," Jim said.

The figure laughed and cursed at him.

"Leave this house."

"You dare try to make me leave?"

"The blood of Christ covers me and my sins and my family's sins."

"Your family?" The figure laughed. It hurt Jim to listen to it. The face was twisted and grotesque as it mocked him.

"You have no family left. No God left. No faith left."

"You're wrong," Jim said.

"I feel your doubt, your fears."

"I'm not afraid. Not anymore."

"I know you're afraid. You can't hide it. Your God is dead. As you will be."

"He is not dead," Jim said.

The figure cursed and stayed where he was.

"God is real and alive, and He is protecting my family."

"And where was He when I took the last breath of your son's life?"

"My son is alive."

Again, a foul curse sounded through the room.

"He's alive and well. And the blood of Christ covers him."

⌒

Suddenly the door behind Jim opened. He heard his wife's voice calling out for Zachary, but it was too late. His son stood at the base of the bed, near Jim.

"Zach, no. Go back in," Jim said, keeping his eyes on Paul.

Something amazing was happening. Paul's face held a look of astonishment and fear and horror.

"No."

"God is alive, and He loves and protects us," Jim said.

"No."

Jim tried to think of a Bible verse, any Bible verse. But his mind went blank.

The figure just stood, looking at Zachary, waiting.

Jim couldn't think of anything to say.

A voice came from his side, from the boy at his side.

"And we know that God causes everything to work together for the good of those who love God and are called according to his purpose for them," Zach said, recalling a section of Romans that Jim and Zach had memorized months ago.

He still remembers. The Word has stuck with him. He remembers.

The figure barked out a curse but didn't move.

For a moment Zach looked like he was trying to remember the rest.

Zach paused.

Jim knew the words. "What shall we say about such wonderful things as these? If God is for us, who can ever be against us? Since he did not spare even his own Son but gave him up for us all, won't he also give us everything else?"

Never before had reciting Scripture given him so much peace and security. Never before had the words meant so much to him. The figure he spoke them to laughed and scoffed. But he didn't refute the words.

Jim didn't look at Zach. He knew Zach was protected. He knew they were all protected. He continued. "Can anything ever separate us from Christ's love?" he asked, he demanded, he shouted to the demon. "Does it mean he no longer loves us if we have trouble or calamity, or are persecuted, or hungry, or destitute, or in danger, or threatened with death? As the Scriptures say,

'For your sake we are killed every day; we are being slaughtered like sheep.' No."

He stopped. The man who once was Paul, the demon that he was now, stood frozen, unable to say anything, unable to do anything.

"No," Jim said again.

The demon flinched.

"No, despite all these things, overwhelming victory is ours through Christ, who loved us."

The words stunned the demon, hurt him, angered him, burned him, scolded him, wounded him.

He looked at Zach with confusion, fright, disbelief.

"It cannot be," the demon said. "I killed him with my own hands. How?"

Jim continued, his voice now roaring the words so the whole house could hear them. "And I am convinced that nothing can ever separate us from God's love. Neither death nor life, neither angels nor demons, neither our fears for today nor our worries about to-morrow—not even the powers of hell can separate us from God's love. No power in the sky above or in the earth below—indeed, nothing in all creation will ever be able to separate us from the love of God that is revealed in Christ Jesus our Lord."

The words gave him new life and new hope. They were real, they were true, they were life.

"Let Paul go," Jim said. "Let him go in the name of the Father and the Son and the Holy Ghost. Let him be. Leave the man alone."

The figure tore out his hair and screamed, a violent, vicious scream, and Jim took Zachary in his arms to protect him.

The man fell to the ground, his body crumbling to the car-peted floor beneath him.

"Zach, go to the closet," Jim told his son.

"Dad?"

"It's okay. Please, Zach, do as I ask."

"Okay."

Jim heard the door of the closet open and shut, and he went to Paul. He stood there for a moment and prayed.

Heavenly Father, please protect me and my family as You have already done. Please protect me. Cover me with Your Spirit. Please, God.

He felt Paul's face. Then he held a finger to his neck to check for a pulse.

Just like that, the spirit

or spirits

inside of Paul had left him. And with the only energy and life that had been sustaining him now gone, Paul lay there as still as a corpse.

There was nothing Jim could do. He stood over Paul for a long time, waiting and watching.

And praying.

And then he took the body of the dead man into his arms and carried him downstairs.

This time, the body he carried would stay there.

And he would go back upstairs and lock the door and pray that morning would come soon—and with it, help.

God was listening.

And morning and help would come.

80

Dreams

Sometime during the night or early morning, the snow stopped and the clouds opened up and a heaven full of stars could be seen from the mountain below. When the sun rose, the flakes glittered like a fairy tale, a snapshot from a Christmas Day album or a New Year's dream.

In her dream, she is sandwiched by her daughter and her son. Her husband sits in a chair next to the bed, watching them, unable to sleep, unable to close his eyes out of fear that he might lose them. She sleeps soundly and peacefully, knowing they are all together. The kerosene heater has gone out and hasn't been refilled, but warm sunlight creeps into the room.

In this dream, she can hear the sound of engines. Of snow-mobiles. Of knocking on the door. Of the main door being broken down with an ax. And of policemen rushing inside to find them.

In her dream she sees Ashley, so beautiful and so peaceful and young enough not to be scarred by their living nightmare. She sees her loving daughter and knows she wants her to be the woman she longs to be herself, without the wreckage of a family that doesn't know the Lord. Ashley will be protected and while she won't be perfect, she will be loved. And loved well.

In this dream she sees Zachary, who is going to be a great

man for the Lord. She knows he has the faith to move mountains—even to move the very mountain they're on right now. He might not understand what happened on this night, and maybe none of them ever will. But he will carry the mark of a man forever changed by God's love and grace. And he will carry the love of parents who almost lost him. Who *did* lose him, but received him back again.

In this dream her husband comes alongside her and whispers for her to wake up. He whispers in her ear that she's not dreaming, that she's okay, that they're okay, that someone is here for them.

She opens her eyes and sees him looking down at her, full of life and joy and something else.

"Someone's here?" she asks.

Because she doesn't want to be dreaming. She wants to know all of this is real.

"Yes, somebody's here," Jim tells her, kissing her on the forehead. "God saved us. He brought us through the night."

He looks tired, but he also looks—different. Tired and worn down but also—

Can that be peace?

She looks up and knows she's not dreaming. Her dreams have left her. They have left her the reality surrounding her—the family she loves, the only family she has ever loved.

She has been protected.

She has been rescued.

And more than that, more than anything else, she has been—and is—loved.

Six months later

It is evening and he sits by a fire. Beads of sweat dot the man's forehead, but he doesn't wipe them away. He enjoys the sensation.

He watches the boy walk toward him and notices he's grown several inches in these last few months. He longs to take the years, all nine years, and relive them.

His son greets him, and he is thankful to God for his son's ninth birthday.

For a moment, they both stare at the fire and listen to the crackling wood. The night is humid, with no breeze. North Carolina with its snow and ice and cold seems like a lifetime away.

And yet it all could have happened yesterday.

"Dad?"

"What is it?" Jim asks.

"I've been wanting to tell you about something."

"Okay." Jim waits, giving his son time.

"There was something that happened in North Carolina—at the house—something I never told Mom and you."

Jim nods and watches Zach, who stares into the fire and acts as though he's searching for the right words to say.

"Remember when Uncle Paul—when that man—had me? When he had me in that room—"

The wave of sadness and hurt crashes over him, the bitterness of those memories burning his still raw and open wounds. Jim knows they will take a long time to heal.

He fights back tears as he listens to Zach.

"When I was in that room, I remember praying. And something happened. And I haven't been able—I haven't known—I'm not sure how to say it—"

"Just tell me," Jim says.

"Remember the Bible story about Shadrach, Meshach, and Abednego in the blazing furnace? How they were put in the fire, and there was a fourth man in there who was an angel protecting them?"

Jim nods, watching Zach, waiting to hear.

"When I was in that black room, with my eyes closed, I remember someone touching me. At first I thought it was Uncle Paul—that man—but then the touch was warm, and it didn't hurt me. I opened my eyes and couldn't really see anything but the outline of someone. It was like the light shone on the outside of this person—making him glow or something. And he took me in his arms, and I felt okay. I remember I felt warm and safe, and I knew I didn't have to worry. I never felt anything after that."

For a moment, Jim tries to understand the meaning behind this. He knows now that anything is possible, and he believes his son. He just wants to understand exactly what happened.

"So you never felt—when Uncle Paul hurt you—you never—"

Zachary shakes his head and looks at him. "No. I never felt any pain. I knew things were going to be okay. I was told that everything was going to be okay."

Jim feels the tears falling down his cheek, and he doesn't mind them or try to hide them. He thinks of the Pattersons, Bob and Evelyn, who didn't deserve to die, whose deaths Jim still doesn't understand.

I want to tell Zach there was a reason for the Pattersons to die, but I can't. All I know is that God saved us.

He smiles at his son, then nods and tries to find the right words.

He has more faith than I do. And it's not just the faith of a child. It's deeper, more profound.

He wipes the tears off his face and looks into the fire and feels helpless before God. Nothing in this world was ever in Jim's control, not the fire nor plans for today or tomorrow. Not his life or his son's life.

He feels Zach's hand clutching his own.

"And everything was okay, Dad. Everything was okay."

Jim feels a downpour of regret wash over him, knowing he doubted God and dared God and spit in the face of God and yet God still loved him.

I'm sorry, God, for failing You, for losing my faith in You, for turning my back on You.

Jim puts his arm around his son and gives him a hug. His eyes well with tears.

"Zach," he says, pulling away and looking at his son. "I want you to know something. I want you to know how much I love you and how proud I am of you. And how . . ."

He tries to compose himself.

God, I love this boy. God, do I love him. And to let him go, to give him up, to let him die . . .

He doesn't understand how a father can watch his son die and not give up every ounce of hope he has.

He doesn't understand God and never will.

But I don't have to.

"Dad?"

"I'm okay," he says, laughing through his tears. "I want you to know I'm overwhelmed by what a gift from God you and Ashley are. And I want you never to change, Zach. Don't ever change. Don't ever lose that faith you have deep inside your heart. Okay? Because—"

He takes in Zach's dark inquisitive eyes and his boyish, caring face.

He knows his son will one day be used mightily for God.

He already has been.

"Because what?" Zach asks.

"Because—because just like you found out in that room in that awful house—you're not alone. We're not alone. We'll never be alone."

"I know, Dad."

He hugs his son and knows he will remember this moment and these words for the rest of his life. A simple peace fills him, peace that has been absent for many years. He thanks God for that peace, and for his son, and for His Son.

The long winter is over.

Acknowledgments

I'd like to thank the following people for helping make this book happen:

Andy McGuire, for saying yes. Steve Lyon, for saying no. And Anne Goldsmith Horch, for unbelievably saying yes. What an amazing journey it's been with this story.

Sharon—I know you won't read this story because it's too scary for you, but thank you for continuing to endure living life with a novelist. Thankfully we're not locked up in a mountain lodge in the middle of winter.

Mom and Dad—I hope you know you helped inspire this story. I know what it's like to live on top of a mountain in North Carolina. And I'm glad for it.

Claudia Cross, for helping find a home for this baby.

L. B. Norton, for your valued edits (during round one).

Barry Smith, for your valued partnership.

And finally, a big thanks to an author who has influenced my writing more than any other—Stephen King. During those months of living on top of that mountain and discovering I was a writer, I read a lot of your stories. Thanks for sleepless nights and for helping inspire my love of writing.

About the Author

*T*ravis Thrasher is the author of nine previous novels. In third grade, while attending school in Munich, Germany, Travis decided he wanted to be a writer. He wrote his first novel in ninth grade when he lived in the Smoky Mountains of western North Carolina. He currently lives with his wife and daughter in a suburb of Chicago.

When his first novel, *The Promise Remains,* was released in 2000, *Publishers Weekly* called it "one of the nicest surprises in CBA fiction." Never one to repeat the same old formula, Travis has written novels in several genres including suspense, adventure, and drama. He strives not to be put into an artistic box, both with his faith and with his stories.

Having worked in the publishing field for over thirteen years, Travis is a fulltime writer and speaker. For more information about Travis, visit www.travisthrasher.com.

A Conversation with Travis Thrasher

Q: What prompted you to write *Isolation*?

A: Some ideas grow slowly and don't come to fruition until many years pass. Some ideas, like the story for *Isolation*, come quickly. I can remember the exact moment when the idea came upon me.

My wife and I were part of a very special small group for about ten years with four other couples. One of these couples was a missionary family. One winter while they were on furlough, we visited them while they were staying at a large home that often housed missionary families. They had been on the mission field for a couple of years, and they spoke about some of the spiritual warfare they had gone through. As they gave us a tour of this unique house (with several staircases and multiple levels), I remember the idea hitting me. I even said it out loud to my friends: "Here's an idea for you—a family like yourself under spiritual attack in a large and spooky house."

That was where the initial idea was born.

The setting is in North Carolina, where I lived from fifth to tenth grades. My family lived high on a mountaintop, and there were many times during those years when I felt isolated. Don't get me wrong—I adore the Smoky Mountains. They're romantic and picturesque and inspiring. But on wintry nights, they can also feel very remote, at least where we lived close to the border of Tennessee, way up in the hills.

This story idea along with my love of scary novels and movies prompted me to write the book.

Q: *Isolation* is quite a departure from your first novel set in North Carolina, *The Promise Remains*. Why the change in genres?

A: My wife keeps asking me when I'm going to write another love story. It's not that I don't want to—it's just that I have so many other stories I'm longing to tell. Some authors find a certain type of story and they stick with it, book after book, year after year. Readers sometimes like this, as do authors, but I don't. I don't want to keep telling the same story. I want to explore different characters, different themes, and different moods. If you read my first couple of novels and then read *Isolation,* you might wonder if they were written by the same person. But my stories are all character-driven, with main characters who are flawed and searching. At the core, I want to write about real people who are searching, who are failing, and who are stuck in some drama (supernatural, suspenseful, romantic) which forces them to change.

Q: What was the writing process like for *Isolation?*

A: One word: grim. I knew early on that I was going to kill off one of the family members. I dreaded writing that scene the way one might dread having to clean up a dead animal stuck in a crawl space. The worst part about that was that when I finally worked my way up to the climactic moments, the family snowbound and under attack, I was writing in the warm glow of springtime. *Ah, yes, look outside and see the blooming leaves and the playing children.* Meanwhile I was stuck having to kill a poor, helpless child. It doesn't put you in the best mood. I have to say this was the hardest book to write for many reasons. But I'm pleased with the result.

Q: Who are some of your influences in writing?

A: I mention my biggest writing influence in my acknowledgements: Stephen King. He influenced not only this book but my writing career in general. Even back when I was unpublished, I believed that one day I would have a shelf full of my own books out there. Not because I'm so talented. I just believed this could happen. Look at Stephen King, who has always been writing and *has* to write. Some of his books aren't the best, but some of them are classics. He's written so many novels, and he's done so because he wanted to—not for another paycheck or out of going through the motions. I can relate to him because he has so many stories he wants to tell.

Q: How do you share your worldview in your book, and what are your thoughts on Christian fiction?

A: I tell people this—I don't consider myself a "Christian novelist" but rather a novelist who happens to be a Christian. So of course I write from a Christian worldview, but I don't view myself as writing Christian fiction, which is a genre unto itself. My goal as a writer is to tell these stories in the best way I can. I want everybody to read them and be entertained. *Isolation* is all about God and Satan—the forces of good and evil battling each other. And while this is a "horror" novel, it also affirms what I firmly believe: God is in control, and He is all powerful. It's a scary journey for the characters to finally see this.

Q: What are your thoughts on spiritual warfare?

A: I know it's real. Talk to any missionary or research it online, and you'll find countless firsthand accounts of demonic activity. Some of my research was so graphic that I knew I could never begin to describe those stories. But one of the scariest things to me, even more than gore and violence, is the thought of being alone. When you have faith in God, that doesn't always mean you'll hear from Him or understand why He does what He does. I think it's easy for those in ministry, especially those who have seen the dark sides of spiritual warfare, to feel isolated. And that's the basic premise of the book: when you let your guard down and don't rely on God, you're prone to attack. Not just physically, but emotionally and spiritually.

Q: The adults in _Isolation_ are both having spiritual doubts, while Zachary, an eight-year-old, has more faith than both of them. Why did you choose to portray the family like this?

A: For one, I believe that when you're a child, it's easier to have a wide-eyed sort of faith. When you get older, you understand the world better. There are more temptations, more ways to falter. It's easy to become jaded, even in your spiritual walk. I wanted to show missionaries as real people, with real doubts and questions that couldn't easily be answered. I found it ironic that this eight-year-old could teach his father a few lessons about faith.

Q: Tell us a little about your next supernatural thriller, entitled _Ghostwriter_.

A: It's a story about a bestselling novelist who writes ghost stories but doesn't believe in them. His wife has been deceased for four years, and both of his children have gone off to college, leaving him alone for the first time. When he gets writer's block, things start to go bad. It's a story with quite a few shocks and surprises. I'm hoping to build on the positive reaction I've received for _Isolation,_ yet create another unique story that fits into my body of work.

Turn the page for a sneak peek at
Travis Thrasher's next riveting novel:

Ghostwriter

Coming May 2009

Not Too Long Ago . . .

They carried the body up the hill. Light from the moon dripped through the blowing branches, revealing the dead leaves they stepped on. The pale, bare heels of the corpse scraped the ground. The load was heavy. Too heavy.

"Pick it back up," a low growl ordered.

"Just a minute. I need to catch my breath."

"Catch your breath back home, woman."

"I'll catch my breath now if I want to, so help me God."

The wind howled. The woman hobbled over to the tree and leaned against it.

"Where is he?" she called out.

"I told you. You never listen to me."

"Listen to what? What's there to listen to?"

"He's bringing the car around."

The gangly figure stepped closer to the woman. He still carried the hammer in his left hand.

"We need to leave."

"I'm too old for this."

"Now."

The moan from the body was low at first but then continued into a deep wail, until it finally erupted into an enraged scream.

The tall figure lumbered back over to the stirring body. Its head was moving, its body jerking as it tried to sit up.

He brought the hammer over its head methodically, again, and again, and even when the head was back on the ground, he kept pounding. Soon there was nothing hard to strike against.

"Pick him up," he ordered.

They continued up the hill where lights from a waiting car penetrated the darkness.

They shoved the body into the trunk; then the doors opened and shut and the engine roared to life.

The car disappeared into the black pit of night.

1

Time

Dennis Shore made a living telling ghost stories—a very good living, in fact—but that didn't mean he believed in them.

So when the fifty-one-year-old author of nine *New York Times* bestselling novels heard the crash above his bedroom in the middle of that September night, he wasn't spooked. He couldn't remember the last time he had been genuinely spooked. Shocked, yes, such as the time he came home to find Audrey with a broken arm, or more recently when he learned that Lucy had cancer. Shocked but not frightened. He sometimes wondered what it would take to scare a man who made a living scaring others.

Something extreme, he knew that.

It sounded like a lamp had fallen, a bulb bursting. The cracking of floorboards made it seem like someone was in the room above his, one of the two rooms on the third floor of the hundred-year-old Victorian mansion. This renovated house made all kinds of creaks and noises, however, so this wasn't anything new. Perhaps he had left a window open. The early fall night was warm, and he could hear the wind gently blowing outside.

The alarm clock said 1:25 A.M. Wearing only boxer shorts, he walked over to the stairs. His knee still bothered him from spraining it a few weeks ago playing softball. No more sliding into bases for him. Golf fit him just fine. If only he could learn how to hit the ball, it would fit him even better.

The wooden stairs wound up toward the third floor. He rubbed his eyes as he ascended. He could remember climbing these stairs one night to discover a squirrel had gotten in and made a little home in the room Lucy and he designated the nursery. It was a joke, of course. First off, neither of them wanted another child. All he had ever wanted was a boy and a girl, and they got both, so they were content. Second, if they were to have had another baby, this would have been the last room in the house to set up the nursery. The stairs were steep and narrow, and climbing them took a toll on your legs, not to mention the rest of your body. The thought of making this trek several times a night, the way they used to in the old house to soothe Patrick and Audrey, was pure torture.

They had decorated the room and made it into one of three guest bedrooms. The view was amazing, overlooking the Fox River down the hill. Guests often picked this room when given a choice. Across from it was a room that was mostly used for storage. They had talked about other plans for it—it could be a memory room, Lucy had said, with photos and memorabilia from their life together. She probably would have fixed it up, too, if the cancer hadn't taken her four years ago.

As Dennis neared the top of the steps, he noticed the flicker of a light. Then it disappeared.

It looked like a flashlight.

He was more confused than anything else. No one was in the house. He had just come back from flying with Audrey to Biola University in Southern California, staying with her over the Labor Day weekend. She was a freshman and approximately two thousand miles away from him. The weekend had been wonderful and it hadn't really sunk in yet that he was here in this house by himself for the first time. Ever.

Reaching the top of the stairs, he turned on the hall light.

Something inside the guest room moved. Motion. A blur. He didn't jerk in fear but rather went to the doorway and flicked on the switch.

No light came on.

The floor squeaked. Then came the sound of rustling covers.

Is this a joke? Maybe Tom's pulling one on me. Maybe he knows I'm alone and he's trying to have a jolly time.

"Tom, is that you? 'Cause if it is, I'm throwing you out that window."

He moved forward, flinching when he stepped on the lamp. He picked it up and put it back on its table next to the bed. There was another on the opposite side that he walked over to.

"I swear, Tom, if you're trying to—"

A hand grabbed his ankle and pulled it. He jerked, and jerked hard, his left leg tugging away from the cold, clammy grip.

"What the—"

Dennis quickly turned on the lamp.

"Let's go. Come on," he said, believing it was his friend Tom, who enjoyed pulling pranks.

But he saw the arm extending out from underneath the old bed. The first thing he noticed was how pale it was. And how slender it looked.

That's not Tom's arm. That doesn't belong to a man.

"Hey—who's that?" he called out.

And a quick, piercing thought ran through his mind.

It's Lucy. She's back.

"Come on out," he said again.

Another arm emerged.

And then he saw the hair. Long, dark hair.

And a pair of eyes.

And he suddenly grew very afraid.